WHEN SHE WAS OURS

WHEN SHE WAS OURS

A NOVEL

ANNA NORDBERG

LAKE UNION
PUBLISHING

This is a work of fiction. Names, characters, organizations, places, events, and incidents are either products of the author's imagination or are used fictitiously.

Published by Lake Union Publishing, Seattle

www.apub.com

Amazon, the Amazon logo, and Lake Union Publishing are trademarks of Amazon.com, Inc., or its affiliates.

EU product safety contact:
Amazon Media EU S. à r.l.
38, avenue John F. Kennedy, L-1855 Luxembourg
amazonpublishing-gpsr@amazon.com

ISBN-13: 9781662539183 (hardcover)
ISBN-13: 9781662539206 (paperback)
ISBN-13: 9781662539190 (digital)

Cover design by Faceout Studio, Addie Lutzo
Cover image: © Donatella Loi / ArcAngel Images

Printed in the United States of America

First edition

For Mom and Dad, the first storytellers

. . . the presence of my mother obsessed me. I could hear her voice, see her, imagine what she would do or say as I went about my day's doings. She was one of the invisible presences who after all plays so important a part in every life.

—Virginia Woolf

Prologue

When Astra was nine and traveling with her mother to Chicago, the passenger in front of them had a panic attack. Astra didn't know what a panic attack was then; she just sat frozen in her seat as the woman screamed that she couldn't breathe and ran into the galley, then turned on her heel and sprinted back down the aisle.

"Everything's going to be okay, sweetheart," her mother said. "Just wait here—I'll be right back." Then she unclipped her seat belt and stood.

A steward rushed over and told Astra's mother to sit down, but she put a hand on his arm and said calmly, "It's all right, I'm a doctor." And with those magical words, he stepped aside. Astra watched her mother walk into the aisle and toward the woman; she was wearing high-waisted grey wool pants and a creamy white blouse with buttons down the front. Astra's mother always dressed well on airplanes. Perhaps she knew she might be called on in an emergency.

"I need to get off! I need to get off!" the passenger screamed, her mouth stretched unnaturally wide. To Astra, it felt like she was screaming at her mother, and she wondered if her mother was scared.

All of a sudden, just before her mother reached her, the woman lunged across two men sitting in the emergency exit row and tried to grab onto the handle to open the door. Her mother moved with speed to pull her back, and then she took the woman's hands in her own and told her to breathe.

Astra felt both terrified and dreadfully sorry for this woman. She could not imagine any situation where she would expose herself in this way in front of strangers.

"Put people in front of all the exits," her mother said to a crew member, in the kind of voice Astra figured she must use in the operating room. He rushed down the aisle toward the galley. Later, Astra's mother would tell her the passenger would never have gotten the door open, the pressure outside was too great, and the door was not designed to open in the air. And yet, even this after-the-fact information could not blur the edges of that sharp memory, the charge it carried.

Her mother continued to take long, slow breaths, clasping the woman's hands. "You were panicking, so you weren't breathing deeply enough to get oxygen. You're doing great now, just count in and out with me." The airplane cabin was completely silent. Astra saw a man come out of the lavatory, freeze, and just stand in the galley, watching the two women. There was a look on his face that Astra didn't understand then, but later, she would.

When she thought back to that day, Astra realized something she had always known but hadn't been able to put into words, and it was this: Her mother was capable. Astra had a capable, unflappable mother, a brave mother, and other people saw this as well. It gave her mother an authority that other women, Astra noticed, often weren't given.

After the incident on the plane, whenever other terrifying situations presented themselves, a sort of low calm would come over Astra, a sense of what needed to be done. In high school, when her friend started choking on a piece of steak, she leaped across the table and performed the Heimlich they had been taught in CPR class. One summer, at the pool near her grandparents' house, she saw a small child jump into the deep end, feet first, like he was jumping into a puddle, and sink to the bottom. She sprinted to the side and saw him standing under the water, holding up his arms, a look of surprise on his face. She lay flat on the ground and pulled him out so quickly that he scraped his stomach against the rough concrete lip of the pool.

When his mother ran over, she had such a plain and naked look of fear on her face that Astra had to turn away, it felt too private. Then she walked behind the clubhouse and sobbed.

The crying afterward, her fear for that tiny child, that was Astra. But this other part of her, the part that could act in an emergency—that was her mother. It was as if the day in the plane, her mother's calmness, her authority, had imprinted on her.

But somebody had to be in danger. That was how it worked.

Part I: The Wedding

Chapter One

February 1996
Longfellow College

It was a ten-minute taxi ride to her dorm from the train station. Astra watched the Gothic silhouette of Longfellow rising like a crag in the distance, sullen yet lovely, and felt a wash of relief. When she had left for home three weeks ago, scrambling for the train, frantically wondering if driving to Manhattan would be faster, she had thought she might not come back to college this year. But here she was. She liked to work. This was how she was built.

The race back to the city had been to see her mother, following a lung embolism that put her in the hospital. For years Astra had stayed near, in case of just this moment, but it had come when she was away. This brutal, unremarkable business of her mother's dying, it had been so slow, and then in the end, still a rush.

The taxi pulled up outside her residential college, which was a spruced-up term Longfellow used for its ancient, decrepit dorms, and she thanked the driver and paid. "Did you have a fun weekend in the city?" he asked as he pulled her saggy duffel out of the back—no one she knew in college had luggage on wheels, including her, because it felt too corporate.

"I did," she said, and smiled. She had friends who would have told him the truth, that she was coming from her mother's funeral. But she could not do such a thing to this kind-faced man. She had learned, early, that her job as a girl with a dying mother was to put others at ease.

There was no one in the courtyard. It was February, the trees stripped of their leaves, the grass faded and cut close to the bone. She walked up the three flights of stairs to the room she shared with Sonia, her roommate since freshman year. Sonia had come to the funeral wearing a long-sleeved black dress with a short ruffled skirt, the kind of thing you might wear to a sweet sixteen. "It's the only black dress I own," Sonia had said, and made a face, and Astra had felt a surge of tenderness toward her.

Sonia's mother, Audrey Chen, a famous psychology professor who studied stigma at Harvard, had also come. In the receiving line she had formally shaken Astra's hand instead of hugging her. "Oh, don't worry, she does the same to me." Sonia told her this later, and yet the fact that Professor Chen had made the trip from Boston to Manhattan humbled Astra. People surprised you.

She stepped inside her room and was struck by the smell of water and petals. The deep window seat—the pride of their room, which otherwise had the faded, slightly embarrassed feel of a penniless count—was filled with flower arrangements in various states of decay. It had never occurred to Astra that her friends might send flowers. She realized almost none of them had her home address.

She sat down and read the cards one by one. They all said variations of the same thing, as if drafting off the same set of talking points—*so sorry for your loss*; *so sorry to hear about your mother's passing*—and these scripted, well-intentioned words of comfort moved her deeply. People tended to talk about going through the motions as if it were a bad thing, but Astra understood, each time she encountered these rote phrases, how much going through the motions still mattered.

There was a note from Sonia too. *Welcome back, roomie. I missed you so much. I'm on science hill all afternoon, but let's get dinner, my treat, no dismal cafeteria fare, okay? Hope you like the flowers—it kind of feels like we're going to the prom. Love you to the moon and back.*

Sonia had been one of the great gifts of Longfellow. She dressed in frayed jeans with faded ultrasoft T-shirts and thrift store cardigans, and she was instinctively cooler than Astra, introducing her to indie bands like Luna, Belle and Sebastian, and Sonic Youth. They both loved the Beatles and Liz Phair. That was enough to start a friendship. Astra had never before had a friend who was both so different from her and yet, at her core, so compatible.

Astra unpacked, then stood in the middle of the room, looking out over the flowers into the barren courtyard. She had no classes to go to; it was still a few hours until dinner. During the past three weeks there had always been so much to do, so many people to see, so many decisions to make. Now her arms hung at her side, and in her first quiet space of free time, she felt something close to fear. She decided to check her mail, and put on her coat and scarf.

The post office was on old campus, where the freshman dorms were, and she had a hard time getting her box open, it was so stuffed with mail—envelopes and junk mail rubber banded into thick tubes, and then, wedged on top, a pale-blue envelope.

She recognized the writing immediately.

She felt a fizziness in her joints, a sense of almost painful elation. She walked straight back to her dorm, into the narrow closet of her bedroom and shut the door. Then she opened the letter from her mother.

> Dear Astra,
>
> I miss you and love you. I just wanted you to know how proud of you I am. Lately I've been wondering if I've said things as plainly as I feel them, and so I wanted there to be no confusion.
>
> This summer, at the wedding, you showed such courage. You've always had courage, but I worry about the toll it took on you, how you always just keep going, in your quiet way. I don't want that to be your lot, but I worry it will, because people have a

way of figuring out, quickly, what people can handle and what they can't. Just remember your kindness is a strength, even if people underestimate it.

I know these thoughts are not my most organized. I'm here at the hospital—Dad has gone to pick up a few things I need at the pharmacy, as well as my thick socks and an extra blanket, because I'm always freezing—and I asked him to get me some stationery first so I could write you.

I'm feeling tired now so I'm going to rest up. I love you and I will always love you.

Mom

Astra read the letter again, and then a third time. It was like pricking herself with a pin, and it made her feel better. Her mother must have sent it the day she went into the hospital.

Why did her mother decide to write to her about the wedding now? Astra usually pushed away thoughts of that night, but they came swarming back now—the sliver of moon, her mother kneeling on the wet dock, her aunt screaming. She remembered running, running for the tent faster than she had ever run in her life, thinking if she could just get there in time, it would be okay. Astra lay down on her bed, pulled her knees into her stomach, and only then did she let herself cry.

Chapter Two

June 1995
New Jersey

From the window of the upstairs bedroom, Astra and her mother looked out at the wedding tent going up in the lower field, inflating like some huge white whale.

"My god, it's the size of Rhode Island," her mother said. "All it needs is some elephants."

As she spoke, the wind picked up one of the tent flaps, not yet harpooned to the ground, and it started snapping vigorously. Astra watched two men catch the rope tether and wrestle it down. This kind of competence always impressed her.

A few yards away from the tent Astra could see her sister Phoebe, in canvas shorts and a light-blue peasant blouse, talking to a small clutch of people—directing, really. The wind gusted even stronger, the tent heaved at its ropes, and Phoebe took a few steps toward it. Astra imagined the whole thing pulling from its anchors, soaring up over the pond, the house, and away over the horizon.

"Should I go down there and help?" she asked her mother.

"Help Phoebe?" her mother said, and laughed. "That's like asking if you should help Napoleon. Only if you dare." Her mother patted a spot on the bed next to her, and Astra climbed on and laid her head down on her mother's shoulder. "It's been so nice having you girls here all to myself for a few days," she said. "And you have been such a help to Phoebe, Astra. She doesn't show it, but she needs you."

Astra knew her mother, whose own wedding reception consisted of champagne and cake, sensibly wrapped up by midafternoon, viewed the extent of these wedding preparations as preposterous, but she had been absolutely loving and supportive from the get-go. When their grandmother called up to ask why Phoebe was having an evening wedding in the country—"Did you mix up *a.m.* and *p.m.* on the invitation?" she'd said—Astra's mother had stood staunchly in her daughter's corner. "An evening wedding is quite a racy thing for Grandy," she'd told the girls. "But I know she can handle it."

Downstairs the screen door banged, and they heard Phoebe's quick step on the stairs. "Mommy! Astra! Eek!" She rushed in, flushed and smiling. Both Astra and Phoebe still called their mother Mommy, something no one else they knew still did, though this lay between them, undiscussed. "Where's the Fels-Naptha soap? I just waded through an entire patch of poison ivy."

"There should be some in the bathroom down the hall," her mother said, making a movement to stand up.

"Don't worry, I'll help her find it," said Astra, gesturing her back down, and the sisters hurried down the hall together.

"What were you thinking?" Astra said. "You've got cuts from the brambles all over your legs."

"I was trying to show them where to set up the catering tent," she said. "At least my dress is long." They giggled together as they poked around the remedies on the blue-tile shelves. Domeboro for drying out rashes. Pepto-Bismol. Hydrogen peroxide. Gauze. Tylenol. Some bright-orange stuff in a bottle their mother used to put on their cuts. Everything but the large bar of yellow soap that the Erickson family had used since time immemorial to prevent poison ivy.

Astra ran back to her mother's bedroom. "We can't find it, Mommy!"

"All right, let me help," Astra's mother said slowly, and Astra's stomach gave a strange little jerk as she watched her mother start to push herself up from the bed.

~

Thea saw her younger daughter's face change, the moment of joy curdle into worry. Astra said, "No, Mommy, you stay, we're fine, please don't get up." It was always the same. Stay, rest, please don't exert yourself.

"It's okay, sweetheart," Thea said, and Astra protested no further, something Thea had become more and more grateful for. She used the IV pole to slowly stand up, and Astra took her other arm. Her daughter was so matter-of-fact about the physical help Thea needed, so different from the well-intentioned flailing of most of Thea's friends, who acted as if they were going to get cancer, too, when they were around her.

Thea was wearing her light-green summer robe, and her hair was still a short stubborn grey, like a marine sergeant. Not exactly the mother-of-the-bride look she had envisioned. She and Astra had gone together to the Garment District a few weeks ago to buy her a wig for the wedding. "You don't need one!"

Her daughters had insisted, and Thea had said quietly, "It's not for my vanity, my loves, it's to put other people at ease."

When they got to the bathroom, the IV pole clunking along behind them, Astra helped her mother up the step, and Thea looked around. "Up there, in the basket," she said, pointing to the highest shelf, where a dark-brown wicker basket nestled.

Phoebe, with her enviable height, pulled it down. "You're a lifesaver, Mommy. I'm getting in the shower right now!" she said, shucking off the canvas shorts and blouse and turning on the water.

If Phoebe wasn't her daughter, there would have been something embarrassing, shocking almost, about seeing such a healthy, youthful body next to her own, Thea thought. But this was her child, and while people tended to talk more about the emotional aspects of parenting these days, raising a child was also a completely physical act. From the moment she'd held them as babies, she'd known every freckle and curve, and as they grew, she'd felt proud of their health and strength, their physical bravery.

She still remembered that afternoon they'd heard Phoebe screaming in the playhouse. Before she and Tom could get there—she remembered running in her heavy gardening clogs, running as if her lungs would burst—Astra had raced back inside to see a bobcat standing between Phoebe and the door. Rabies was a big deal in the '80s, and Thea and Tom had warned the girls about any wild animal out in the daytime. Astra had grabbed the toy broom, swatted the cat away from her sister, and they had sprinted outside into Tom's arms.

Later, after they had put the girls to bed, she and Tom had a drink. He'd poured them each four fingers of scotch and placed the bottle between them.

"I don't know if I'm up for this," he'd said. "The thought of something getting at Phoebe or Astra. I go crazy." She had put her hand over his and squeezed it as they both took a long pull of scotch.

"Luckily, I'm sure something will happen to us first," she said, and they'd laughed.

"No, but really, Thea, I'm serious. I wanted our children to be like you, and they are."

All that seemed so long ago.

Phoebe was in the shower now and the girls were laughing about something or other. Astra had her back turned to Thea, and she noticed how long her daughter's hair had gotten, long and thick and slashed with red, like Tom's. Instinctively she reached out and put her hand on her daughter's head, let it slide down the ponytail. "Mommy, don't pet me!" Astra said.

"It's just your hair is getting so long," Thea said. "We'll have to figure out how to put it up for the wedding."

"You can do it. We could braid it?"

"Yes, of course." One of Thea's great accomplishments as a mother had been to hide, from both her long-haired daughters, how much she loathed doing French braids, the near impossible two-step of trying to pull the hair back so it didn't poof up on top while keeping the braid straight. Suddenly, Thea felt exhausted. In healthy people, fatigue creeps up over time, but for her it was like stubbing a toe—a sharp, quick pain. "Astra, can you help me back to bed?" she said, more sharply than she meant to, and her daughter turned, with that look of hers—panic mixed with guilt, quickly hidden away—and took her arm.

Astra helped her mother back to bed, asked if she wanted any water or one of the books piled up next to the nightstand. People sent so many books, and half of them were about dying. Thea had seen every kind of death—young, old, sudden, protracted, grieved and ungrieved. She was afraid of death, of course. What in god's name did it mean to not be afraid of death? But she was also matter-of-fact about it. She left those books in a pile, and reread *Pride and Prejudice* and *Jane Eyre*, the novels of her girlhood.

Chapter Three

Astra pulled up the covers over her mother, turned off the bedside light, and drew the shades. Her mother was already asleep. Under the light summer quilt, she looked tiny as a child.

Phoebe poked her head in, wearing a towel. "Hey Astra," she said, her voice quiet and sweet. "Could you run and grab me a fresh set of clothes? I don't want to put the poison ivy ones back on."

Astra nodded, leaving the room and closing the door behind her without making a sound. She smiled at Phoebe, who was waiting in the hall, and mouthed "be right back," then padded down the stairs and through the hallway to her sister's room. Phoebe had left the window open—her parents had never put in air conditioning, a fact that Phoebe and Astra's friends, with their ice box houses in the Hamptons, had always marveled at—and the breeze from outside smelled warm and green, the way it did before a heat wave. The wedding was going to be scorching.

Everything in Phoebe's room was neat and orderly—the sheets on the twin bed tight as a drum, no clothes lying around on the chairs. It was as if the room already understood that Phoebe didn't live here. Of course, that had been true for years, since the awful year when Astra was thirteen and her sister went off to college. But her marriage—to a man Astra truly liked—was another ending, a different ending.

Since her sister's engagement to Eli, Astra had probed all the places where envy or sadness might lurk and hadn't found any. There was none of the jealousy her friends had told her to expect, perhaps because she was so young that the idea of getting married now—or frankly ever—seemed absurd. Phoebe, serious, beautiful, mature Phoebe, was getting married at twenty-five, which to Astra basically seemed like a child bride, but it made sense for her sister. Phoebe would marry young, and Astra would never marry, and thus they would balance each other out.

As she rustled through the drawers, the thin T-shirts folded neatly as a stack of napkins, Phoebe's piles of faded khaki and twill shorts, the intimacy of it felt suddenly overwhelming and she had to stop and steady herself, taking deep breaths. She plucked out a shirt and shorts and ran upstairs.

~

At 5 p.m. it was hotter than it had been at noon, with the sun beating sideways and the heat of the day trapped in the long grass. Astra sat with her sister on the stone wall by the driveway, the way they did when they were kids, waiting for their father and Eli to drive up.

"I haven't seen Mom like that since her first surgery," Phoebe said quietly. "I'm worried the wedding is too much for her."

"Stop that right now," said Astra, and she put her arms around Phoebe's shoulders and shook her gently, until her sister started smiling. "Your wedding is what's keeping her going. First it was my high school graduation, now it's this. She said so."

"Now we'll just have to find someone for you to marry," Phoebe said, "to keep Mom motivated." They both laughed.

"That will be perfect," Astra said. "She'll have to live another twenty-five years, at least."

Phoebe was silent for a moment, and Astra felt her sister shifting on the wall, turning slightly away from her, the way she did when she had something important to say. "You know how much Eli likes you, right? Like, not just because he has to?"

"Of course. You know I adore Eli."

"I just don't want you to worry."

"I know, I know, you're not going to abandon me," Astra said in a light voice. Right at that moment they heard the crunch of tires on the gravel and jumped up. "Here they come!" Astra said, and they jumped up and down and waved their arms wildly, the way they used to do when they were kids.

~

Tom saw the girls before Eli did.

He could tell they had been waiting on the stone wall, and it brought back the summers when they were children, and he and Thea commuted into the city for work while the girls stayed out at the farm with his parents, and later, an au pair.

How he looked forward to those nights when, after a sweltering day in the city, exhausted by the commute, he would see the way their faces split open in joy when they first spotted the car and galloped down to meet them. Each girl would fling themselves into a parent's arms, smelling of grass and sweat and the sweetness of Coppertone sun lotion, and he would catch Thea's eye over the roof of the station wagon, and she would smile at him. That was happiness.

"Looks like the welcome wagon has arrived," Eli said.

It startled Tom that this young man who was marrying Phoebe was sitting next to him and not his wife. But he gave a good-natured laugh, and said, "From how relaxed they look, you wouldn't guess there are going to be one hundred and fifty people here in forty-eight hours. God help us." Sometimes he did this, played the hapless father, even though he was the one who had gone through the budget and the guest list with Phoebe line by line.

As Tom folded himself out of the car, his quarterback height still impressive in his late fifties, Phoebe came and hugged him. His throat felt hot; he realized his daughter had come to him first, not her fiancé, and the sweetness of this moved him deeply.

~

Tom always said Thea fell in love with him because he'd had a happy childhood. But that was not exactly it. It was how he had been loved—the dinners his parents cooked, the pride on their faces at his high school graduation, and when he got a scholarship to college. Tom was a man who had been held in his mother's arms as a child, and Thea could tell that.

He did not call it love at first sight when he first laid eyes on Thea, because he understood that to admit such a thing was to appear, in New York in the '70s, like a bumpkin. But that's what it was.

When it started getting serious, his friends back home ribbed him for dating a blue blood, making references to the hoi polloi and whether he was eating finger sandwiches on yachts. Their teasing slid off him like water. "What is her house like?" his friend Danny asked him—Danny who had gotten a job right out of high school at the Kenvil Power Plant, the largest smokeless power plant in the country, and bought a Cadillac with fins.

"Well, it's huge, but everything looks old, and a bit battered," Tom had said. "You're always hungry after dinner." His friends were disappointed. They expected something shiny and energetic, not this frugal, austere corner of American wealth.

What still astonished him is that Thea loved the house in New Jersey, this wooded, sloping land that used to belong to his parents. She loved tromping around in the woods with him, and there were times, before she got sick, that she would just run through the big field—the field where Phoebe's wedding tent was currently inflating like the Hindenburg—with her arms thrown wide. He could not believe his luck.

And then, when Phoebe was in college and Astra was in her junior year of high school, their luck had changed. "I guess the universe is trying to even the score," Thea said to him, after her diagnosis, back when they still believed she would beat the cancer. He had told her she was being ridiculous, but deep down he felt the same way. How he had managed to get this woman to fall in love with him he never fully understood. And now he was paying the price of too much happiness.

Chapter Four

Thea heard the car come up the driveway, she saw the girls waving from on top of the low stone wall, the way they used to when she and Tom commuted in during the summer and they stayed with an au pair, usually one of Thea's young English cousins who thought the notion of spending a summer in New Jersey sounded mysterious and exciting.

She lay back and closed her eyes. She knew Tom would be up here soon, checking on her, perhaps telling her she was wearing herself out. The other night, seeing a full glass next to her in bed, he had started yelling. "You're not drinking enough water, Thea! Dr. Kelly has told us how important it is—if you get dehydrated, you'll have to go back to the hospital again!" It was the same voice he used in those rare times he yelled at the girls when they were doing something unsafe, and she knew underneath the anger, it was only fear.

When the doctors had told her she had only two more years to live, Thea had driven to Long Island to see an old medical school classmate, David Wanabo. She and David had not been particularly close in med school and had gone in different directions since then—David into the wilderness of private practice, while she had become chief surgical resident at Columbia Presbyterian. Many years later he had floated back onto her radar when she heard colleagues talking about him—he had opened a clinic that performed radical surgeries for colon cancer patients, removing several organs, months in a hospital bed, permanent colostomy bag—but some of them did live, even after being given terminal diagnoses.

"He's a quack," Teddy Wilson, chief of oncology, had told her.

"Well, I suppose there's something to a surgery that can cure you as long as it doesn't kill you," Thea had said, and they'd laughed.

And yet, a few years later, here she was, driving up to Providence, to the hospital where David Wanabo worked, a hulking, ugly building, with yellowish walls and windows that looked like rows of teeth. It reminded her of a prison.

David had been so warm when she arrived, coming to the lobby to greet her. She had found herself liking him in return. This had happened since her diagnosis—a reordering of what made her actually want to spend time with a person.

He had shown her around, taken her through the ward, and though it was what Thea had prepared herself for, it still struck her, looking at the patients in the beds, how impossible it felt that this could be her. She, with her terminal cancer, felt healthy next to them.

"Assuming I actually survive the surgery, is it always a six-month recovery?" she'd asked David.

"Yes," he'd said simply. "Sometimes longer." She was surprised. Most people didn't know how to stop talking after they said the thing that mattered.

"Well, thanks for being so candid, David. I appreciate it."

He had reached out and squeezed her arm, nodded. "It's a lot on the patient, and the family," he said. "What do Tom and your daughters say?"

Thea had told him they were very supportive, but it wasn't the full truth. Tom, Phoebe, her sister, they were all encouraging her to do this; it was the magic bullet they'd all been waiting for. But Astra had told her—begged her—not to have it.

Thea could remember Astra's face, when she told her what the operation would involve. A look of worry, but underneath that, a wince. "I don't want you to have it," Astra said quietly.

"Sweetheart, this is the best chance I have—"

"But what if it kills you? Or what if you're in bed for the rest of your life? You don't have to do this for us."

"I know that, sweetheart. I want to do this. I want to feel like I've tried everything," she said.

Astra looked down at the ground. "It sounds like you've already made up your mind," she said. "So I don't know why you're asking me." There was an edge to her words, a touch of sandpaper in her tone that Thea had not heard for a long time.

"It means a lot to me, Astra, that you want to make sure this is what I want," she said. Her daughter looked at her, almost angrily.

"Would you let me have this operation?" Astra said. Thea was startled into silence for several seconds.

"That's not a fair comparison, Astra. It's a specific operation, for colon cancer—"

"Can you just listen to me!" Astra said, her voice rising. "You always just—you always shut conversations like this down, with your doctor card. I hate it."

Thea was silent for a few seconds, digesting this idea her daughter had never shared before. "I'm listening," she said.

"If for whatever reason, doctors were saying I needed this operation, would you let me have it?" Astra said.

Thea thought about all the things she could say, all the ways she could answer this question.

"No," she said.

"Well, that's how I feel about you," Astra said.

And then Astra's face crumpled up the way it used to when she was a child, and Thea put her arms around her daughter as she cried. She understood now how Astra felt, and it broke her heart. But she would have the operation anyway. She knew this.

~

She told none of this to David Wanabo, at least not then.

What she did tell David, on her second visit, was that she had to do everything, absolutely everything, she could to stick around for her family.

"I understand," said David. "But I must admit I'm still surprised. I know you're close with Ted Wilson, and he thinks this is scorched-earth surgery, with limited payoff."

"Well, maybe you appreciate a limited payoff more when you're dying," she'd said. "My girls still feel so young. I don't want to think there's something I haven't tried."

He'd nodded. "I get it," he said. "It was the same with Marcy. That's why I started doing this." In that moment she realized, perfectly and completely, that his wife, Marcy (she would never have remembered her name), had died, and she'd had no idea. She had to close her eyes, and when she opened them, she took David's hand.

"David, I didn't know. I'm so sorry for you and your family." He raised his hand as if to wave her apology away, but she said, "No, David, let me say this, please. You are doing really important work here, and I never—I never gave you the credit you were due."

In the end, she hadn't been able to do the surgery. They discovered an offshoot of cancer in her leg, and David wouldn't perform the surgery if it had spread. But they still talked about once a month, and she often asked him about his kids, trying, without asking directly, to get the answer to the question that burned within her—are they okay? Are they okay without their mother?

Finally, David had said gently. "Thea, I know what you want me to say. And I can't say it. They're not okay. But they also had enough time with Marcy for me to know that they will eventually be okay. And I believe that for your daughters as well."

She had cried, and she knew David was crying on the other end. It was strange, how out of the ashes had come this extraordinary, humbling friendship with David Wanabo, a man who had counted so little to her when her ambition burned hot.

Chapter Five

One of Astra's earliest memories was driving out from Manhattan to her grandparents' house in the country, taking the George Washington Bridge to Route 80, the highway melting away into narrow country roads and a night sky where the Big Dipper blazed below the moon. In the city, she could never see any stars.

When she was fourteen, her grandparents had died, suddenly and within months of each other. How young they had seemed, in their mid-seventies, and how healthy, until a heart attack and a stroke had carried them away. Her father had worn his grief so quietly, but they had talked, often, of how it was hard because it felt like Grandma and Grandpa were going to live so much longer. That was before her mother got sick.

Amid the warm hubbub of her father and Eli's arrival, Astra had slipped away for a walk, alone. When she'd come back with Phoebe's clothes, she'd found her sister crying. "Mommy is so weak, I was thinking—how are we going to get through the wedding? What if she collapses? I'm scared, but I also feel—I feel embarrassed." Astra had tried to comfort her, but Phoebe had shaken her head. "I think maybe I'm a bad person," she said quietly.

Astra had tried to tell Phoebe these feelings were normal, that grief made you think weird and horrible things. What she didn't say was that it was not Phoebe, but her, who she sometimes thought was the bad person.

Ever since the operation in Rhode Island that never happened, Astra had felt a small but distinct space between her and the rest of her family. They had all rooted for this procedure to happen, and she had not. It had hurt, to go against them, and it had scared her too. Didn't she want her mother to get better, want that more than anything in the world? Yes, but not like that. And when the operation was called off, a hot, violent guilt flamed inside her. What if her thoughts had some crazy, destructive power? Astra was too young to understand that the universe didn't actually care at all about what she felt, it just moved forward, random and inexorable.

~

Astra had been walking for half an hour now, in the cool, deep woods that surrounded her grandparents' farm, an old-growth forest filled with beech and ash and hickory. She could feel herself getting calmer, the way she always did when she was outside. She swung her arms by her sides, she kicked a small rock, she galloped up the rocky slope of the trail like she was a child. No one could see her. She felt the quiet, indescribable pleasure of being alone.

And then, out of the corner of her eye, she saw something move, something huge and dark.

She froze. Whatever it was, it was at least fifty yards away. She tried to tell herself it was a dog, a huge black shaggy dog. But it moved differently from a dog, slower, more powerfully. In all her years coming to the house in New Jersey she had never once seen a bear, but she knew they were here—at least once a year they went marauding in the bird feeders and knocked over the beehives. Her father had seen them growing up.

She took a step back, as quietly as possible, but the animal heard, and its movements changed. It was hard to see through the trees, but Astra thought it was standing up on its hind legs, as if angling for a better look.

The fear she felt was astonishing. It was cold and plain, so different from the anxiety and worry of the past years. She took another step backward but willed herself not to turn and run. Her father had told her and Phoebe, when they were girls, that people make that mistake in the wild. It marks them out for prey.

The animal made a huffing sound, and she had a brief, electrifying thought that it was going to start charging her, and this bright hot fear for her own life felt strange and invigorating.

Then the animal turned and started to move away, with a slowness that Astra understood. Anything that large had nothing to fear in these woods. She watched as it slouched out of view, and then she ran. She followed no path, leaping over rocks and tree trunks and tearing through brambles that drew blood. She kept running and running, with an adrenaline rush that made her feel like she could run forever. After a few minutes, she started to see green through the trees, the suggestion of open fields, and safety. It was her parents' property line, ringed by a tall fence with a gate they never used.

The gate was metal, anchored by heavy wooden posts, and a thick sweep of dead leaves had piled up on each side of it. When she reached it, she saw cobwebs on the latch.

She grabbed the latch and pulled. It grudgingly gave an inch. She moved it up and down, trying to breathe life back into it, then pulled again. She knew the bear wasn't following her, and yet she could not look behind her. She thought if she did, she might conjure it.

She gave the latch one last yank, and it sprang free, and she put her shoulder into the gate, pushing against the mound of leaves, until it opened about a foot, enough for her to slip through.

She had crossed to safety.

Astra did not know it then, but this would not be the first door that would be shut against her during a moment of danger. Years later, she would think of it as a sort of dress rehearsal, a muscle memory she could call open, when the situation required it.

Chapter Six

Thea could hear a ruckus outside, the sound of someone running. Her windows overlooked the driveway and pond but not the porch, so she could not see what was happening, though she could hear the screen door banging as people ran in and out. With effort she lifted her legs and swung them to the side of the bed. She took a few deep breaths, then reached down to unhook the IV from the back of her hand.

Slowly she made her way to the door, and then the top of the stairs, gripping the doorknob and then the banister, like a person fumbling in the dark. She was just contemplating her first step when up barreled her daughter, straight into her arms. Thea just stood there, Astra's cheek fitted into the curve of her shoulder, as her daughter managed to choke out what happened. She could feel the fear in Astra's voice, even though she said, several times, that she wasn't sure what she saw, that it might have just been a dog. It was not a dog. Thea knew her daughter, and a dog would never have made her this scared.

Astra was bleeding from several cuts in her legs, and a few drops had run down her calves in livid streaks, staining her socks. Thea said nothing. She just kept rocking her daughter back and forth, a ritual left over from childhood they had never let go of.

Chapter Seven

In the first flush of planning the rehearsal dinner with Eli, Phoebe had not realized that a courtyard filled with fine gravel might be a terrible choice for a bride whose mother was in a wheelchair. When she had realized, her mother assured her it would be fine, and anyway, it was too late, the deposit in, the invitations in the mail.

Last night she had lain in bed awake for half the night, imagining her mother marooned amid the finely raked sea of pebbles. But they had arrived early, her father maneuvering the wheelchair into a corner with a little ring of chairs. Every time Phoebe looked over, her mother seemed happy, as old friends came over to sit by her and say hello.

"See, Phoebs, it's all going great."

Astra had come up beside her, holding a glass of champagne.

"Aw, thanks, lil' sis," Phoebe said. "By the way, you look smoking in that dress." They had bought it together, at Bergdorf's with their mother's credit card. Astra had refused at first to spend so much on an outfit, but Phoebe had pulled rank and overruled her. It was a Ralph Lauren cocktail dress, with a sweetheart neckline and elegant puff sleeves, the nipped waist accentuated by a full tea-length skirt. It had an old-world feel to it, which was not trendy right now in a sea of spaghetti strap dresses and baby doll shirts, but the style suited her sister.

"Well, since you twisted my arm to wear it, I will tell you, on the eve of your wedding day, that I am kind of obsessed with it," she said.

Then she clinked her glass with Phoebe and said, "I'm going to go check on Mom."

Phoebe was not as close to Astra as many of her friends were with their sisters—the five years that separated them had loomed large, particularly during adolescence—but of all the sisters she knew, they liked each other the most. She could tell Astra had been genuinely happy for her when she'd called to tell her, a year ago, the news that she was engaged.

Phoebe's friends had been more skeptical. Allison, who she had known since kindergarten and thus took more liberties than her college friends, had straight out said what she assumed most of her friends were thinking.

"Is this because your mother is dying?" Allison had said. "You can live together for a couple years first. This is the decade you're supposed to make stupid mistakes and learn from them, I get that, but not on this level."

Allison's words had hurt her deeply. It was not that Allison had doubts but how she had put it, and the friendship had not ended but it had been bruised. Worse, she was worried Allison might be right. When Eli had asked her—down on one knee with an actual ring, completely out of the blue—her unqualified, joyous yes had surprised her.

She had not said yes because her mother was dying, but the knowledge made her assess Eli differently. She was terrified of what her family would look like after their mother was gone, and she evaluated Eli not just as a lover but as her family.

As she was thinking this, she turned, and Eli was in front of her. "I saw you talking to Astra. She looks beautiful tonight."

"Well, don't let your friends get carried away by any wild notions about the maid of honor catching the bouquet," Phoebe said.

Eli laughed, a warm, wonderful laugh. "I would never. Though Charlie already asked me if she was single."

"You know what Astra said to me, after our engagement? She said how happy she was, and how perfect you were for me, and then I said

I couldn't wait for this to happen to her, and she said, 'Oh no, Phoebs, don't you know marriage is the place where all interesting stories end?'"

"She said that?" Eli said.

"She did."

Eli took a minute for the words to sink in. "Wow," he said. "I'll be sure to let her know that I can't wait for my life to get super boring with the woman of my dreams." Phoebe laughed, and then he picked her up, swung her around wildly, and said, "How boring is *this*!"

Phoebe usually hated public displays of affection, but she was so caught off guard, so stunned by Eli's complete inability to be embarrassed by how in love he was, that she could say nothing. She saw the surprised looks of her friends and family, the way their faces all opened like flowers into the exact same expression of delight, and she thought, *Fuck you, Allison. I know what I'm doing.*

Chapter Eight

Astra watched Eli put Phoebe down and kiss her. A clatter of applause followed, and she smiled in spite of herself. She and Phoebe usually hated over-the-top displays of affection, but Eli could pull them off, because he had a deep and instinctive comfort with himself. The sisters sometimes talked about this with a kind of wonder.

"Wow, that dude is really in love with your sister." It was Jordan, her godmother's son, who she had known since she was little. In a quirk that delighted their mothers—sometimes they joked it had been an arranged marriage—Astra and Jordan both attended Longfellow, though Jordan was a year older.

"He is. Phoebe had to talk him out of setting off fireworks after the vows," she said.

Jordan laughed. "Thank god. Your mom looks good, too—she seems really happy."

Jordan knew everything about her mother's illness; with him she had always felt the deep comfort of someone who was almost a sibling. "She is really happy," Astra said. "Making it to the wedding was one of her goals."

Jordan took her hand and gave it a squeeze.

Farris brought Thea a very small glass of champagne.

"I'm not sure Ted Wilson would approve," Thea said, and Farris laughed.

"Tough patooties for Teddy," she said. Ted had been their classmate in medical school, and while he had not been able to come to the wedding, he'd sent Phoebe and Eli a charming set of sea urchin salt and pepper shakers from Tiffany. *Marissa did not pick these out; I did,* he wrote on the card.

Farris was Thea's dearest friend, and Astra's godmother. They had met in college and then been roommates in medical school, part of only a handful of women in their year. Farris had been the only Black woman, and when people asked Thea how it was having Farris as her roommate (always polite, always smiling), Thea would reply, "Well, it's very hard, because she's smarter than me." After a while, people stopped asking.

Once, Farris had found Thea sobbing in the break room after a senior resident had dressed her down during clinical rounds, and she had put her arm on her friend's shoulder and said, "I'm going to give you ten more seconds to cry, and then you're done. It's absolutely no help at all."

Thea had watched Farris's face when Phoebe and Eli had their little Hollywood moment.

"You think he's a little much," Thea said.

"Did I say anything?" Farris said. She reached over and took Thea's hand, bringing it back over to her lap and holding it lightly.

"He's good for her," Thea said.

"I know," Farris said. "And you know I'll make sure that whoever Astra ends up with, they love her like this crazy boy loves Phoebe?"

"I do, Farris," she said. "After all, you're the only person I know who would be brave enough to speak out during the 'speak now or forever hold your peace' part."

"Brave enough or crazy enough, you mean," she said.

"Sometimes they're the same thing."

~

When Thea became an attending surgeon, her first patient cried when she saw her. It was a woman in her late forties, attractive and well maintained, wearing a St. John suit and scarf with a lovely pattern of peacock feathers.

"She can't be the right person," the woman said, when Thea walked through the door. "What can she know that Dr. Lodge doesn't? She looks like she's in high school." These questions were directed at her husband, who was wearing a grey windowpane suit and had slicked back hair.

"I'm Dr. Erickson," Thea said. "It's very nice to meet you. Dr. Lodge was one of the doctors who trained me during my residency. He's an internist, but I specialize in cardiothoracic surgery, which is why he's referred me to you." The woman turned away and said nothing, but her husband stuck out his hand and shook hers with great warmth.

At conferences, Thea wore shapeless black pantsuits and put her long hair in an ugly bun at the nape of her neck. "Who are you trying to be? Yentl?" Farris said, the first time she saw this getup. Farris's figure was curvy and beautiful to Thea's upright coat hook, but then Farris wore her own armor—high-necked formfitting dresses in brilliant colors like lapis and emerald and royal purple.

And then, one day, a new patient came in for a consultation, a woman in her late sixties. It was Mrs. Schneider, her mother's close friend from Bryn Mawr. "Oh, Thea, I can't wait to tell your mother what good hands I'm in," she said.

"Mrs. Schneider, I'm so glad to see you," she said. "Does my mother know you're here?"

"Oh no! I just remember a conversation we had, when you were in medical school, and I said it must be so hard for you. She just looked at me and said, 'Thea will make a competent doctor,' which, for your mother, was such high praise I understood what she actually meant, which is that you would become one of the best doctors in the world." And then Mrs. Schneider held out both her hands, and Thea took them, and in the warm silence that followed, neither of them cried.

Her career could be divided into pre– and post–Mrs. Schneider. Post–Mrs. Schneider Thea developed a reputation for taking on the hardest cases, and her outcomes were better than those of any of her peers at the hospital. She allowed herself to be what she had always known she was—better than the competition. When the hospital's chief of staff backed her for chief of surgery against her better-liked rival, a neurosurgeon named Peter Stillman, he'd told her, "You work hard, you're ambitious, but for the patients, not yourself." He'd paused then, as if considering whether to keep speaking. "Ego in the operating room cuts both ways. You need the right kind, and you have it."

And then she had gotten sick. Thea had never been sick, not in all her life. She had never stayed the night in the hospital except for when she delivered the girls, both births that had gone so quickly Tom had said, "We can't have another, or we won't make it to the hospital." She had felt secret pride in this, and she wondered sometimes, if that thrill of satisfaction she'd gotten from her body's strength was being punished now.

She shared this idea with Farris, and then Farris had told her that she must see someone, a therapist.

"But I have you," she said.

"I am not your therapist," Farris said. "I am your friend. You need someone else, and I will find her for you." Farris was the chief of psychiatry at a hospital in Nashville.

"Her?" said Thea, amused.

"Oh, yes."

And Farris had found her, a Dr. Stone who she characterized as *not a nincompoop* and who had an office in a brownstone on the West 70s, the little bronze nameplate next to the door the only indication that Thea was not walking into someone's apartment.

"Thea, hello, how are you? Please come take a seat," Dr. Stone said when she entered the sunny office.

Dr. Stone was small and tidy looking. She was dressed all in black, with a chunky necklace and big brassy earrings that were clip-ons, which Thea recognized because she also wore clip-ons. She had never gotten her ears pierced.

They discussed the reasons Thea was there—her diagnosis, her fear of leaving her daughters in the lurch, the strangeness of being a patient after decades of standing on the other side. Thea thought Dr. Stone had good bedside manner.

"Can you tell me more about your early relationships?" Dr. Stone asked during their second session. "With your siblings, your parents?"

"My parents?" Thea asked.

"Yes."

"Well, they were very correct, we would think of them as old-fashioned, today. My father—he was very kind, he was generous enough to let things slide. My mother was basically descended from the Victorians."

Dr. Stone smiled.

"Tell me more about that," she said.

"Well, she never really said, 'I love you,' to me or my sister growing up. I think she thought that was—over the top."

She saw Dr. Stone writing something down on a yellow legal pad.

"But there were no—hardships or anything like that. My mother just wasn't very effusive."

"Is there a particular memory, something you think of really positively, when it comes to her?" Dr. Stone asked.

Thea thought back to the Christmas when she was fifteen, and her mother gave her a green silk leisure suit from Lord & Taylor. Thea had admired the suit in the window months ago, walking past the department store with her mother, and as she opened the slim black box and parted the tissue, she'd cried out in pleasure at the sight of the emerald silk folds.

"I was so touched she'd remembered," Thea told Dr. Stone. "The idea that she'd gone back to get it for me. There was such a sweetness to that. It wasn't—it wasn't really like her. I was so excited to try it on for her."

Thea remembered holding the suit up to her body, smiling while her mother smiled too, and then realizing the trouser legs were so long they pooled at her feet, while the arms hung down almost to her knees. How excited she'd been, for this gift from her mother, that now somehow became humiliating, turning her into a child playing dress-up. As the memory broke upon her, Thea started crying, a fit of crying so violent she thought Dr. Stone would be alarmed. But Dr. Stone was not alarmed. She just quietly passed Thea some tissues.

When she was finally done, Thea looked up at Dr. Stone.

"What mother doesn't know the size of her own child?" Thea said.

When she left, Dr. Stone put her hand on Thea's shoulder, nodded, and said, "You're doing real work here. See you next week." Thea had glowed from the praise, glowed from the idea that, by talking about how she never felt fully loved by her mother, she was healing herself just in time to die.

Chapter Nine

Thea was wearing her wig, and a beautiful sapphire-blue pantsuit she and Astra had picked out together at Saks. Despite the heat, it was long sleeved, to hide the marks from the IV. Her veins had been pricked so many times they had bloomed into a delicate purple skein, and while she was not vain about it, she'd trained herself to remember that people who did not work in hospitals could be stunned by the ways an illness asserted itself.

Eli's mother was wearing a lovely suit in a creamy beige, alarmingly close to white, and Farris had whispered, "Who's the other bride?" and raised her eyebrows as she stood next to Thea before the ceremony. "Farris, behave," Thea had said, laughing, and then she had clasped Mrs. Friedman's hand in welcome and told her how nice she looked. It was true.

Two months ago, Dr. Kelly had agreed they could pause chemo treatments before the wedding to try to build up her strength, so the strange truth was, Thea had woken up on the morning of the wedding feeling as close to healthy as she had felt in a year. She had decided to walk down the aisle and not use a wheelchair.

Now, she wondered if this was a mistake. Eli stepped up next to her, gave her his arm, and smiled. "Showtime?" he said, and she nodded.

It was about fifteen yards of grass that could have been cut a little shorter, but as they set off at a stately pace, Thea felt strong. She nodded at family friends and colleagues, smiled at Phoebe's college and high school friends. She did not know all Eli's friends, but she liked that there were a lot of them. She trusted a man who had real friends.

She remembered her own wedding, at the tiny Episcopal church downtown, her family's church, where there was a plaque with her great-grandfather's name on the wall. White lilies tied to the pews, the men in morning suits. She had thought, as her father walked down the aisle—her father who she loved so much and who occupied so little of her thoughts—that there was a chance she was pregnant, and she was right. It was so early that everyone simply remarked on their "honeymoon baby," but Tom always referred to it as their mild shotgun wedding, one of the inside jokes of early marriage that bound them together.

Eli was handing her off now; she had made it to her chair. The bridesmaids came after with the groomsmen, Astra in a lapis-colored taffeta dress that looked remarkably well on her. And then it was Tom and Phoebe, and a hush fell over the guests, followed by the whoosh of more than one hundred people standing at the same time. Thea was not a softie, and yet she loved this part of weddings, the collective ritual that still remained.

Phoebe wore the same veil Thea had worn—a piece of family lace that had almost dissolved when they'd had it pressed, but an ancient seamstress who looked like she predated the sewing machine had repaired it. Thea had told her of course she didn't have to wear it, but Phoebe had insisted, and Thea had been touched.

She thought if this feeling of strength could hold for the day, she would not be greedy for anything again.

~

Astra was in front of the band, dancing with Phoebe and their cousins. Robby, Thea's nephew on Tom's side, started twirling Astra and then did an acrobatic dip all the way to the ground that Tom once tried with her and she had never returned from. But Astra emerged laughing and light. She looked different tonight, to Thea. Both her daughters were wonderful dancers, thanks to Tom, and she had not realized what a pleasure it would be to be able to simply sit and watch them.

While it was Phoebe's wedding day, Thea found herself drawn again and again to her younger daughter, the one whose wedding she would never see. Astra had never even had a serious boyfriend, and while Thea had a sense of the kind of man her daughter might fall in love with (or woman, she corrected herself, though she thought it unlikely), she didn't know for sure. Well, she did know this. It would be a good person. Astra, who had such a hard time standing up for herself, who would rather wait twenty minutes in line than tell someone they cut in front of her, could be utterly ferocious defending her ideas, her principles, and of course, the people she loved.

She remembered when Astra was twelve, how kind she was to the new girl in school, Eleanor. Eleanor was too smart and too pretty to be liked by the ruling clique, but Astra refused to bully her or join the "boycott Eleanor" club, and she invited Eleanor over to the house, included her in her birthday party. Thea hoped her girls—who worked so hard, who had never, since they were seven years old, had to be nagged to do their homework—knew that it was this part of them that she was most proud of. Had she told them this enough? She wasn't sure.

While she was watching the girls dance, she noticed a young man she hadn't seen before. He was standing at the edge of the dance floor, staring at Astra, and it took her a moment to recognize him. He was Nick, the son of her college roommate, Patty Rosenfeld. He had become remarkably handsome, just like his father, a big shot partner at a white-shoe law firm, whom Patty had been in a difficult marriage with for twenty-five years. Nick was close to six feet, with brown hair that looked like it would curl at the end if he grew it long.

It took her a while to understand what the expression on his face meant, but when she finally did, she looked down at her hands and saw that they had turned white from gripping the sides of her chair. The look on his face was awe.

Astra had noticed someone looking at her. At first, she couldn't place him, but when he started walking toward her, she realized who it was. Nicky Rosenfeld. The last time she had seen him was at his bar mitzvah, when she was ten. Her mother had bought her a grown-up dress—green, with an empire waist and shoulder pads—and they had gone just the two of them. The other girls were in sparkly dresses with full skirts and wore makeup, and though they were only thirteen, they looked like adults to Astra.

During the ceremony in the synagogue, she had watched Nick read the Torah, his voice falling up and down, calm and clear. This was her first bar mitzvah, and she hadn't known what to expect. What she saw astonished her. Watching him perform in front of all these people, in Hebrew, she felt the respect she always experienced when seeing someone do a thing she could not.

She had stuck close to her mother during the party, drinking Shirley Temples, and when the band had started playing in earnest, she'd looked longingly at the dance floor, which was circular and rotated slowly under a spray of colored lights. Her mom had put her arm around her, pulled her close, and said, "I bet you thought this would be a little more fun."

"It's okay, Mom. I really enjoyed the service. I want to congratulate Nicky for doing such a good job."

"Of course," she had said. "I'll come with you."

He was on the dance floor surrounded by school friends, so they had waited until he came off, and then her mother had said, "Nicky, it's Dr. Erickson, an old friend of your mother's. Congratulations. You did a wonderful job."

Then Astra had stepped forward and put out her hand; he had taken it, looking a little surprised. "I really enjoyed your Torah reading," she said. "I can't believe you learned all that. It was beautiful."

He smiled, shook his head. "I made about ninety-seven mistakes, but thank you for saying you liked it. I'm glad you came." He returned the pressure on her hand, looked right at her, then said goodbye politely to them and folded back into his crowd of friends. They had left soon after, thanking Patty and her husband, John.

Now, she looked at him—taller, even better looking than when he was thirteen—and gave him a little wave of recognition. "Nicky!" she said, as he got close.

He smiled. "It's Nick now, but you can be grandfathered in. How are you, Astra? I realized that must be you, dancing with your sister."

"It's so nice of you to come," she said.

"How could I miss this after you and your mom came to my bar mitzvah? On a boat, no less."

"Well, it was the day you became a man," she said.

He laughed hard at this, surprised, and then he reached out his hand and took hers. "Let's dance," he said.

They danced to the last of "Superstition" and then the band shifted into a slower number, "I Will" by the Beatles. It was a song Astra loved.

Nick took her in his arms, one hand on her back, the other hand holding hers. Then he smiled at her, with such a genuine look of pleasure it took her aback. She wondered if there was something about her tonight—dancing with her family, celebrating Phoebe—that made him think she was a different person than she was.

"So, you've graduated now," she said. She knew from her mother that he went to Brown. "Are you one of those people who has a job and everything figured out, or are you just going to improvise into adulthood?"

"I'm one of the very boring people who have a plan," he said, and then in a conspiratorial whisper, "law school." She laughed, and he joined in.

"I'll be going to NYU in the fall and working as a paralegal in the city over the summer," he said.

"I'll be working in the city too," she said. She had an internship with a small book publisher on Canal Street.

"Well, maybe we can meet at Dorrian's," he said, and grinned. Dorrian's was a bar on the Upper East Side where high school kids went, and she wondered if he was teasing her, ever so slightly, for being younger.

"Why stop there? We could go big—CBGBs, the Tunnel?"

"Right," he said. "And when was the last time you were at the Tunnel, Astra?"

"I've never been. But I'd like to be one of those people who talk about going."

He laughed again, and then he said, "I'm so glad I came tonight." There was no turn to his voice—he said it as if it was simply a piece of information he wanted her to have. Astra thought about how a few months after the bar mitzvah, Nick and his family had visited them out in New Jersey for the weekend. She had developed a crush on him, while he'd had eyes only for Phoebe, who looked like a brunette version of Alicia Silverstone. Nick's parents had been so unpleasant with each other that weekend even Astra had felt the strain, and afterward, as her parents were cleaning up Sunday lunch and getting ready to pack the car, her dad had said to her mom, "Well, let's never do that again." And they hadn't. While her mother and Patty had stayed close, Astra hadn't seen Nick for ten years.

"It means a lot to my mom that you and your mother came," she said, and he smiled.

"Your mom is so great," he said. "I think my mother would have been happier if she had just stayed roommates with her forever instead of marrying my dad."

"Oh, don't say that!" Astra said. She couldn't imagine ever saying anything disloyal about her parents and their marriage.

"It's okay," Nick said. "It's true. They're getting a divorce. No one knows yet."

She looked at him, and his pain, in its newness, its strange shape, somehow felt worse than her own. But she could tell from his face he wished he hadn't said it. He looked embarrassed, or not embarrassed, not exactly, but ashamed.

"I'm really sorry about your mom," Nick said quickly. "I've only heard a little from my mother about her illness, but I can't imagine what that must be like."

She understood now what the look on his face meant. He was ashamed to mention his parents' divorce when her mother was dying. It was how she would have felt, had their roles been reversed. This had never happened to her before with a man.

"Thank you," Astra said in the steady, serious-sounding voice she reserved for inquiries into her mother's health. "It's just really wonderful she's able to be here, at Phoebe's wedding."

Nick looked at her and said nothing. So many times she had practiced saying the right thing to put people at ease—"I'm so grateful for the time we have" she would say, or, even worse, "My mom is a fighter," polishing these banal, courageous-sounding phrases to a high sheen. But she sensed Nick didn't want this.

"Actually, when I try to think about what our life looks like without her, it's like one of those old maps, where the world just ends in a mass of nothing," she said. "I guess I don't even know how to be scared of something I cannot even imagine. It's just a hard blank in my mind." She had never spoken this way about her mother's illness to anyone.

Nick looked at her the whole time she said this, and then he pulled her into him and wrapped his arms around her and laid his head on top of hers.

"Thank you for telling me that, Astra," he said.

It was the only time in the four years since her mother was diagnosed that a person had done the exact thing that made her feel comforted, and she let him hold her, stunned.

"And I promise I won't tell anyone about your parents getting divorced, not even my mom."

Astra thought of her parents, how she once saw them get out of a cab together down the street, laughing and holding hands, when she was walking home from school in the eighth grade. Growing up, she didn't realize what a rare thing that was.

"I know you won't," Nick said. "My mom once said it was almost infuriating how little your mom liked to talk about other people, and I bet you're the same."

"Well, I'm not my mom," said Astra. "She's like a different species than the rest of us. But I'm also not, you know, the town crier."

"Though you would look great in a tricorne hat," said Nick, and they laughed.

The song was almost over, and Nick pulled back and smiled. "Let's get a drink," he said. "We need to lighten the mood." And then he put his hand lightly on the small of her back and they walked toward the bar, the bottles of liquor like gemstones under the lights of the tent, the glasses sparkling at attention. A wedding bar always felt young and hopeful.

They both ordered champagne.

"So how have the last few days been?" Nick said. "Was it pretty crazy, getting everything ready for the wedding?"

"It was, but Phoebe is like a field marshal, so we haven't had any real catastrophes yet. And I was able to outrun a bear that I thought was going to maul me to death, which would have been very awkward, so that was good."

"Excuse me?"

"I'm making it sound more dramatic than it was. But literally I was out walking two days ago in the woods, and I saw a bear, maybe fifty yards away from me. I've never run so fast in my life."

"Holy shit."

"Yes. Honestly, I think what kept me together was the thought that here we were, worried about guest list drama and whether it was going to rain on the wedding day, and none of us had considered the possibility of the maid of honor getting eaten by a bear. I couldn't do that to my family."

"So basically, the fear of a WASP breach of etiquette is what kept you alive?"

"I knew you'd understand."

He was laughing so hard he had to put down his champagne, and when he finally stopped, he put his hand on her arm. "You know I'm not laughing at the idea of a bear attacking you, right? And now you need to tell me the whole story immediately."

She did. It felt good to spool out the whole story from a position of safety. Astra was a good storyteller, and she could feel Nick leaning into her, sometimes laughing, sometimes grabbing her arm. She embellished a little, made the bear feel closer than it was.

When she was done, he said, "Can I tell you something? I am so fucking glad that bear didn't eat you." And then he picked her up and swung her around. Her drink had gone straight to her head, and she could not remember a time in the last two years when she had felt so unbearably happy.

~

If Nick could see the look on his face while he watched Astra give her toast, he would have been embarrassed for himself. He felt relieved none of his friends were here tonight, thinking how amused they'd be at how hard he was falling for this girl. When Astra finished, her family clustered around her and Nick stood back, waiting. That's when he noticed a man, a few feet away, looking right at him.

"Hi, I'm Nick," he said, and stuck out his hand. The man was in a morning suit, clearly one of Eli's groomsmen, not the one who had made the speech.

"Oh, hello," the man said, shaking Nick's hand. "Charlie. I assume you're with the bride?"

"Yes, she's a family friend."

"Of course. Family friends all around," he said in an amused voice, and gestured to the boutonniere in his lapel.

"Are you a college friend of Eli's?" Nick said. "He's a lucky guy." The words sounded pathetic to him.

"Eli's ridiculous luck has been a source of consternation to us all for quite some time," Charlie said. "But you are the one everyone envies tonight. I didn't see it, until last night—you weren't there, I think?—but the little sister has her own thing going. Maid of honor, always a coup."

Nick knew this kind of person. When he was in middle school, the Eighty-Sixth Street gang—a bunch of private school kids who used to take off their clip-on ties and shake down younger kids for their allowance and bus passes—had pushed him around a couple of times, once throwing him up against a wall and giving him a concussion after he tried to fight back. When he had seen one of his tormentors at a high school party years later, the kid had whispered, "Hey there, Bus Pass," as he walked by, and Nick had punched him in the face. Unlike what he told his parents, the parents of the host, his friends, and on some level, himself, he had never actually regretted it. Nick knew a sucker punch was wrong, and yet he also knew that Tim Sevetti was an asshole.

"Wow, it's so surprising Eli didn't pick you to give the best man speech," Nick said.

Charlie laughed and then put his hands up in mock surrender.

"Okay, sorry, I'm only giving you a hard time because you're dancing with the girl I want to dance with. In another life, I think we actually might like one another. You take care, Nick." And then he raised his glass and walked away.

Nick could see Astra now, making her way back to him, and he felt a sense of victory, white hot and keen.

Chapter Ten

Eli's best man Matthew had given the first speech—a solid toast on Eli's absurd decency, including the time he drove twenty miles out of their way to deliver a squirrel they had hit with their car to an animal hospital. "By the time we got there the squirrel had a name, Edmund, and Eli's hardened fraternity brothers were basically in tears rooting for this little guy to survive," Matthew said, to warm laughter. Astra went next.

She told a very funny story about when she and Phoebe dressed up as a shower for Halloween—Phoebe wore a bathing suit and carried an old-fashioned back scrubber, and Astra wore a Hula-Hoop on shoulder straps that had a shower curtain strung around it, and a shower nozzle on her head. ("Phoebe looked daring and cool, even in a shower cap, and I was a faucet, which basically sums up our childhood," Astra said to laughter.)

The costume had been a huge hit, until the Hula-Hoop got stuck in the elevator and Astra had fallen on top of Phoebe, who had to go to the ER for stitches. "I remember going into her hospital room, feeling terrible, like I ruined Halloween, and Phoebe just looked at me and said, 'it was worth it.'" Thea remembered that moment, how surprised she'd been by Phoebe's generosity to her sister, when she was being a horror to her parents.

Then it was Thea and Tom's turn to speak. They walked slowly to the microphone the band leader was holding out with a smile. He handed it to Tom, who passed it immediately to Thea.

"When two people are in love, willing to bind their lives together the way Eli and Phoebe did tonight, they may feel invincible at first, but at some point it becomes clear—in two years, or ten, or forty—that we cannot get on without our people, our friends. Every family knows this . . ."

Thea thought this was the way she could refer to her illness, without bringing it to the center.

"Both Eli and Phoebe understand something fundamental about friendship, which is that it is an action, and when life gets hard, those actions can get harder—sending notes, showing up at life events, gathering around a meal. Tom and I shared that work, and I see that same partnership in Phoebe in Eli."

She looked at her daughter and her husband—the word felt fresh minted and strange—and Eli's face was hard to describe. He was happy, of course, but there was something else. What it reminded her of most was the look on a family member's face whenever she gave them good news after a surgery. An almost radical relief. How much this man wanted to be loved by their family. It was the thing, selfishly, she liked the most about him, because she knew it would make a difference, when the time came.

~

When the speeches were done, Astra thought they might go to the dance floor again, but Nick made no move toward it. Instead, he looked closely at her, and then said, "Do you want to go outside and get a little air?"

She was going to say no, she was fine, she wanted to stay in the tent with her family. But when she opened her mouth, what she actually said was "I'd love to."

Nick took her hand, and they walked toward the exit. He walked quickly, as if he thought she would change her mind, pulling her into the summer night.

Outside it was dark and surprisingly warm, as if the daylight had shut off too quickly. The sounds of the wedding disappeared almost instantly. Nick and Astra heard the frogs, the low whirring of insects. The moon was yellow and skinny and gave off almost no light.

Nick held her hand but nothing more. Astra waited for him to speak.

"What your mother said about friendship," Nick said. "I really loved that. After all, I wouldn't be here if she hadn't stayed friends with my mom."

"She cares about your mom a lot," Astra said. "She has this hilarious story about when she was in the hospital, after giving birth to me, and they wouldn't let her eat yet, and your mother dressed up as a candy striper and snuck her an entire gallon of melted Häagen-Dazs."

"My mother dressed up as a candy striper?"

"That's how the story goes."

Nick was quiet. "I would have never in a million years thought my mom would do something like that," he said. "It's just—I've struggled a bit with my mom lately. I want to support her, but she can be—she can be needy."

Astra had thought, with a sort of vibrating heat, that they would start kissing the moment they stepped outside. But this was somehow more intimate.

Nick spoke again. "I know a lot of it has to do with the shit she's put up with from my dad. And I'm not always a picnic either. But I can't say to her the things she wants me to say. I can't say those things about my dad, to her."

Astra took a step closer to Nick, laid a hand on his arm. "I don't think it's your job, Nick, to make things okay for your parents."

"But it's what you try to do," he said. "Your family doesn't put you in that position, I know that, but I can tell—I saw the way you went to your mom, before dinner, because you knew she needed to sit down. You *care* so much. You're so—you're so good-natured. I couldn't stop watching you during the wedding. I saw you dancing with your sister and your cousins and I just thought—"

He trailed off. They were standing so close together, and she felt the years since she had last seen him, remembering the crush she had had on him back then and how young she'd felt. She wondered if it was the wedding that was giving her this sway over him—if he was drawn not to her but to her proximity to happiness. She didn't care, she could feel her power, the fact that he wanted her, and a current of anticipation, and fear, went through her.

She turned her face up to his, aware of the way he towered above her and how much she liked that. He kissed her, slowly at first, one arm around her waist and the other wrapped around her shoulders. He ran his fingers through her hair and then pulled her head back gently as he kissed her harder. It went on like this for minutes, in total silence, neither of them saying anything, except for the sound of their breathing. When they finally broke apart, Nick looked at her and said, "You kiss just like I thought you would kiss." Then he stepped back and put his hands in his pockets, like a boarding school boy in a novel.

Astra didn't trust herself to speak, so she stepped forward, toward him. He caught her hungrily, and suddenly it was different, not gentle or exploratory. He put his hand on her waist, and tipped her head back to kiss her jaw, her throat, her earlobe. She made a sound that did not seem like it could have come from her, and he wrapped his arms around her so tightly she was surprised by how strong he was. In his suit, he looked so slender, reedlike.

They broke apart, both breathing hard as if they'd been running. "Astra," Nick said, and her name sounded different, new, in his voice. "Is there some place we could go?"

She could feel it, his gentleness covering an urgency, one she felt too. But it was different for her. Through high school, and then college, the thing that set her apart one by one from her friends is that she'd never had sex. Nick felt like the first person she could even imagine sleeping with, and still, alongside her desire she felt a small, low terror. It was always this way.

What she could not tell her friends was that when she hooked up with boys, what stopped her was not prudishness, but a sense that she simply could not go on, a feeling that was not shame but just as powerful as shame, scalding and absolute. This past year at college, a boy she had had a crush on for months had finally kissed her, they were alone in his room, and then he had dropped to his knees to kiss her stomach above the waistband of her jeans. The moment he went to take her shirt off, she froze. She could not be this close to another human being. She wanted to be alone, in her own bed. With Nick, it was the first time she had not felt, physically, like a fraud.

But there was none of that fear or hesitation in her voice when she finally said, "There's a gazebo by the pond. Well, actually, it's more of a shed. But you don't seem to be in a picky mood." Nick smiled.

"We've definitely reached the gazebo point in the evening," he said, taking her hand and swinging it wildly, like a little boy. "Lead the way."

"And Nick," she said, laughing. "You know I can't stay long. My sister might need me—they'll be cutting the cake soon."

"Got it, cake cutting, sister, of course," he said, but the way he said it, she could tell that the cake, the tent, the wedding no longer really existed for him. For her, it was the opposite. Even as she leaned into him and started to walk down to the dark smoothness of the water, part of her was still in the tent, thinking about her family.

They walked to the gazebo, which had a little dock stretching out in front of it about ten feet into the water—a dock for diving into the murky water on hot days, and fishing, and rowing bright little boats. There was a teak bench with a cushion upholstered in faded green and white stripes, and in silence, she walked to it holding Nick's hand. They sat down, and she folded herself into him, her head on his chest and her legs tucked to the side. He stroked her hair, starting from her scalp and letting the long strands slide through his fingers. When he slowly lowered her down onto the cushions, they barely fit.

The whole length of him was pressed against her; she could feel his belt buckle against the light fabric of her dress, knew it would leave a mark on her skin. One of his arms was around the back of her head and the other he ran down the side of her body, slowly, then back up, passing lightly over her breasts, but not cupping them. He ran his thumb along the heart-shaped neckline of her dress. "Your skin is so smooth," he said. "I can't stop touching it."

It was something other boys had told her, but with Nick it sounded new, as if he was the first person to ever say such a thing in the world. He made no move to try to lift up her dress, but ran his hand up her bare leg, skimming the edge of her underwear. This was the place she usually froze, shut down, but she found she did not want him to stop. She shifted her body so that one of his legs was between hers and he pressed it against her. She felt, lying underneath him, that if her mother's illness was the first real thing that ever happened to her, this was the second.

They kept kissing, it could have been a few minutes or thirty. His hands were lightly tracing her body, his thumb brushing over her nipple under the stiff taffeta, but he seemed in no hurry for anything more.

Then he lifted her up so that she was facing him and they kissed like that, her legs wrapped around his waist. She began moving against him and he froze, his breathing changed. He wound a hand into her hair and gripped it tightly. "Astra," he said, in a hoarse voice. "If you keep doing that, I am going to lose my mind."

He held her, and she was glad it was dark. Her face burned from the words he had just said, the intoxicating idea he had of her, that she was the kind of girl who could turn him on in this way. Not the kind of girl. The girl. It was a new feeling for her, she could feel it straining against her other beliefs, the ones she had polished so silently until they became her core truths. This hot grasping in the dark, it was for other people, who weren't trying to hide the slumbering, broken things inside of them. It was not supposed to be for her.

As Nick started kissing her again, she wondered how long they had been gone. Swimming up from the heaviness of her desire was another feeling, a fear that her family was looking for her, that they didn't know where she was, because she had left the tent during her sister's wedding reception.

She'd felt that way only once before, at her thirteenth birthday party, held at a rollerblading rink downtown. Two of her friends, Veronica and Shelly, thought the party was babyish, and convinced Astra to sneak outside with them. Veronica boasted she would bum a cigarette, and then, the moment she was asking someone for a light, Astra's mother appeared, walking toward them with an anger on her face Astra had never seen.

"Girls, inside, now!" she said, and they silently complied, Veronica letting the cigarette slide from her fingers and fall to the ground.

Astra had never forgotten that feeling of wet misery as her mother talked to her that night. "All those people showed up for you," she said. "How unkind is it to act like you don't even want to be there? What you did was disrespectful to your guests—to your friends, your family, and yourself."

Astra heard a ragged cheer from the tent, the sounds of a celebration happening without her. How could she have left her family, and come outside in the dark? An almost-frantic guilt cut through her desire.

~

Nick felt Astra shift in his arms, and her mouth became sharp and tense under his. He pulled back and looked at her. She was smiling, but she looked like a different girl.

For Nick, who had gone to this wedding grudgingly and at his father's request, so his mother wouldn't have to go alone, the night had stunned him. He'd had one serious girlfriend at Brown—a premed student from the Midwest who was small and pretty and much more experienced than him—and then he'd dated around. He was looking forward to his summer in New York, single and headed to law school. Girls liked him, he knew that, though he wasn't an asshole about it.

And then he'd seen Astra. He loved the way she looked, frankly he burned for her, but it was the way she wore happiness that attracted him most. When he first saw her on the dance floor, it felt like he could tell everything about her in that moment—her kindness, her capacity for joy, her quick-wittedness. And when she gave him that first smile of recognition, that small wave, he'd felt actual joy inside him, tight as a spring. And the way she looked at him after he kissed her—my god.

But she was not looking at him that way now. She seemed hesitant, worried.

"Nick," she said. "I think I have to get back to the reception. They're probably wondering where I've gone."

"It's only been ten minutes or so. We can go back in a little bit," he said, and smiled, and reached out to take her face in his hands.

She was smiling, too, but she gently disentangled herself from his arms, stood, and started smoothing down the skirt of her dress.

"Wait, did I do something?" he said.

"No, no—everything is—everything is amazing. If it weren't my sister's wedding I would Irish goodbye with you this second. But I think—I think I need to be with my family right now. I mean, they might send out a search party."

Her tone was light, but he could hear the stress under her voice. She felt so far ahead of him, adjusting her clothes, talking away, while he sat there on the bench, in a daze.

"Nick, once everything is done, all I want is to be with you. That's all I want. Okay?"

She said it with a simplicity that took him aback. None of the girls he'd dated had ever spoken to him in this way, in its vulnerability and plainness. He was pretty sure Astra didn't usually speak this way either; she'd been so sharp and playful at the beginning of the night. He loved the earnestness on her face, the way her hair had come out of its half-up braid, making her somehow more lovely.

He understood her need to return to her family; he respected it. He wanted to be the kind of guy who was totally cool about it, and he even thought of himself, until this moment, as that kind of guy. But the truth was, he did not want her to go. He didn't care if she never returned to the tent and missed the cake cutting and the bouquet toss and whatever else was planned. He wanted her to stay with the strength of a physical need.

"Okay," he said, and he stood, almost groggily, and reached for her again, thinking they would kiss and then he would take her hand and walk back to the tent. But Astra stepped away from him, as if she needed to put distance between them. "Nick," she said. "Come on, we need to get back."

He felt a shiver of rejection. A few minutes ago, he thought they were going to have sex, and now she was standing in front of him, a worried frown on her face, looking at him like he was a kid who was late to class. The tiny kernel of rejection flamed hotter.

He took a deep breath and forced himself to smile. "Of course," he said. "I'm sorry, you sort of swept me off of my feet." He smiled again, his best smile.

She gave him such a look of honest happiness, his heart jerked sideways.

"Go and find Phoebe. I'm just going to take a minute out here to regroup, okay? I'll see you soon."

She smiled at him, and then she turned and walked back into the tent. He watched her go.

In the years to come, Nick would realize that this moment—the evening unfolding in front of him with all of its delicate, electric possibility—was a hinge. There was another life for him waiting, he could feel it, could see it as a thing more real than his own. All he had to do was follow her into the tent, take her hand, stay with her. But he did not. Something held him back. And it was that decision that changed everything. Those minutes, standing in the dark after she left, were the last moments of the first part of his life. He wished he had known.

Chapter Eleven

When Nick walked back into the tent, he saw his mother, sitting at a table with a few other women about her age—trim, stylish, fierce-looking women who all looked like New Yorkers. The husbands had all wandered off, or maybe not come in the first place. Or maybe they didn't exist. This always occurred to him last, despite the disintegration of his own parents' marriage.

He walked over to say hello, and he could tell the pleasure it gave his mother to introduce him; her tall, polite son. He shook their hands, said the same things over and over.

"I saw you dancing with Astra," his mother said, loud enough for the others to hear.

He could see the eagerness on his mother's face, and he had to get away, immediately. He could not, would not explain to her the truth—that he was dazzled by Astra. That his feelings astonished him. He could not have her vibrating around him, turning this perfect moment into currency for herself.

"Yes. She's the only person here I know, other than the bride. It's nice to see her." He smiled again at the table, put his hand on his mother's arm, and said, "I'm going to head to the bar."

It made him feel guilty, sometimes, the way he kept things from his mother. When he was thirteen, and his family had spent a weekend with the Ericksons in the country, it was Phoebe, who was three years older and preposterously hot, who he'd had a crush on. When his mother had found him that Saturday night after dinner, red faced and curled up in a ball in his bed in the tiny guest room, she had for once not overdone it. "Well, Phoebe is a very beautiful girl and it's normal that might bring up some feelings for you," she had said, with a matter-of-factness that had come at the exact right time and never returned throughout the entirety of his adolescence, like a stranger passing through town.

He went to the bar, ordered a Jack Daniels and coke, and when he turned to scan the room for Astra, there was a girl standing in front of him, a girl who looked exactly like the girls he had known in high school, with her little black dress and her bone-straight dark hair swinging in her face. She was wearing CK One perfume.

"Hi," she said. "Get me one of those too?" she said, pointing at his glass.

"Maybe in about five years," he replied, and she laughed and made a face. "You looked more fun than that," she said. "I saw you dancing with my cousin."

"You're Astra's cousin?" he said, and she nodded.

"Oh, yes. First cousin," she said, and smiled. "Astra and Phoebe, the golden girls."

He took another sip of his drink. "Why do you say that?"

"Well, look at them. All perfect and with their shit together. I'm like the little black sheep of the family."

He laughed in spite of himself.

"And what's your name, first cousin?"

"Allie."

"I'm Nick."

"I know," she said. "Astra had a huge crush on you after your bar mitzvah."

He was startled. He knew this cousin should probably not be spilling the beans, but it also felt unbearably sweet to hear this; it even soothed him, after the rejection he'd felt at the gazebo.

"Well, I did kill it during my Torah reading," Nick said. "Exodus, always a crowd-pleaser." Allie laughed.

"Just so you know, she doesn't have a boyfriend," she said. He could tell she enjoyed the mantle of authority it gave her, to dole out this information.

"Yes, I figured that out."

"She never has. She's never even really dated anyone."

"Really? Why do you think that is?" He tried to make it sound casual.

"My mother says it's because my aunt has been sick for so long, that Astra isn't able to fully separate, the way you normally would as a teenager. My mom's a shrink, by the way."

"She sounds like one," Nick said, and Allie laughed again, and leaned into him. He had a clear, cold thought, even with the bourbon pleasantly burning inside him, and it was, *What the fuck are you doing, Nick?*

"Or maybe it's because no one's good enough, right? Now, are you going to get me that drink or what?" Allie said.

Nick shrugged. "What the hell. I'm not your mom," he said. "And you're not in, like, eighth grade, right?"

"I'm eighteen, okay?"

He turned to the bartender and ordered a Jack and Coke for each of them. She picked up the cold glass and sipped it like it was something she did all the time.

He raised his glass. "Cheers, little black sheep. It was nice chatting. I'm going to head back to my table now."

Her face fell. "To look for Astra? Just so you know, when guys run after her, she gets nervous."

"Thanks for the tip," he said, keeping his voice neutral. Then he turned and walked away.

"Wait! I'm sorry, I'm sorry I said that," she said, following him and putting a hand on his arm. "Sometimes I just say these things, I don't even know why. It's just hard to be here, with all this happy wedding shit. My parents hate each other and are getting divorced."

The word *divorce* had the power to stop him. It was like a password, a code.

"I'm sorry," he said slowly. "I actually know how that feels."

She looked up at him eagerly.

"Really?"

"Really. Why don't you put that drink down and we can go find Astra together."

"I don't want to find Astra," she said, and there was a bitterness in her voice. "Astra, who's so perfect she took the SATs the day after she learned her mother had cancer, and I can't even keep it together during a good old American divorce." There was no flirtatiousness in her voice now, it was just raw and ragged with distress. "I know that's what my mom is thinking, every time she tells me how fucking strong they are."

Nick could feel the pain coming off this girl, real pain mixed in with alcohol and the knowledge, clear to them both, that she was trying to manipulate him into staying with her.

"Could you just come out for a cigarette with me?" she said. "Please? I just need to like, take a time out from all of this." She waved her hands in front of her and twisted up her face in a funny expression, and for a moment, she reminded him of Astra. "It's so hot in here. When we were kids, we used to jump in the pond after dessert on summer nights. Sounds tempting, right?"

Nick hesitated. He didn't smoke, but he liked a cigarette at parties, and he felt sorry for this girl.

"Okay, one cigarette," he said. She smiled, and the first look of actual happiness flashed across her face.

Outside the tent, she took out a pack of Parliaments and a lighter. He watched as she lit her own cigarette and then held the pack out to him. He took one, expecting her to pass him the lighter but instead she leaned forward, offering him her own lit cigarette, and he bent down and lit his off hers. The small intimacy of this act made him uneasy.

She exhaled the smoke through her nose, then took another drag.

"Jesus, I've been wanting one of these all night," she said. "I wish my dad were here; he's actually fun at parties. But my parents—god, they're trying so hard to be mature about this, like they want to win the divorce sweepstakes. They split this weekend, with my dad going to the rehearsal dinner and my mom going to the wedding, and I feel like that's going to be every event for the rest of my life."

"I know how much it sucks—navigating the events," Nick said. "But at least it sounds like they're trying to be civil about it," Nick said.

"Oh, just in public. You should hear what they say to each other at home."

Nick felt like he was traveling further down this conversation than he wanted to, but there was a small part of him that really wanted to hear what it was like for her. It was hard to talk about it with his friends, whose parents all seemed to be in startlingly healthy marriages.

"Do they try to hide it from you when they fight, or is it all out in the open?"

"Oh, they try to hide it. My mother is always so careful with how she talks about my dad to me, she's always using her therapist voice, except once, when I came home from school and she was reading something on her computer and crying, and she just turned to me and said, 'Your father is such a piece of shit.'"

"God, I'm so sorry, Allie."

She looked at him. "You're a nice person, Nick," she said, and she took a step toward him.

Nick threw down his half-smoked cigarette and crushed it with his shoe.

"I think we should get back inside," he said, but he didn't move, and she was so close to him now that as she blew smoke out the side of her mouth, he could breathe it in.

"Allie," he said, stepping back. "I need to get back."

She looked at him. "What, are you afraid the hall monitor is gonna come find us and tell your girlfriend?"

He laughed. There was something so ridiculous about it, this girl with her jaded poseur act, and he suddenly just wanted to be away. "No, Allie," he said. "But I do think you've had too much to drink and we should go find your family." He knew how sanctimonious he sounded, but he didn't care.

She stared at him, and as a look of such hurt flashed over her face he felt a stab of guilt, and then it vanished. "Oh, I haven't had too much to drink," she said, in a flat voice. She sloshed the last of the watery ice in her glass out onto the grass and then reached for his bourbon. "But don't worry, I can fix that. I'm gonna walk down to the pond, and I'm taking this for the road."

"Suit yourself, Allie," he said. He let her take it. He wanted to be done with this girl; he wanted to be with Astra.

"Last chance," she said, raising her drink and smiling an off-kilter smile, and then she disappeared into the darkness.

Chapter Twelve

When Astra entered the tent, blazing with flowers and lights, it felt almost as if the time in the dark with Nick hadn't happened. She saw Phoebe at the edge of the dance floor and ran over, throwing her arms around her sister.

"Oh, thank god you're here," Phoebe said. "There's finally a lull so let's go to the bathroom, I need you to hold my dress while I pee." Astra followed her into the luxurious porta-potty ("it even has carpeting," her mother had marveled) and gathered up the creamy handfuls of fabric while Phoebe sat on the toilet. She felt a relief as instinctive as breathing. Her sister had needed her; she had come back.

"I saw you dancing with Nicky," said Phoebe. "He's certainly gotten handsome."

"Yes," Astra said. The idea of trying to tell Phoebe what had happened, of trying to put words to it, felt impossible right now. "I don't think he knows anyone else here."

"Well, you're the maid of honor, so that makes you extra sexy—I bet he's super into you."

"As I remember, the only person he's had a crush on in this family is you," Astra said.

Phoebe laughed. "You know what Eli told me?"

"What?"

"He said, 'I was so worried you'd look like some meringue with poofy hair, like not yourself, and instead you just look like the perfect version of you.'"

"Jesus."

"I know."

"Marry that man, Phoebe!" she said, and they laughed again.

When they came out of the bathroom, the band was playing "Billie Jean," and Astra watched as a circle of Eli's college classmates formed around him. Eli was an excellent dancer; he didn't take himself too seriously. Matthew joined him in the middle and started doing the Russian squat, kicking out his legs with a look of total seriousness that made everyone crack up. There was a playfulness, an affection between these men that Astra found incredibly moving.

The wedding was in its final stages now. Astra had noticed a few of her parents' older friends leaving, even though the cake hadn't been cut yet. That was the final signpost, and then it would be over.

Astra stood just to the side as Eli and Phoebe gamely held on to a large silver knife together, sawing through the thick hide of frosting. The guests cheered, and then the cake was wheeled away. A minute later, a small dark-suited army of servers fanned out, carrying dainty slices on small white plates.

Astra smiled as a server offered her a slice, and then started to scan the room for Nick. She felt a hand on her shoulder and turned.

"Astra, have you seen Allie?" It was her aunt, Elizabeth. "I've been looking all over for her."

"Not since the speeches," said Astra. "Let me ask my mom—I saw them talking a little while ago." She'd actually seen them together before she and Nick left the tent, when Allie had caught her eye and raised her eyebrows, gesturing to Nick, and then given her a thumbs-up.

"Thanks, sweetheart. If you see her, just let her know I'm looking for her."

"Of course."

Allie was four years younger than Astra. They'd been very close growing up, but high school, when four years stretches to its farthest possible length, had created a distance.

She found her mother sitting with Eli's parents, and quickly explained she was looking for Allie.

"Your niece?" Eli's mother, Mrs. Friedman, said, looking at Thea. "I saw her leave the tent a few minutes ago."

"Thanks so much, Sarah. I just need to go say goodbye to a few guests," her mother said. "Astra, can you help me up?"

Thea hooked her arm over her daughter's and stood slowly. The way she leaned on her, Astra could tell how tired her mother was. "I can go find her, Mommy, there's no need for you to get up," said Astra.

"Honestly, I could use the break," her mother said. "Let's step outside and get some fresh air."

Outside the tent a line of tiki torches led back up toward the house, where the cars and shuttle buses were parked.

"Not that way," her mother said, turning them away from the torches and into the cool dark. "I'm not sure I can handle any more well-wishers right now. Let's just walk toward the pond and take the back way to the house. I think maybe I'm done for tonight."

"Of course, it's probably past all our bedtimes," Astra said. Inside, she felt nervous, leading her mother as she walked so slowly next to her. What if she didn't get back in time to say goodbye to Nick? She'd glimpsed him once, back in the tent, and felt such a secret, fierce happiness she'd blushed.

About twenty feet from the tent, the ground began to slope, and Astra navigated it carefully. She could feel her mother leaning more and more on her arm. As they got closer to the pond, she could hear a splash in the water, followed by another rhythmic splash. Someone was swimming.

"Oh, god, has the skinny dipping started already?" Astra said. "I heard some of Eli's friends joking about it earlier, when they were sweating through their jackets."

But her mother didn't say anything. She was silent, listening. Astra could still hear someone kicking through the water, but no shouts or joking around. It sounded like it was just one person, and Astra thought of the one rule that, from when they were small, had been beaten into the girls. Never go swimming alone.

"Astra, can you still hear the splashing?" her mother asked.

"I can, Mommy," she said.

"Okay then," her mother said. "Let's go embarrass this poor person and get them out."

They walked down toward the water, and Astra's mother started calling, "Hello, whoever is in there, could you come out please?" But the sound had stopped.

"I think you scared them, Mommy," Astra said. "They're probably just hiding by the ladder."

"I'm sure they are," her mother said. "I'll wait here, but I need you to run back to the tent, sweetheart. Try to find your father, or Elizabeth, and bring them down here now."

"What? I can't leave you," Astra said, confused.

"You'll be too slow saddled with me. Go now, Astra—run." Her mother's voice changed and shifted in register—urgent, clear, with no grace note at the end. Astra knew this voice, it was the one her mother used on the phone with the hospital, the voice of the surgeon.

She turned and ran.

Chapter Thirteen

Once Astra was gone, it felt even darker to Thea than before. She almost regretted sending Astra back. She should have asked her daughter to run down to the dock and look for the swimmer, but instead, Thea had sent her back to get the grown-ups. Not because Thea didn't trust her daughter's competence, but because she'd felt a reflexive parental impulse to protect her. What had occurred to Thea when she heard the splashes, but apparently not to Astra, was that they still hadn't found Allie.

Recently, Elizabeth had confided in Thea about how hard it had been with Allie since she and William had told her they were getting separated.

"It's a little embarrassing," she said. "Your girls are keeping it together while you're sick, and Allie is screaming at me that her life is ruined because her dad has moved to a house five blocks away."

"It's good she feels like she can get mad at you," Thea said. "No one yells at me anymore because, you know, I have *cancer*. I miss the fights, frankly."

Thea took another few steps toward the water.

"Whoever is in there, please come out now!" she called. Nothing.

"Allie, is that you swimming? Can you come out now?"

Thea felt the same feeling she would have in the operating room when a surgery that was supposed to be routine suddenly skidded sideways. Those were always the scariest—the look on the resident's face, the urgent conversation with a bewildered family member or spouse. She felt that now. What she had expected, when they'd first heard the splashing, was to embarrass some young person. Instead, all she saw was the awful, calm surface of the water.

How long had it been since Thea had been in an operating room? Two years? Her vision narrowed, sharp and precise, she looked at each swath of the water as if it were a grid. Her eyes had adjusted to the dark, she could make out the short, narrow dock. And then she saw Allie, floating face down by one of the wooden pilings. She must have swum under the dock without realizing it, come up, hit her head, and knocked herself out.

"Elizabeth! Astra!" she yelled and then she walked toward the dock. She must not fall; she must not pass out. She could do this.

She reached the railing by the small gazebo and held on, pulling herself arm over arm, until she heard the sound of running behind her.

Chapter Fourteen

Nick could not find Astra. Inside, the crowd was beginning to thin out, and he could see Phoebe and Eli hugging and saying goodbye to a knot of older guests.

Then he saw her, running into the tent from the same exit where they had left together an hour ago, clearly looking for someone. He waved, and when she saw him, he realized he was not the person she was looking for.

"Astra!" he called, and she stopped. Her face looked strained. "Hey," he said, when he reached her. "I've been looking for you. My mom and I are leaving soon and I wanted—"

"Nick, can you go outside, back to the pond"—her voice caught a little, he thought she was going to tell him to wait for her there, he could feel his face flushing—"and find my mom? She's down there, and I need to find my aunt. Please, just can you run down there and make sure she's okay?"

"Of course, Astra—"

"Thank you!" She grabbed his hands; she looked so serious, and then she was gone, weaving through the crowd.

Nick walked outside, retracing his steps from earlier in the evening. It felt darker now, as if the night had come on in earnest. A lantern with one skinny bulb hung off the gazebo, throwing off a shallow pool of light. And then he saw Astra's mother, holding onto the railing of the dock and pulling herself along, one hand over the other. He could tell, even at this distance, the effort it was taking, and he wondered why she was so determined, where she was trying to go. He sprinted toward her.

~

Thea realized it was Nick Rosenfeld, not Astra or Elizabeth, emerging from the dark.

"Nick!" she cried, before he could say anything. "There! By the far side of the dock! My niece is in the water, you have to pull her out!"

"Allie?" he said, and there was a look of panic on his face, and then he shucked off his blazer and dove into the water. Allie was about thirty feet away, and Thea thought it would be fastest if Nick ran down the dock, but as he cut through the water, his arms flashing up and down, she thought she had never seen someone swim so fast.

Thea continued pulling herself along, hanging onto the railing. "Elizabeth!" she yelled again. By the time she got to the end of the dock, Nick had dragged Allie out of the water. She saw him hold his hand over her mouth to check her breathing, the way they taught it now in CPR. "She's not breathing!" he yelled, and she saw him thread a fist through the fingers of her other hand, preparing to do chest compressions.

"Run to the house and call 911," Thea said, her voice taking on natural authority the way it did in her operating room. "It's 43 Farmington Road, tell them it's a half mile from the Texaco."

"I need to do CPR," Nick said.

"I'm going to do the CPR," she said. "Now help me down alongside her, then go to the house and call 911."

He froze. "Now!" she yelled, and he jumped up and held her arm, steadying her as she knelt. He was surprisingly strong. Thea tilted back her niece's head, did two breaths—people never tilted the head back far enough, they were afraid of shutting off the airway, a common misconception—then started the compressions. Nick sprinted to where his jacket lay crumpled up on the dock, and when he came back, he was carrying a cell phone. "It's my dad's; he let me borrow it," he said, and Thea heard him make the call and say the address correctly. She was almost at thirty compressions, and she realized she was going to run out of strength.

"Nick, come over here."

"They want me to stay on the line," he said.

"You can do both," she said, and he came over. "Sit next to me, and take over doing the compressions," she said, after she had done the breaths. He did. "You're going too slow, do it to my count, you need to compress her chest more, it doesn't matter if you break some ribs. We've got to keep the blood circulating and keep her alive."

She counted to thirty. "Okay, stop, I'm doing the breaths," she said. "Okay, start again." And he did. "That's better," she said. "Good. Keep it up."

Her niece smelled of pond water and bourbon. If Allie had alcohol in her system, it was even worse than she thought, and she willed the ambulance to come, even as she knew the narrow, one-lane roads it had to travel meant it would be several more minutes.

She heard steps on the dock. Astra and Elizabeth. "Alexandra!" She heard her sister scream, and it was perhaps the most terrible sound she had ever heard. For the last few years, she and Elizabeth had struggled with her diagnosis, why one sister was marked for this horror and another wasn't, but now, in a moment, everything felt reversed.

"The paramedics are on their way," she said to her sister.

"Thea, please save her. Please save her." Next to her Thea could feel Nick shaking; his face as white as paper, but he kept up with the chest compressions. It had been about two minutes. Without saying anything, Astra turned and sprinted back toward the tent. Thea had no chance to call after her.

She did two more breaths. Nick started the compressions. Two and a half minutes.

"Move over," she said to Nick, and he looked up, startled, but did as he was told. She thought, for the first time, that her niece was going to die, and she didn't want Nick to be the one doing CPR when it happened. He looked so young, and stricken, she felt she had to spare him.

Then Astra was back, carrying a small square box. "It's the defibrillator," she said. "There was one in the tent." She could have wept at her daughter who had been so responsible, so grave in emergencies, ever since she was small.

The AED was in the tent because Thea had insisted on it—it was the only thing she ever told the wedding planner was a nonnegotiable, the need for a defibrillator in the tent if her daughter was getting married at least thirty minutes from a good hospital. And Astra remembered, when Thea had forgotten.

"Bring it here," Thea said, and she noticed that Astra's hands were steady while she put it down next to her mother, and Thea attached the pads to Allie's chest and turned the machine on. She delivered the first shock. Nothing.

Her sister had now started to keen, a low, wordless wailing. "Elizabeth, go up and wait for the ambulance, so they know where to come," Thea said, but her sister shook her head.

"I can't leave," she said.

"I'll go," said Astra, and as she stood, Thea's eyes filled with tears. She was known for her unsentimentality in the operating room ("hard as nails, that one," the attending physician had said during her residency, and she could tell he did not mean it as a compliment), but when it came time to deliver bad news to families, she always did it herself.

She delivered another shock. Nothing.

"Come on, Allie," Thea yelled, and she made a fist with her hand and brought it down on Allie's chest. It was like hitting a sack of grain. The driveway was silent, no red flashing lights, no sirens, and Astra, instead of running up to the house, had frozen next to her mother. They were all waiting.

"Goddammit, Allie, come on!" Thea yelled, bringing her fist down a second time. "Don't you die on us!" She raised her arm again, and then Allie's chest rose on its own, a deep, shuddering breath. She started coughing up water and Elizabeth ran to her daughter and cradled her in her arms, sobbing, while Thea slumped back, exhausted. Astra put her arms around her, and she leaned back into her daughter.

"You saved her, Mom," Astra said. "You saved her." Thea knew it was the AED, and not her fist, that had brought her niece back, but she said nothing. She would give her daughter, and herself, this moment. Astra was looking at her, and in her face burned something she had not seen since her daughter was a child, a look of love so fierce, and absolute, that it seemed impossible another human being could love you this way. "We saved her," Thea said, and she put her hand over her daughter's, and closed her eyes.

Chapter Fifteen

Nick stood at the end of the dock. He had run up and met the EMTs—most of the guests were already gone, at least the Ericksons had been spared that—and brought them down to the dock. They had put Allie on a stretcher and taken her and Elizabeth to the hospital in an ambulance. Afterward, Astra's mother had put her hand on his arm and said, "You did well."

He looked back at the dock, the gazebo, the bench. What was it, two hours ago, an hour ago, that he had held Astra there? The thought was too painful, he could only brush against it before skittering away.

And Astra. She had thrown her arms around him and whispered, "Thank you," before walking up to the ambulance with her mother. She didn't know yet. No one knew yet.

Suit yourself. That's what he'd said to her when she plucked the drink out of his hand. He hadn't tried to stop her; he'd let her walk off in the dark, to the pond. He, Nick, had done that.

He looked back at the water. God, what Astra's mother had done. Kneeling there on the dock as her sister screamed, keeping her voice steady as an airline pilot's as she told him what to do, bringing her niece back—that was real. It could have been the only thing she had done in her life, and it would have made it a good life, a worthy life. He now understood why he had fallen so hard for Astra. She had grown up in this family, and that had made her a good person, strong and not brittle—he could tell this the way any child who has not grown up in a happy family can tell. And in those moments when he could have followed her back into the tent, but did not, he had felt, amid all his desire for her, a tiny prick of envy.

Someone was standing behind him. He turned, and saw Astra, about ten feet away. She no longer looked as she did at the wedding. The joy on her face was replaced by exhaustion, and she looked plainer, falling just to the other side of pretty. Her wilted dress, her bare feet, her hair falling out of its pinned-up braid—it was like a caricature of the messy beauty of girls at the end of a party. Instead of the carefree look of someone who had danced the night away at her sister's wedding, Astra looked like a woman whose girlhood had ended that night.

He longed for her, even then.

~

"Hey, you," he said.

"Hey," she said back. "Nick, you were amazing back there—" He tried to cut her off, part of him couldn't bear to hear her praise him, but she held up her hand. "No, just let me say this. You were amazing. You helped save Allie. I know that was a lot more than you bargained for when I asked you to look for my mom, and I'm just so sorry you got pulled into all of this."

The way she was looking at him, it killed him. "Your mom was the amazing one," he said, and it was the truth. "She saved her. She saved all of us." He meant it. If Allie had died, that was not something he could have come back from.

She took another step toward him, and he caught her in his arms and kissed her, feeling how warm she was against his body. He didn't even realize until then how chilled he was in his wet clothes.

He kissed her neck, the delicate skin of her collarbone above the neckline of her dress, and then he wrapped her into him and just held her against him. He could feel the damp from his shirt soaking into her dress, but neither of them moved.

Nick finally stepped back. “It’s late,” he said. “Let me walk you up to the house. Can I call you tomorrow?”

“Yes,” she said. “I would love that. Or we can make a plan right now, because tomorrow’s already here, I think.” She smiled, this sweet smile, and Nick smiled back. He felt wild, drunk. Were you allowed to feel this happy after something so terrible had happened? He didn’t know.

“And I’m going to let Allie know what you did,” Astra said. “I’ll make sure my mom calls as well to let you know how she’s doing.”

Nick felt his body change. He didn’t answer, and Astra stopped and looked at him with a worried expression.

“What is it?”

“Nothing,” he said. “It’s nothing, I just—it was just so horrible tonight, what almost happened.”

“I know,” she said. “And what scares me so much is we actually got the good version of the ending.” She made a face. “I imagine this isn’t the fun wedding fling you were hoping for.” She was trying to be funny, but her voice sounded strained.

Nick stopped, took her in his arms, and kissed her so hard he could tell he startled her. She tried to say something, but he just kept kissing her until finally she was kissing him back, meeting his intensity, and he was the one who finally broke it off.

She was looking up at him with a look of such unguarded desire, he wanted to fix it in his mind forever. “Nick, thank you,” she said. “I know I keep saying it but—thank you. I don’t know what we would’ve done if you hadn’t pulled her out.”

Nick looked past Astra, to the tent still lit up against the night, bright and blazing like a carnival. He hated lying. Not because he was such a good person, but because it was like biting into something rotten. Even his father, when he started having an affair, had come right home and told Nick’s mother about it. Nick had been furious at him, but his father had looked at him and said, “I’m already doing one terrible thing, Nick. I don’t want to do two.”

"I gave Allie the drinks," Nick said, turning back to Astra and looking straight at her. "Not at first, I told her no, but she was persistent, and I thought, it's a wedding, she's been drinking already," he said. Astra was looking at him, her face arranged in an expression of understanding, as if she were trying to figure out what he was saying.

"And then—she asked me to come outside for a cigarette, and I did. She was really upset over her parents' divorce. I tried to get her to come back inside, but she wouldn't." His voice was vibrating with pain, and Astra took his hands in hers. He told her how Allie said she was going to the pond, but he didn't believe her, didn't think she'd do it. How he'd just walked away. He was surprised, how little he tried to defend himself. But it was almost as if telling the story was a way to actually confront what he'd done. He hadn't stopped Allie. He hadn't stopped her from going to the water.

Nick saw the words register on her face, and what he held on to was—even as the way she looked at him changed, and even as it broke his heart—he didn't regret telling her. He didn't regret it at all.

~

The look of misery on Nick's face was so profound Astra's first thought was to comfort him.

"Nick, Allie was already drinking. She's not a stranger to a cocktail. And we don't know what happened when she went into the pond."

He was silent, and in that silence she felt awful. She imagined trying to tell her mother and aunt what Nick had done. *She would have gotten the drinks anyway, Aunt Elizabeth. We don't know what happened . . .* But they did know. Allie almost drowned. Astra felt a hot, bright shame.

And yet, the thought that made her feel sick was how much, in that moment, she wanted to be the person who didn't care. She wanted to be the person who didn't care that the man she was falling for had done this. Didn't care that he'd let Allie wander off drunk into the dark. That's how much she wanted to be with him.

He had told her, and that had taken guts. She could tell her mother what happened, explain Nick's side, give him credit for being honest. If Allie woke up and had a different version, well, they would deal with that then.

But as her brain churned through what he'd said, another thought took hold of her. What had actually happened between Nick and Allie? Why was he out in the dark, talking to Allie about her parents' divorce? He had just been outside with Astra. He'd told no one but her about his parents' divorce, and then fifteen minutes later he's drinking and smoking and communing with Allie, sharing with Allie? Her conversation with Nick that night had seemed like something precious and rare, that was only for her. Maybe that wasn't true.

She leaned over and put her hands on her knees.

Nick was beside her instantly, holding her shoulders. "Are you okay?" She didn't answer.

"I'm so sorry, Astra," he said. "I know it's a lot to take in." But his voice had changed, he sounded relieved. She had told him it was okay, and he had believed her.

"I think I might throw up," she said, but she started to cry instead, long, strangling sobs. He put his arms around her. She let him, and it felt good. She wanted to just stay here, sobbing, with him holding her.

"I wish I didn't know. I wish you hadn't told me," she said. "She's my cousin."

Nick rubbed her back in small circles, while his other arm was around her shoulders. "I know Astra," he said. "I know. But like you said, she'd already been drinking."

This was the point when she could have turned to him, let him hold her. What would come would come. Instead, she straightened and stepped away from him.

"Nick, she's only sixteen," she said.

Nick opened his mouth to say something, then changed his mind. After a few seconds he said, "She said she was eighteen," he said. And then softly, "I'm so sorry, Astra."

"Why were you even talking with her?" she said, more sharply than she intended. It was as if she had to punish him, after her earlier disloyalty to Allie. She felt, side by side, her desire for Nick and her need to be loyal to her family tearing at each other.

Nick stepped back. He looked miserable, but also confused.

"Well, if she's only sixteen, where the hell were her parents!"

She almost hated him for saying it, though he had a point, she knew it, and this made her angrier.

"I don't know!" she said. "I don't know what they were doing. But I mean, what were you doing? Why were you turning her into your drinking buddy?" She knew this was unfair, and yet it made her feel good, to say it.

Nick looked away. "Astra, the only person I've wanted to be with, this entire night, is you."

She thought of the expression that had flashed over Nick's face when she had told him she had to leave the gazebo to go back to the wedding, to her sister. It was arrogant, hard, like a mask. But then it had melted away and he had taken her hand. This person, cut open, standing in front of her now, this is who he really was.

"Can I still call you, when I'm back in New York?" he said.

She knew, if she said yes, that he would wrap her in his arms, crush her against him, that he would put his mouth on hers and kiss her out of adoration, and relief, and gratitude.

Standing there in the dark, she felt the power she had over him, and she hated it. She would throw it off her if she could. But he just stood there, waiting for her answer, in the dark.

Part II: The Promise

Chapter Sixteen

November 1995
New York City

Nick woke up in his childhood bedroom, with the same white cube of an alarm clock he'd had since elementary school, blinking at him.

He got dressed and brushed his teeth. As always, it took a few minutes for the surprise to wear off that he was here, at home on the Upper West Side, and not downtown. He had deferred from NYU Law for a year, told his parents he wanted to work as a paralegal in order to get some experience before going back to school, but it was a stall. His old self—intact, confident, dealing with the unremarkable catastrophe of his parents' divorce—that person would be at NYU right now. But he was not that person anymore. He wasn't even interested in pretending to be.

He remembered Astra standing in front of him, waiting for her to speak, after he'd confessed to giving Allie the drinks. She looked so hurt, but also there was such a look of compassion on her face, he thought she was going to forgive him. It was like a door swinging back open.

"Nick? Are you there?"

It was his mother calling.

"Yes, Mom? I'm up—you can come in."

She opened the door tentatively, with a look on her face he couldn't read.

"What is it?" he said.

"Thea Erickson is on the phone for you," she said.

Chapter Seventeen

Thea put down the thermometer and recorded her temperature in the notebook she kept by the bed. She had done this for two years now—her cancer diary, she called it—a list of her daily temperature, medications, procedures, doctor's visits. Occasionally she scribbled little notes: *felt especially poked and prodded today—also why is the temperature in the imaging rooms like the arctic tundra? Dr. Kelly is so brisk in his manner. I know he must be a good doctor or else he wouldn't have any patients.* The pages had a comforting monotony to them, but she knew one day the notebook would just end in a blank page, like a ship's log lost at sea.

As a doctor, she couldn't tolerate wild hopes. She realized now she would have liked to, to keep hoping straight up to the end, like a car flying off a cliff.

The phone on Thea's bedside table rang. She picked up.

"Mrs. Erickson?" a voice said. "My name is Betty. I'm with the hospital scheduling office?"

"It's Dr. Erickson. Yes?"

"I'm so sorry, Dr. Erickson, that's what I meant."

"Not a problem at all, how can I help?" Though it felt like a little bit of a problem. This was Columbia Presbyterian, the hospital where she had worked for decades. And now she was just Mrs. Erickson, cancer patient. She would tell Teddy, not because she wanted to get this Betty person in trouble, but because they could share a dark laugh over it.

"I'm calling to schedule you to come in for your chemo pump replacement. Would Monday, November 10 work?"

"No, that won't work. How about the Tuesday of that week?"

Monday of course would work; she had no social calendar these days. But Tuesdays were a better day for surgical procedures, even small ones. People were fresh from the weekend, they had time to get readjusted to work on Monday, and it was far enough from Friday that Dr. Kelly would be in town if anything went wrong. Thea knew this, and it felt good to know it, the accumulated wisdom of three decades of practicing medicine.

About five minutes later, the phone rang again. It was her mother. She called Thea weekly, on Fridays, and Thea had forgotten. Most people she knew called their mothers, but in her life it was the opposite. Her mother preferred to do the calling herself.

"Hello, dear, how are you?"

"I'm not great today, actually," she said. Why she felt moved to speak plainly with her eighty-year-old mother, after a lifetime of speaking in code, she couldn't say.

"Oh?" her mother said. "I'm sorry to hear that. Why?"

Because I'm dying. "I'm not sure. I guess I feel a little low today."

There was a pause on the other end of the line. Thea knew every flavor of silence with her mother—the silence of withheld praise; the avoidance of loving words, given so easily by other people's mothers; the lack of talk about any function of the body, including dying. Thea's illness was a strictly forbidden topic between them. She waited for her mother to say something cheery as she glided onto the next subject.

"You do sound low. I'm coming over."

"Oh, Mom, it's okay. You don't need to come over. You're still recovering from your hip surgery."

"Don't make me sound so old. I'm on my way now. I'm going to put on my coat and take a taxi crosstown and I'll be there in fifteen minutes." Her mother said *crosstown* even though she was traveling from Park Avenue to East End.

When the bell rang, Thea rose slowly to get it. It took her so much time to walk to the door she thought her mother might ring again, but she didn't.

She opened her door, and there was her tall, bony mother, in her tweed skirt and the sensible shoes that a nurse might've worn in a World War II medic ward. She was carrying the same purse she'd had for thirty-five years, a beige leather half-moon with a buckle and long strap. The first time Farris had seen her parents' vast prewar apartment on Park Avenue, when she traveled home with Thea for Thanksgiving, she'd said, "Mrs. Loomis, why do you carry that tatty purse every day when you have all this money? Are you worried someone's going to find out?" There had been a stunned pause, and then everyone had howled with laughter. How she missed Farris.

"Althea," her mother said. It was her real name, though only her mother used it. "How are you?"

"I'm okay, Mom. It's good to see you."

It was. Here she was, in her fifties, glad to see her mother.

"Well, I thought you might need a little pick-me-up," said her mother, walking in. "Why don't you put your feet up in the living room while I make us some tea? Do you still keep the Earl Grey above the toaster?" Thea nodded, then sank into the chintz sofa and immediately regretted it. The pillows were so deep she wondered if she would be able to get up again.

"How are the girls doing?" her mother called from the kitchen, where Thea heard her filling the kettle, the delicate clink of teacups on a tray. "How's Tom?"

"They're good," Thea said, and then, when her mother appeared with the tea things, she was gripped by a sudden wild desire to tell the truth.

Early on in her diagnosis, her mother had seemed offended at the idea that Thea could die, as if it reflected poorly on both of them. "Oh, that's ridiculous," she had said, when Thea broached the topic. "You're not some tubercular woman in a novel." Since then, they rarely spoke about her illness, and when Thea did give her mother an update, she used her surgeon's voice. But something shifted in her now.

"I'm worried about all of them, actually," she said. "The girls, but especially Tom. I feel like I'm leaving him holding the bag."

"Because you're the one who has colon cancer?" her mother said, as she added sugar and milk to Thea's cup and handed it to her. "Do you think he wants to swap places with you?"

"That's not what I meant—"

"I know what you meant," her mother said. "Have you talked to him about it?"

"A little. We talk about the girls a lot, but as for what happens after"—she made a circular motion with her hands—"he doesn't really want to get into it."

"Well, that sounds reasonable," said her mother. "I'm not sure how much is to be gained by talking about it, but I understand why you are worried. You're the center of the family. It's not like after you are gone it will be the same family, just muddling along with a vacancy. They'll have to figure out who they are without you."

Thea looked at her mother. Never in her life had she spoken in this way, a way that suggested she observed Thea's life closely, in a meaningful way.

"I hadn't thought about it like that," she said finally.

"Do you think Tom can become the center of the family?" her mother asked. The way her mother said it, it was clear what she thought, and Thea's loyalty forced her to speak sharply.

"He can do it. He's always been very engaged with the girls. He takes parenting seriously."

Thea remembered early on in her illness, during her first stay in the hospital, when Tom brought a little canvas tote with all the things she had asked for—shampoo, toothpaste, and extra socks—and how pleased with himself he was. Tom was not normally oriented to detail, but she could tell he was trying to be the good patient's good husband.

"He's incredibly loyal, yes," her mother said in a neutral voice. "But he'll have to become the decision-maker. That might be hard for him."

Thea understood this; it was something she worried about too. Tom had been a wonderful husband and father, but he could be passive. Maybe it was easier for men to be passive because either way, people assumed they were in charge.

"Well, the girls are grown," said Thea. "It's not like he has to schedule the pediatrician appointments."

"What a relief," said her mother with a smile. "I always knew if I got hit by a bus, you children would never go to the dentist again. Can you imagine your father, hustling you up to Dr. Strife's office?" Her mother laughed. She rarely did, but when it happened, it had a generous, headlong quality, lasting long after others' subsided.

"You've raised two girls who take after you, Thea, and that's going to serve them well," her mother continued. "They don't make a big fuss over things, the way that's so fashionable now. They get on with things. They have a sense of themselves to fall back on."

"But maybe that's what I'm worried about, Mom," Thea said, and there was a vulnerability in her voice as she leaned forward, holding her teacup, that felt new and unfamiliar. "How hard they will work, especially Astra, to hold it all together. They should know they don't have to do that."

"Would you prefer they just lie in bed all day?"

"No, but there's a balance."

"Ah," her mother said slowly. "And you think I know nothing about that?"

"Oh, Mom," Thea said, and she laughed. "You think talking about feelings is vulgar. Let's be honest."

Her mother watched her closely, and Thea found herself wondering, not for the first time, what kind of doctor her mother would have been, if that path had been open to her.

"I think talking about feelings in a certain way is vulgar, yes," her mother said.

"Well, I never knew there was a distinction," Thea said, and she looked down, and then back at her mother. "I wish we talked like this more, Mom."

"We talk every week."

"Like this, about real things." She paused, and when she realized her mother was not going to speak, she plunged on. "We never talk about my illness."

"What's the point of doing that? Is it going to make you feel better?"

Thea suddenly felt so tired she thought she might just lean back, into the pillowy cushions, and go to sleep. The fact is, talking about her illness with her mother probably wouldn't make her feel better.

"Well, you never talk about how you're feeling either, Mom," Thea said. "I'd love to hear about that, too, and while it may sound ridiculous, in my current state, I worry about you. You lost Dad last year, and now I'm sick. Who's going to take care of you?"

"Do I seem, to you, like a person who needs someone else to take care of them?"

"Actually, no," Thea said. "But there will come a time when you will. And it would be nice, for once, to hear about how it makes you feel that I'm sick." After all this time, she still longed for her mother's love, for her to express it fiercely. Maybe everyone did. "I know you think I indulged Phoebe and Astra sometimes, but they know, down to their bones, how I feel about them."

Her mother looked at her frankly. "Why would I need to say it? Why does everything need to be said? You are my child, of course I love you."

"Well, Mom," Thea said. "I cannot tell you how much it means to me to hear that." And she stared down at her hands and started crying, crying with great heaving sobs. After a moment of stunned quiet, her mother stood, and Thea almost expected her to let herself out in the face of such ungovernable emotion. Instead, she came and sat beside her.

"I am going to say this so you hear it, Thea. My heart will break when you are gone."

Chapter Eighteen

Ever since the wedding, Thea had been having strange dreams.

One specific dream she had several times. She saw Astra running, alone, through a kind of overripe, fairytale garden. Something was behind her, something Thea couldn't see, and there was a look of such raw fear on Astra's face that Thea always cried out, waking Tom, who told her she was having a nightmare.

But the dream did not feel like a nightmare. It felt—and as a woman of science she knew how ridiculous this sounded, but there it was—it felt like a sign. During her long illness, Thea had come to understand that maybe she'd dismissed too quickly the other ways the body tried to communicate.

For instance, she had seen so many patients in pain—real pain—for which she could find no medical cause. And she could not explain why, when someone touched a certain spot on Thea's foot—she had done regular therapeutic massages since she had gotten sick; a colleague in the oncology department had recommended them—she felt like she might scream out.

Her massage therapist, a kind young woman with tattoos all down her arms that Thea did not understand, had told her this was the part of her foot that correlates to the reproductive system, and that in some of her patients, it became sensitive after they lost their mothers. Had that happened to Thea recently, she asked. And Thea, lying there on the table, thought the question both incredibly moving and unprofessional at the same time.

The doctors had warned her that the medications she was on could have these kinds of side effects. But still, deep down, she felt the dream about Astra was a message. A warning, but of what, Thea didn't know.

~

The week before Thanksgiving, Thea finally made up her mind to call Patty. She and Patty had spoken only once since Phoebe's wedding, when Thea called to let her friend know Allie was going to be fine. Patty had broken down into a fit of crying, which Thea thought was a bit much—it was her niece who had almost died, after all. But Thea also understood. Patty was crying for Nick. There would be no long-lasting consequences for his role in that terrible night. At least not medical ones.

She dialed the number, expecting to leave a message, but Patty picked up.

"Hello, Patty, it's Thea," she said, after a moment. "How are you?"

"Thea," Patty said, her voice warm and a bit uncertain. "It's so nice to hear from you. How are you?"

"I'm doing okay," said Thea. The inadequacy of the word hung between them, but Patty did not push. "How are things going for you?"

"Work is work. John is John," Patty said briskly.

"And Nick?" Thea asked. "I was hoping to get his number at law school from you, actually. I need to ask him about something."

Patty was quiet. "Nick is actually still here, at home. He deferred for a year, decided to stay in the city and work as a paralegal."

"Oh, I didn't know," Thea said.

"John's taking it about as well as you can imagine."

"I'm sorry to hear that, Patty, I know that must be hard."

"He hasn't really been the same since the summer," said Patty, and then trailed off. Thea wondered if her friend was going to start crying.

"Patty, he'll get through this," she said.

But the moment of vulnerability had passed. Patty's voice cooled, and she told Thea she would go see if Nick was home. They both understood what she was actually saying, which was she would see whether or not Nick would come to the phone.

About ten seconds later she heard quick steps, and could imagine Nick crossing the scuffed parquet of Patty's entryway, picking up the phone that sat on the little chinoiserie table where her friend kept the mail in a silver tray. It had been years since she had been to their apartment on West End, but she could picture it perfectly.

"Hello, Dr. Erickson. How are you?" came Nick's voice. "My mom said you wanted to speak with me?"

"Hello, Nick," she said. "Yes. I was hoping you might be able to meet me for dinner next week, would that be possible? I have something I need to ask you."

He paused for a second. "Yes, of course," he said, sounding surprised. "What night works for you?"

As Thea hung up the phone, she thought, whatever you might say of Nick, he was not a coward.

~

Thea had only learned the full story of what happened between Nick and Astra the morning after the wedding, when Astra appeared at her door at 7:30 a.m. and crawled wordlessly into bed beside her.

She could still see her daughter's face, the anguish on it.

"What's wrong, honeybunch?" she said.

"I couldn't sleep at all last night. My legs kept shaking," Astra said.

"That's the adrenaline," Thea said. "It used to happen to me after surgeries." She started stroking her daughter's hair. "Last night was a lot, sweetheart—it's going to take a while for all the emotions to settle."

Her daughter said nothing. "My plan is to stay in bed all day and read, if you want to join me," Thea said.

"Okay, Mommy," Astra said, and then, "Have you heard anything about Allie?"

"Yes. Elizabeth called this morning. They're keeping her one more night for observation, but she's going to be okay."

What Elizabeth had also told her, and Thea did not share with Astra, is that a social worker had come that morning and asked to speak to Allie alone. "Her blood alcohol level was twice the legal limit," Elizabeth had explained, in a devastated voice. "Allie told the social worker she didn't remember anything." Thea had felt deep compassion for her sister, and under that, a ping of satisfaction that the hospital was doing its job.

"So, she's going to be okay," Astra said. "Thank god." And then she moved her head slightly, so that Thea's hand slid off it. "There's something else, too, I need to tell you—"

"Okay," Thea said.

And then her daughter told her about Nick giving Allie the drinks, and not stopping her when she ran off toward the pond.

"Are you disappointed in me?" Astra said, when she was finished.

"Disappointed in you? Why would you ever say that?"

"Because I liked him. Because—because I still like him. Even after this horrible thing."

Thea looked at her daughter closely. She was surprised to hear this of Nick, but she had also seen him on the dock and on the dance floor with Astra. She knew he was so much more than this one thing. But she could tell from her daughter's face that it was different for Astra; she was stunned into rethinking him entirely.

"Astra—" she said. "I know this is a shock, but remember Nick pulled Allie out of the water too. There's a lot of blame to go around here—Elizabeth, me and your father, too, frankly, as the hosts."

Her daughter shook her head fiercely, as if refusing to allow that. And then she burst into sobs.

"I just felt so happy, Mommy," Astra said. "He helped save Allie, he seemed to care about me so much, I couldn't believe it was happening, that something amazing might come out of that night of horrors."

Thea remembered watching Nick's face when he was with Astra. She had felt—what had she felt? Such happiness, but underneath that, a sort of longing. In addition to being present at Phoebe's wedding, she thought she might get the chance to see who Astra would love. She had been too greedy, she thought.

"Sweetheart, of course you were happy. Anyone could see how taken with you he was. Nick made a mistake, but you don't have to cast him off into the wilderness."

Astra looked at her almost angrily. "What if Allie had died?"

"Let's just be so grateful, for everyone, that she didn't."

"But Dad would never do anything like that. You would never do anything like that."

Not like that, Thea thought. But she had done things that were wrong, things that would surprise her daughter. Her daughter's goodness was beautiful, but it was also black and white, and Thea had always thought she'd have more time to guide Astra, to help her be a little less rigid in her thinking. This unfinished work, it haunted her.

"What did you tell him?" she asked gently.

"I told him not to call me. I said I wished I was the kind of person who could get over what he did, but I'm not," Astra said, and her voice became soft and trembly like a child's. "I'm just not that person, Mommy, but sometimes I wish I was."

She put her arms around Astra. Thea had known Nick since he was a child. After last night, she'd had a new understanding of him—he handled himself well; he could stay calm when he was scared. That told you something about a person. He had a seriousness about him that she appreciated. And yet this new revelation from Astra shifted that understanding again; it surprised her. And Astra could tell. She could always sense Thea's emotions, ever since she was a little girl, as if there were still threads that connected them.

"Astra, if you want to be with him, it doesn't make you less of a good person. Not to me. Do you understand that?"

What she wanted her daughter to know is that if this was the person she wanted to be with, Thea understood. She would back her.

But Astra said nothing. She just shook her head and then lay down next to Thea, turning her face to the wall.

Chapter Nineteen

The restaurant Thea picked for her dinner with Nick was a small Italian spot on the Upper East Side, nice but not too nice, a family place that would be quiet on a Tuesday night. She and Tom used to come here with the kids on Sunday nights, after driving back from his parents' house in New Jersey, but as she walked in now, with her cane and her soft grey fuzz of hair, no one recognized her. She had made an effort to put on a nice sweater, an English cardigan with puffed shoulders and simple brass buttons, over a navy-blue blouse, but the sweatpants she had on made any actual appearance of togetherness impossible. They couldn't be helped. Normal pants wouldn't fit over her chemo pump, which was the shape and size of a hockey puck.

"Reservation for Erickson," she told the maître d', Armand, and smiled.

"Of course, right this way," he said, nodding pleasantly. "Dr. Erickson isn't here yet."

"Actually, I am Dr. Erickson," she said, and it gave her pain to have to tell this kind man, who had known her children since they were in elementary school, this fact. She knew she was altered beyond recognition—her grey skim of hair, the skin pulled so tight against the bones of her face it looked like a mask. Vanity had not completely been washed away this late in the game, and she wondered again if she were being punished for that tiny coil of satisfaction she'd always felt for looking younger than her age, for her strong body that had made her breezy pregnancies and deliveries things of legend. Her body had never failed her, not once, until it failed her utterly.

"Oh, my goodness, of course," Armand said, and he came around the podium, took her hand in both of his, and said, "It's so good to see you again."

"It's lovely to see you again, too, Armand." And when she said his name, his eyes filled with tears.

She had arrived early, so she could be seated when Nick came in. She did not want him to see how long it took her to cross the room to their table in the back, the one in the alcove she had requested. Armand walked her over himself, and helped her, with enormous delicacy, get into her chair. It was these moments she feared, the idea that she would keel over, the knot of worry that would ignite around her. She had become a doctor because she had wanted to do that for others, not draw it on herself.

The maître d' bravely handed her the wine list. "I'll hold on to it, just in case," she said. She had stopped drinking after her diagnosis, but it felt like it would be impolite, another blow, to refuse.

Just before 7 p.m. Nick walked in. He was wearing a suit with what looked like a school tie, and instead of carrying a briefcase he had one of those soft nylon messenger bags slung over his shoulder. It reminded her of the school bags Astra and Phoebe had insisted on for school instead of backpacks—canvas saddlebags in camo green with one long strap that sawed into their shoulder and made them walk tilted slightly to the side. All the girls had them.

"Dr. Erickson, hello," he said. His hair had grown; he somehow looked younger than he had at the wedding. "It's very nice to see you."

He settled in across from her. "I haven't been here in years," he said. "Not since I was a kid. I used to love the chicken parmesan."

"Well, the menu has remained delightfully unchanged since the Carter administration, so you can still order it," she said.

He laughed. "I think I will."

He looked at her expectantly. He had, after all, no idea why he was here. She had not elaborated on the phone, and she could tell that under his polite manners, he was nervous. Perhaps he thought she was here to berate him, though what she felt for him most, when she thought about it, was compassion.

"Thank you so much for coming, Nick. I really appreciate it."

"Yes," he paused. "How is Astra?" He looked down at his plate, and then back at her.

"She's doing pretty well," she said. "I'm looking forward to her coming home, at Thanksgiving." He nodded; she could feel his disappointment, and his desire to ask more. What could she say? *She never called you, but she thinks about you all the time?*

"I'm here to ask for your help," she said.

"My help?"

"Yes."

He looked at her with interest.

She went on. "But first, I just want to say how sorry I am about everything that happened. I know, from your mom, that it's been hard for you—"

"Please," Nick said. "You don't have to say that."

He looked so sad, and she felt for him, in that moment, what she might have felt for a son.

"Nick, I'm not sure Allie would have survived if you hadn't gotten her out of the water that quickly," she said. "You stayed calm on the dock. Those things mattered."

Nick tried to say something, but she waved him off and kept talking. "And yes, I know, Astra told me about the drinks, about Allie running off to the pond. That's not what I'm here to talk about."

"You were the one who saved her," Nick said quietly. "And you also saved me, frankly. You gave me a life that is recoverable. I never thanked you for that."

Thea sat back and watched him.

"Nick, it may not be fair of me to do this," she said. "But I am going to ask you to promise me something." He looked at her, almost eagerly.

"It's something that may never come to pass," she said. "In fact, it most likely won't. But it will give me peace of mind knowing I have your word, if it does."

"Yes," he said again, and he sounded excited. Thea understood. He wanted a chance to atone. Was it fair for her to use this knowledge to extract a promise? Probably not, but she would do it anyway.

Thea told him what she wanted from him. She laid it out carefully, not caring how wild it sounded, and when she had finished, he simply looked at her. It was not what he was expecting, she knew this, but he gave her his promise. He looked right at her, and said, with emotion in his voice, that he would do this thing she asked of him. She reached out her hand, and he took it, and she told him thank you. She felt the sense of lightness that comes after discharging a burden.

Their food arrived—chicken piccata for her, the chicken parm for him—and they both paused as the plates were put down. For a few minutes they simply ate, unembarrassed by the silence.

"My parents don't know yet, but I'm not going to go to law school," Nick said suddenly. Thea leaned in, the way you do when someone is sharing a confidence. She imagined most of the diners at the tables around them assumed this was her son, this handsome young person, taking his sick mother out to dinner.

"No? If you feel that way, you should tell your mom and dad," Thea said.

"I will," he said. "I just want to give it a little more time before I ruin my mother's year again."

"She worries about you, Nick," Thea said. "Like all mothers."

"I know," he said. "But I guess if any good came out the summer, it's that I'm not sleepwalking into some life another person planned out. I realize I'm not going to make any difference in the world unless I do something I'm really passionate about."

Thea smiled. She could have used a little less of this kind of talk, but she understood it was how young people spoke now—her girls, too, sometimes.

"What will you do instead?" she asked.

"I want to go to medical school. I've started taking postbacc classes at Columbia, so I can apply next fall. Though my dad's gonna freak, obviously."

"Medical school?" Thea could not help the note of genuine pleasure that crept into her voice. Phoebe had wanted to be a doctor since she was in preschool, but the difference between the idea of a thing and the reality of it had become clear to her older daughter in college. Thea had never minded. She was proud of the girls and the different paths they had taken. And yet the way she drew forward when Nick said it, the warmth of her reaction, made her wonder if she had fooled herself all these years.

"Yes." He sounded embarrassed, but also happy. "After the wedding, I thought—that's what I want to be. Like you."

She smiled. "Well, that's very kind of you," she said. "But guilt won't get you through medical school, I can tell you that now."

"No," he said. "It's what I want."

"Well, in that case, I think you would make a good doctor." She never said this lightly, not to anyone.

The happiness on Nick's face made him look so young, so good hearted, she saw again the man her daughter had almost fallen in love with.

"Why don't we have a glass of wine?" she said, and signaled Armand.

Chapter Twenty

Thanksgiving 1995
New Jersey

Thea had put on her long puffy coat—it was like a quilt with sleeves—and walked to the tree outside their kitchen window and back, just to feel the cold on her face. It was no more than twenty yards, but she had to stop and catch her breath several times. She loved this time of year, when the air smelled cold and sharp, like cider.

"Mom! Mommy! I'm up!"

Astra was waving at her, bundled up in the plaid bathrobe she used to wear as a child, topped off by an absurd knit hat that belonged to her father. Her daughter walked out as if she was in no hurry, but Thea knew she was coming to check on her. Her family, always afraid she was about to conk out.

Astra had come home on Sunday, and it was Wednesday, the day before Thanksgiving, but she still looked exhausted. She always looked exhausted when she came home this time of year. To see her daughter's pale skin and the smudges under her eyes made Thea feel the same fierce way she did when the girls were young and hadn't gotten enough sleep—an urgent, physical need to care for them, to put them to bed, to bring them nourishing foods. Her daughter was twenty, and still she felt this way.

With Phoebe the feeling had shifted. Thea did not think of herself as the kind of person who discharged her responsibility once a child was married off, as if she was Mrs. Bennet heaving the load of five unmarried daughters. It was regressive, at best. And yet physically, she felt the care of Phoebe had passed out of her hands. What concerned her, instead, was how early marriage would go for her, with its frightening intimacy and relentless compromise. Would Phoebe think these things, which were just the signposts of the strange, wondrous agreements of marriage, meant something was wrong? She'd tried to speak to her daughter about this, but Phoebe always laughed her off. It worried her.

"Hi, honeybunch!" she said to Astra. "Did you have a good sleep?"

"I did. Totally Rip Van Winkled."

Thea smiled. "Have you had breakfast yet?"

"No, but I will. Do you want to come sit with me?"

"I'd love that."

Astra took her hand. When she was a small child, she'd liked to walk alone, but then, suddenly, they would be in a crowd, and Thea would feel a sharp pull on her handbag, or her sleeve, and it would be Astra, hanging onto her. She was always startled at how strong her daughter was.

Whether Astra actually wanted to have breakfast with her mother, or whether she was just worried Thea was overexerting herself, Thea didn't know. It didn't matter. She would take any opportunity of time with her daughters now. When they were little, the idea of quality time was all the rage among parenting circles, probably because the idea of working moms "having it all" was also in ascendence. It had taken Thea a while to realize that both ideas were absurd.

She would make special plans to take her girls to Serendipity for lunch, and they would invariably have a meltdown from sugar and overexcitement, and then in the car, racing to some appointment, is when they would actually open up to her. You could not program the time, she knew this, even though she also knew, in a moment of brisk honesty, that this was exactly what she was trying to do this Thanksgiving.

Tom hadn't wanted a large Thanksgiving, but she had insisted. They would be thirteen in all. Eli was bringing his parents, his older brother Micah and Micah's wife, Eliza, and their two young children. Elizabeth, her divorce finalized, would be flying in too, and bringing their mother out from the city. Allie would stay with her father. "She's not ready to come back. She says it feels too traumatic," Elizabeth had said, in a weary voice. Thea had not pushed.

The big idea behind this holiday, in Thea's mind, was to create a tradition that could continue without her. Recently, when she'd brought this up to Tom, he'd paused, his face neutral. "I thought it might be nice to just have our family," he said. His expression as he watched her was like the quarterback he used to be, trying to read the play.

"If we start this now, with the Friedmans, then it has precedent," she said. "It's not just a big old pity party next year."

"You mean next year, when you're not here."

"Yes, Tom."

He looked away, and she thought he must be welling up with emotion, and she moved toward him to comfort him.

"Thea, how about instead of trying to stage-manage everything after you're gone, you just try to focus on your health!" he snapped. His tone surprised her, and then she felt relief, that he could actually still get pissed off.

She could see his point, and yet she still said to him, "I'm dying either way, Tom."

She watched him deflate at her words.

"Thea, I just don't want you to wear yourself out hosting a dozen people for Thanksgiving when it can just be us. I don't want this, and Astra doesn't want it either."

"Don't bring her into it," Thea said. "That's not fair."

"Well, she doesn't! You're the one always going on about how I will need to support her when you're gone! And I know you think I'm just going to be a complete mess, and I am, but that doesn't mean I can't hold it together for our daughters."

"I don't think that," she said, but she did, a little bit.

And what Tom said was true. She was always going on about what he would need to do after her death, when Thea and Phoebe were half-orphans. By her bed, Thea kept a notebook where she wrote, night after night, guidelines for the conversations Tom would need to have with their children. She thought it was because she was abdicating her great duty, which was to shepherd them through moments of heartbreak and pain, but it occurred to her now that Tom found it presumptuous. Maybe it was. Maybe it was a monstrous presumption.

She felt how easy it would be to say yes to him, to keep this gathering small.

"Tom, how many more of these am I going to get, really?" she said.

"Okay, Thea," he said, in a soft voice, and she felt a small, sharp thrill of victory.

~

Phoebe surveyed the place cards one more time, wondering if she should move her mother-in-law farther away from her grandmother. "Grandy will be fine," her mother had said. "Noncontroversial dinner table conversation is a sacred law to her."

This was true, and yet it was hard to imagine two women more different from Mrs. Friedman and Grandy. The first time she had met Eli's mother, Mrs. Friedman had proceeded to talk about people Phoebe did not know with such stamina and detail—the Realtor who had sold them a house in Connecticut twenty-five years ago without disclosing the fact that there was mold in the basement; Micah's third-grade teacher who had wanted to put him in remedial math until she intervened—that Phoebe did not actually utter a word until thirty minutes after they sat down at the table. Mrs. Friedman's ability to talk into silences had felt so extraordinary to Phoebe she'd had to excuse herself after the main course, pretend to go to the restroom, and sit alone in the dark in Eli's childhood bedroom. He had found her there, and held out his hand to her, without saying a word. Other people's families.

And then, after that terrible night when her mother had told Phoebe and Astra her cancer was terminal, where Astra had sobbed while Phoebe sat stone faced, everything had changed. They'd made dinner plans with Eli's parents, and Phoebe had told Eli to cancel. That night, Mrs. Friedman showed up with a hamper of food and flowers. She'd hugged Phoebe, pressed her to her like a child, and then gone to the kitchen, put on an apron, and set to work heating chicken soup, chopping vegetables, and stashing various Tupperware dishes in the fridge and freezer, each with taped labels instructing her how long to put them in the oven for at what temperature. Phoebe had gone to her room to lie down, and when she returned, the kitchen was empty, the soup on a low simmer on the stove, the table set. For the next several weeks, every time Phoebe had opened a Tupperware, she had felt loved by this woman who was not her mother.

"You put Mr. Friedman next to Aunt Elizabeth?"

It was Astra, carrying a wooden spoon—she had come in from the kitchen where she was helping her father with the stuffing. Astra always helped with the meal and Phoebe did the table, a division of labor that had formed early and never been revisited.

"What, do you think it's a mistake?"

"No, I just can't picture it," she said.

"To be honest, Astra, I can't picture any of this. It feels weird."

Astra smiled. "I'm so relieved to hear you say that. I feel like it's going to be a disaster. The turkey is about twenty minutes out, I'd say."

"Roger that," Phoebe said.

~

When everyone first sat down to eat, there was no sound but the delicate clinking of knives on plates. Phoebe started to think there would be no conversation, and that she would have to say something, and then her mother-in-law turned to her grandmother and said, "Virginia, you have two daughters as doctors. What is your secret?" Phoebe tensed and waited.

Her grandmother paused and swallowed, folding her napkin. She had beautiful manners, more polished than even her own mother's lovely manners. For a long time, Phoebe had liked that her mother came from so grand a family, until she went to college and realized she should be embarrassed instead. Astra, of course, had always been embarrassed.

"I suppose my secret was doing nothing," her grandmother said. "My daughters found their own way. I could have told them how courageous I thought they were, but I think it's immodest to call your own children courageous. Isn't it just another way of complimenting yourself?"

The table laughed heartily. Phoebe watched her mother, who sat quietly with her lips in a line.

"Mom, I don't think you did nothing," her mother said, and all the heads at the table swiveled down to her end. "You certainly weren't like the other mothers growing up."

"Ah yes, that could probably be my epitaph," her grandmother said. "*Not like the other mothers*. I remember Nancy Bissell saying to me, 'Virginia, how can you march with all those wild-looking people at those Vietnam protests? Aren't you afraid?'" Her grandmother smiled, as if she were picturing Nancy Bissell right that instant.

"Were you afraid?" Eli said, and Phoebe's grandmother turned to him as if she had been waiting eighty years for someone to ask her this question.

"Well, I wasn't afraid that one of my children or nephews would be drafted, like so many people were. All of my nephews were in college or working. We knew all the right people; we could get them exceptions. But it made me feel ill, knowing all these other poor kids were getting blown to bits in the jungle."

A short silence followed this speech, as Grandy picked up her knife and fork and began eating again. Phoebe had never heard her grandmother talk about marching. Under all of Grandy's unspoken rules, did a small flame of radicalism burn? Was it that tiny fire that had pushed her mother out onto her own path? Phoebe didn't know.

Eli caught her eye and smiled. She had not told him how moved she was that his family was here, instead of having their usual traditions and their usual meal up in Connecticut. He would never say it was a sacrifice, but it was. Spending a holiday in a different home always came with an overpowering flavor of strangeness; she realized, with a bracing honesty, that it was not something she would ever have asked of hers. Each family has their own unspoken understandings, and Eli's family had shown up in force not just because they loved Eli, but because they loved her, and it was this revelation that filled her with wonder.

Chapter Twenty-One

Astra's door was closed. Thea stood outside it, leaning on her cane. It was Sunday night, and they were back in the apartment, Tom puttering around with all his prework routines. Even though she hadn't worked in over two years, Thea could still feel the muscle memory of a Sunday night—the way she used to check her calendar, put all the bills she needed to pay in a stack on her desk, make sure the girls had laid out their uniforms. That hint of melancholy at the weekend ending and the adrenaline of the week to come.

She knocked. "Astra, it's me." Astra had decided to stay tonight and drive up to school early next morning for her classes, but right after dinner, she'd gone into her room and shut the door.

Thea knocked again, then pushed the door open slowly. Her daughter was sitting on her bed, reading. It was the same bed, the same frilly yellow gingham bedspread, that Astra had had since she was ten. Thea hated it. Her dear friend, Olivia Rutledge, had been the decorator.

"Hey Mommy, what's up?" Astra said. Her voice was polite, but underneath it, Thea heard a ping of frustration.

"I just wanted to check in, sweetheart."

She walked slowly toward the bed. Thea had not been in this room for months, and she looked around at the balloon curtains that matched the bedspread, the Laura Ashley upholstered window seat with its fringed pillows. "We really should have redecorated this when you went to college," she said.

"It's okay. I don't want to change it."

"I used to worry all this frilly stuff would turn you into a ninny," Thea said. "Olivia told me I couldn't do venetian blinds in a girl's bedroom. That it was too masculine and would make your bedroom look like a bank."

"I know. And you said, 'What's wrong with that? Maybe they'll grow up to be bank presidents,'" Astra said. "And before you ask, I was listening in the hall."

"Well," said Thea, "my fears can now be put to rest." And she smiled. "No one turned into a ninny."

"No one turned into a bank president either," Astra said. "Though Phoebe seems like she might be on track to be one."

Thea heard the little current of distaste in her daughter's voice. She wondered if Astra was just waiting for her to leave.

Thea moved slowly to Astra's bed and lowered herself down onto it, using her cane for balance. Astra sat up to help her, but Thea held up her hand, "it's okay, I'm fine," she said, as she plunked down onto the mattress. For a while now, her legs had not been strong enough to sit or stand smoothly.

"I know Thanksgiving was a lot," Thea said. "There's been a lot of change, now that Phoebe's married—"

Astra's expression changed, a little whisper of contempt flashed across it. She looked like a teenager.

"If you don't want to talk about it, I understand—" Thea went on.

"God, Mom, I'm fine! Phoebe got married. It's not like she's turned into an alien or something."

Thea hesitated. With Astra, she'd always been good at feeling out her moods, but this conversation felt spiky and off-balance. She spread her hands out and smiled.

"I'm sorry, I'm making a mess of this," she said. "Do you want me to just leave you alone?"

She said this directly, without any resentment, and yet immediately, as she saw Astra's face crumple up, she realized her mistake. Her daughter felt guilty. Always, always, her daughter acted as if it was her personal job to keep the universe of this family running smoothly. And then this sense of duty supercharged when Thea got sick. It weighed on her, this burden her daughter heaved upon herself.

"No, Mom, of course not," she said softly, like a penance. "I don't want you to leave."

"Astra, I should have asked you about Thanksgiving, and I didn't," Thea said. "I'm sorry."

Astra looked down and plucked at the duvet. "It's okay, Mom. I get it. I did just want it to be us, though."

Thea nodded. "Thank you for being honest," she said. "I don't want you to ever feel like you have to tiptoe around me."

Astra didn't say anything, she seemed to be curling up into herself, and Thea was trying to search for the right words to tell her that she was allowed to feel whatever she wanted to feel, about Phoebe and holidays and what things might look like after Thea was gone. She thought so much about these conversations with her daughters, but they never came off the way they did in her head.

Instead, what Thea said was, "I'm so sorry I'm not going to be at your wedding."

Why had Thea said this? She thought about making it to Astra's college graduation; she thought about getting strong enough so they could go on a trip together, just the two of them. Her daughter was a junior in college, for god's sake, she didn't think about marriage with her. And yet, she had said it.

Astra stared at her for several seconds. Thea started to say something, but Astra cut her off.

"Don't worry, Mom," she said, in a flat voice. "I'm never going to get married."

Well, Thea thought. *At least she's not tiptoeing around me here.* She took a breath.

"Well, Astra, I understand that feeling," Thea said. "I really do. I used to feel the same way."

Her daughter looked at her now with interest, for the first time that night.

"You felt that way with Dad?" Astra said.

Thea smiled. "Oh no, not your father, I knew I would marry him the moment I met him." That was true. Thea remembered when Tom had proposed, how she'd cried out *Yes!* the minute he reached into his pocket, and how they'd laughed and laughed. *What if I'd only been reaching for my glasses?* he said.

"No, it was with someone before, my college boyfriend," Thea said. "When he got down on one knee, I was so shocked I thought maybe he was having a medical emergency. I could not fathom he was proposing."

She thought of the look on Cutter's face as he held out the ring, the little sideways jolt of fear she'd felt. What she could still recall, as if the shock had frozen the memory in place, is the feeling of having done something wrong. She must have committed some terrible error if he could think she would say yes. They had not even said I love you yet—that would have been the natural inflection point, the moment to take stock. But Cutter had skipped it. And in those first moments of panic, she could feel the need to say yes, to end this discomfort, the politeness and propriety of her whole upbringing rising within her.

"What did you do?" said Astra.

Thea thought of how she had folded Cutter's fingers back over the ring box, and for the briefest second his face had narrowed and sharpened. He looked unfriendly, even aggressive, and she'd thought, *it suits him.*

"I said no," she told her daughter. "We kept dating for a while, though. I broke up with him when I started medical school. He proposed again, one more time, after that."

"Mom!" Astra said. "I can't believe you never told me this."

Thea hesitated.

"Well, I haven't thought about it in a long time, until you said you never wanted to get married. He hasn't been part of my life," Thea said. "But that's how I felt when he asked. Something immovable and absolute telling me no."

She could still see the vase of tulips Cutter had brought her in pieces on the floor, the flowers looking skinny and helpless in a pool of water. His anger had been a relief. She didn't have to feel guilty anymore.

Astra was quiet for a while. "The only time I didn't feel that way was with Nick."

Her daughter was looking down, twisting a section of the frilly yellow duvet in her hands.

"Obviously I didn't think I was going to marry him, that would be ridiculous," Astra said. "I just felt something shifting that night—like I could have a new idea of myself. I felt I could be with someone who really understood me, who got me—because he did, Mommy—and I felt like he *wanted* to be with me, not some other version or other idea of me."

"Why would you ever think someone wouldn't want to be with the real version of you?" Thea asked. She was about to say something else, but she stopped herself. She forced herself just to listen to her daughter.

"This isn't me feeling insecure or wanting to be someone else," Astra said quickly. "And it's not that I don't think I can be loved—I know I'm loved. It's just—even before you got sick, I always felt like dating, relationships, that was more for Phoebe. I'm different; I always have been. And then when you did get sick—" Her voice changed.

"Please tell me," Thea said.

"I felt like there's something wrong with me too," Astra said softly, as if she was worried it would hurt her mother to hear this. "Something inside me that doesn't work right. This broken piece of me. Phoebe doesn't have it, but I do."

Thea looked at her daughter, her beautiful daughter, burning up with health. Thea was a doctor, she knew there was nothing physically wrong with Astra. But even in this wild feeling Astra was expressing,

Thea felt a kinship with her youngest child. Hadn't Thea been formed by her mother's love too? Until she met Tom, she'd believed she could only be loved for her best parts. But Tom loved her flaws just as fiercely. Tom had showed her a different kind of love, and she had made it her own, turned it on her daughters, and loved them to their last atom.

And now Astra, the recipient of that love, felt her mother's illness so keenly she believed something was broken inside her. It made Thea want to weep. She spoke to her daughter now in her gentlest voice.

"But you didn't feel like there was something wrong with you when you spent time with Nick?" Thea said.

"Right," Astra said. "It was different, with him. But then, when it all went off the rails, I was devastated, but I—I was also sort of relieved. Like I could just go back to my old way of thinking, and sort of, shrink back." Astra looked down, like she couldn't meet her mother's eyes. "I know this might not make any sense to you."

Thea thought of the way Nick had looked at her, sitting across the table from her, when she asked him to make that promise. He still cared about Astra, more than cared, that was obvious. And she'd used that, to get him to say yes. She didn't regret it.

Could she tell her daughter Nick still cared? No, not without revealing why she'd seen him, and the promise Nick had made. Thea didn't think he'd ever have to fulfill it, but it was there, just the same, a fail-safe. She did not have to burden Astra with it.

"Astra, I know you're not broken, I know that, but I also understand what you're telling me," Thea said. "I'm listening to you, sweetheart. And I'm so glad you're sharing. I worry, sometimes, that you keep things from me, because you don't want to distress me."

She took a breath and went on. "As for Nick, he did something that didn't fit with your standards," Thea said. "That's hard. But it's not an irredeemable mistake. If he'd lied and we learned about it later from Allie, that would be different. But he didn't."

Astra pressed her lips together and said nothing. She did not look angry; she was thinking.

"But that's not the point I want to make here," Thea said. "This is about you feeling worthy of love, and I happen to know something about that. Maybe you think I always expected to meet someone like your dad, but I didn't. It was a surprise for me too. And I want to say this, so you'll hear it. You are going to be loved. When, or what that looks like, I don't know. But you are loved now, and you are going to be loved, for exactly who you are."

She saw her daughter look at her and put those words away, somewhere inside her.

"Well, you have to say that, because you're my mom," Astra said, but her voice had shifted, the tightness was gone.

Thea reached out and rubbed Astra's back, and Astra leaned into her arms and let Thea hold her.

"You're absolutely right," Thea said. "But that doesn't mean it isn't true."

Chapter Twenty-Two

January 1996
Longfellow College

The door to the lecture hall opened, and Astra saw the dean of her residential college walk in—a man who other classmates greeted robustly in the dining hall as if he were a friend, and who she saw exactly twice a year when he signed her class schedule. He was followed by Sonia, whose look of pale urgency Astra recognized instantly. She started packing up her books, felt her classmates' curious, neutral stares on her as she squeezed by their legs to get to the aisle, and then hurried, without trying to look like she was hurrying, toward the door.

Dean Clancy put a hand on her shoulder and used the other to open the door. Before it had even swung shut behind him, he said, "Something has happened, Astra." And then suddenly she was crying, and this Dean she barely knew quietly and with tremendous kindness put his arms around her as she sobbed, and it was Sonia who had the presence of mind to say, "Astra, there's still time. I'll drive you to the train station."

Chapter Twenty-Three

When Astra's cab pulled up to the doors of Columbia Presbyterian Hospital, the first person she saw was Farris, talking to someone at the desk. Astra couldn't understand how Farris had gotten here before her from Nashville. And then she realized. Phoebe and her father had waited to call her.

She ran up to her godmother, who put her arms around Astra and, for about ten seconds, said nothing, just held her, and then she said quietly, "I'm so glad you're here."

"What's going on?" Astra said. "All they said was Mom had an embolism?"

"Yes, they admitted her for an infection yesterday, and then she had an embolism in the middle of the night. It's a blood clot in her lungs," Farris said. "I just flew in this morning," she said gently.

"Can I see her?"

"Of course. I'll take you right now," said Farris, and paused. "She's under a lot of painkillers, sweetheart. She has moments of lucidity, but they're coming and going."

They rode the elevator to the second floor, and when the doors opened, she saw Eli and Phoebe, her father, her Aunt Elizabeth, and her grandmother. They rose as one when they saw her.

Her mother's door, or what she assumed was her mother's door, was closed.

Her father came over and hugged her.

"Can I see her?" Astra said, and her father took her hand and started to walk toward the door, but Astra stopped and looked up at him. "Can I see her by myself?"

"Of course," he said, surprised, almost apologetic.

Astra opened the door. Her mother looked so small under the hospital sheets. One of her beautiful hands rested on the sheets and the other was tucked under. Astra thought her mother's hands were the only part of her body that still looked the same.

She was sleeping, so Astra went and sat beside her, pulling one of the vinyl chairs up to the right side of the bed. All the contraptions and IVs were hooked up on the left, chirping softly.

Astra looked out the window. Thea had a good room, with a view of the tree-lined street. All the medical literature said that mattered, and she was glad, that after her mother had spent decades working in this hospital, whoever had assigned her to this room had pulled some rank.

"Astra, honey, you're here." Her mother was awake, and her voice was softer than usual, with a stop and go cadence that was unfamiliar.

"Of course I'm here, Mommy," Astra said, and reached for her hand, which was dry and cool.

"I want to talk to you about what is going to happen next," her mother said. "First, when I come home—" Her voice faded away, and Astra nodded. The way her father had put it, it sounded like the doctors did not think her mother would leave the hospital.

She realized her mother was not going to say anything else. She had closed her eyes and was breathing slowly. Astra looked at her mother's arm on top of the sheet, threaded with bruised purple veins from all the blood draws. Her face was slack and puffy, with dark-yellow crescents under her eyes, as if she'd been poisoned. Astra felt a fierce, girlish possession of her.

"Mommy—" she said, and her mother's eyes opened.

"I'm afraid," Astra said. How many times had she said this to her mother, how many different meanings had it carried over her childhood. And now it would be the last time, the last time she could tell her mother she was scared.

"I know you are, sweetheart," her mother said. "It's okay. I am, too, but it's okay."

Her mother's eyes closed again. Astra wondered if it would have been different if she'd arrived earlier. She got out of the chair and knelt by the bed, so she could put her arms around her mother. "I love you so much I'm afraid my world will stop without you," she said, but her mother was asleep and did not answer.

~

Around 2 p.m. a youngish woman with dark hair and a kind manner—Dr. Bass, a more junior doctor at Dr. Kelly's practice—came to give them an update. Astra sat with her father and Farris—everyone else had gone home to rest for a few hours. Dr. Bass sat across from them, on a chair that was the color of orange sherbert. Behind her, a Georgia O'Keeffe print hung on the wall above a vase of flowers made out of cloth.

"We've isolated the infection," Dr. Bass said, with her hands folded in her lap. "That means we can start a course of antibiotics." Astra's mother had gone into the hospital because of an infection, but Astra had forgotten about it until now.

"Once we get the infection under control," she said. "We can start to talk about hospice care. I can discuss options—"

"What is the point of the antibiotics?" Astra said.

The doctor had been looking at her father, but she looked at Astra now. "Well, now that we've determined what kind of infection it is, we can treat it," she said.

"But she's dying," Astra said. "Will the antibiotics change that?"

The doctor paused, reassessing her. Astra was not a person who questioned authority as a rule, and while her throat felt hot as the words came out, her voice was clear and direct. There was no give to it.

"No, but they could give your mother a little more time," she said.

A little more time. Astra wanted a little more time. She wanted all the time, in fact, years and years and years. But not like this. Not with her mother so slow and wasted and tired, in pain every time she started to swim up from the morphine.

Her mother had done everything she could. She had gone as hard at this disease as she could, choosing the most aggressive treatments, the most rigorous schedule. What if the antibiotics worked, and suddenly they were suggesting some new procedure, some other medicine? She thought of her mother lying in the hospital bed, week after week, growing smaller and smaller, her eyes filmed over, talking only in fits and starts. That could not be allowed, not after what her mother had been through. Astra could not allow it, both because the person her mother had been in life demanded they protect her from such a lingering death, and because she, Astra, could not bear it. She could not bear it.

When Astra did not reply right away, Dr. Bass continued, in an authoritative voice. "I really think it's the right course of action. Let's see how she responds, and we can always reassess in a few days."

Astra respected Dr. Bass arguing her case. If her mother were here, would she say yes, absolutely, treat the infection, do everything you can? Astra thought she would. Would she say that because it's what she wanted, or what she felt she owed her family? This, Astra didn't know. But she could do this one last thing for her, which was to say—it's okay to go now. It's okay to rest.

"No," Astra said, and a universe was contained in that word. Her father and Dr. Bass both turned toward her immediately.

"I just don't see why we would do the antibiotics if they're not going to make a difference, and she's already suffered so much," Astra said.

Dr. Bass was quiet. "Well, I understand what you are saying," she said, and then she looked at Astra's father. "Are these your wishes too?"

Astra could see the doctor and her father talking; the doctor nodded her head, but the world had fallen silent to Astra. She just leaned back on the upholstered chair, exhausted, and let the grown-ups talk.

Chapter Twenty-Four

When she finally fell asleep, Thea dreamed of water. Dark, black water rushing down the stairs, out of the door to her bedroom when she opened it, pooling on the floor around the kitchen table. She dreamed she was standing in the ocean with the girls when they were little, and a wave broke over them, pulling hungrily at her legs, dragging at their small bodies. She felt the current try to wrench them away from her and her holding on, holding on, not letting go.

The dream shifted, and she was lying in bed in the apartment, listening for the door, waiting for Phoebe to come home. She heard the front door close softly, hours after curfew, and Phoebe's quick steps in the hall, and then her daughter was next to her under the covers, crying, saying how sorry she was for being late. She was not a teenager but a child, and Thea held her to her small, impossibly warm body to her.

The dream changed again. She heard steps outside her bedroom, and this time it was Astra, looking at her from the doorway, her pale, beloved face watchful and sad. Her daughter stood there soaking wet, not from a rain but as if a torrent had washed over her, as if her child had pulled herself up the banister against a dark tide. Astra wanted to tell Thea something, words she did not know how to speak.

And then in Astra's face, Thea saw it. She saw her family going on. She saw graduations, she saw Tom with a tiny grandchild, and Phoebe and Eli next to him. She saw a man Astra might love, a slender man with his back to Thea, holding her daughter in his arms. She saw a wedding, and realized it was Tom's, and she felt happy. And she understood, most of all, the pain on her daughter's face. It was not for her grief, but for all the living her mother would not be there to see.

During her illness, always, the thing Thea focused on was staying alive for her girls. That was the driving need that consumed everything in its path, like a fire. But now, she was confronted with another idea. There was that part of her that wanted to live for herself, that felt the ache of these lives going on without her.

She knew what her daughter was asking, felt it in her bones. Astra wanted to know if it was okay for her to go on. It was such an easy question, and yet Thea understood, what an impossible business it was. All that living, all that living, she still wanted it so much.

"It's all right, sweetheart," she told her daughter. "It's all right. I want you to."

Chapter Twenty-Five

January 31, 1996
New York City

The day of her mother's memorial service was barren and grey, the leafless branches of the trees like dead things against a pewter sky, and Astra was grateful for this. Her family arrived at the church early but there was still already a small knot of people outside, some of whom Astra recognized and some she didn't. As they got out of the car, Phoebe gripped her hand like they were tiny children wading in the sea. Her sister had stayed the night at their parents' apartment, without Eli, and this kindness, this final act of solidarity with their family as it had been and would never be again, had moved Astra deeply. In the morning, Phoebe had come into her room, holding up two black dresses, one knee-length and one mid-calf, like a pantomime of when they used to get dressed for parties when they were girls. "The longer one," Astra said, and Phoebe nodded, and then they both burst into tears.

The service was being held at the Presbyterian church where Phoebe and Astra had been confirmed, despite their family's spotty attendance, and when they stepped out of the car, the small crowd turned to them, in a coordinated hush. Astra thought of Phoebe's wedding, when the guests all stood for Phoebe to walk down the aisle. It was the same ritual, at the other side of a life.

They said brief, quiet hellos, put hands on people's shoulders. Their father led the way, nodding to some friends, clasping hands with others, and then they were through the group and into the church, the programs with the picture of her mother they had chosen a week ago in tidy stacks. It was a photograph of her standing outside, flushed from a walk, looking at the camera as if she had just finished laughing at a private joke.

"Astra—I didn't realize how many people would be here, how many people we would have to talk to," Phoebe said, coming up next to her. "It's like the world's weirdest cocktail party. I'm not sure I can do this."

Astra squeezed her hand. "I'll stay right next to you, Phoebe."

And Phoebe was right, there were so many people there—friends of Astra's from high school, her old English teacher from eleventh grade, her soccer coach—whom she had not expected to see. She was grateful when the music started playing, signaling the service was going to begin soon. Astra walked down to the front pews with her sister, past the dais, which was awash in flowers—lilies and hydrangea and white roses. A wreath of freesias stood in the center on a stand, with a card below. *With my deepest condolences—Cutter Nesbit.*

"Who's Cutter Nesbit?" she asked her sister. They stood holding hands in front of the greenery, like small children in a fairy tale.

"He was a friend of Mommy's—from college," said Phoebe. "He sent me a wedding gift, some sort of crystal pitcher; it was really nice. I had to ask her who he was."

"Was he at the wedding?" Astra asked.

"No, Mom didn't invite him," Phoebe said. "But this was really kind of him to send. I think he lives in California." Astra wanted to ask more, but the pews were filling up; it was almost time for the service to start.

As they sang the first hymn, "We Gather Together," Astra stood next to her grandmother, who seemed small and stoic in a suit of midnight wool, and held the hymnal for both of them. Her grandmother's voice was surprisingly sweet and thin, and as she sang she gripped Astra's arm. When it was over, and the minister welcomed everyone to a celebration of life for Althea Loomis Erickson, her grandmother said, "Your mother would have liked that."

Since the morning Astra had felt a burning in her throat that spread out into her collarbone.

Ted Wilson was the first to speak. During the opening prayer she saw him, sitting without his wife in a pew near the front, crying visibly. He leaned forward and quietly touched his forehead to the back of the pew in front of him. It had never occurred to her, what the grief of people outside their family would look like.

"Thea Erickson was a force in medicine," Dr. Wilson began, listing her accomplishments as a trailblazer in cardiothoracic surgery.

"When Thea got sick"—and here Dr. Wilson's voice faltered—"she also took a different path than most doctors do. She was aware that doctors tend to have worse outcomes than civilians, because we treat them differently. I remember her looking at me as I was tentatively outlining treatment plans and she said, 'Stop pussyfooting around, Ted. You're the expert here, not me. I want to go as hard at this as I can.' The stakes were high for Thea. Because as anyone who knew her understands, she would do anything—anything—to have one more day with her family. With her husband of over twenty-five years, Tom, and her daughters, Phoebe and Astra."

Astra took her grandmother's hand and started to shake. She could feel the pew shaking, and she wondered if the hymnals would start rattling in their holders. Her grandmother put her hand over Astra's and said, "It's all right now, just let it out," the way you might speak to a small child, and Astra wept through the end of Teddy's remarks, through Farris's and her aunt's.

And then her sister climbed up to the lectern and said, "My mother always told me I had a lovely voice. I hope she was right." Then she started to sing.

Phoebe sang "Pull for the Shore," one of her mother's favorite hymns, and Astra's tears stopped. She raised her head and looked at her sister, her beautiful sister with her beautiful voice, and she felt such love for her, and also, it was unmistakable, a tiny hot current of jealousy. How strange, after a girlhood of standing in the warmth of Phoebe's shadow, she should feel this now. She didn't mind Phoebe being better at sports, or prettier, or more popular. But she minded this.

Astra had put her eulogy off until the last minute, as if delaying was an act of defiance at her mother's death, rather than what it was: an obvious mistake. She'd written about her mother singing lullabies, one of those tiny, comforting rituals that, multiplied by a thousand, made Astra feel secure and loved. She had chosen it because she thought the people in this room wouldn't know that, wouldn't have seen this side of her mother, the surgeon, but as she looked over her words now, they felt slight and childish.

Phoebe finished singing, her beautiful voice dying away, and Astra could feel the room vibrating with withheld applause. When her sister made her way back to the pew, Astra rose and hugged her—"You were amazing, Phoebe," she said—and then she walked up to the lectern, clutching her piece of paper.

She waited. The room was silent, respectful. Many people had their heads bowed. She could hear the occasional loud sob, from a different part of the church than where her family was seated. She unfolded the piece of paper. *Every night, for my entire childhood, my mother sang me lullabies . . .*

Astra took a breath and she got ready to read, and then she stopped. She turned over the piece of paper and looked up at the audience. She did not feel scared she had nothing written down now. For the first time today, she felt like she was doing exactly what she was supposed to be doing.

"When I was a very small child, probably no more than two, I didn't understand that my mother was a doctor, I just thought she was in charge of everything," Astra said. People laughed. "When we were at a museum and a stranger fainted or when she was chaperoning my nursery school field trip and Susie McAllister broke her wrist during the three-legged race, my mother was always the one who helped. It was an extraordinary thing, growing up with a mother like that, but it felt natural to me. I had no concept yet that she had spent decades honing these skills. I just thought people saw her the way I saw her—as someone who always knew what to do."

Astra spoke slowly, letting one sentence thaw into the next. She talked about how the world felt flatter without her mother in it. How the irony of her mother's death was that she had lost the person she most needed to process it with, to help her understand.

As she spoke those words, she saw someone standing in the very back of the church, looking at her.

"Everyone talks about cancer as a fight, and to be frank, this annoyed her. My mother knew she was going to die. I would like to say that changed her, but it didn't. And I see now what strength that took. To not change. To hold on to exactly who you are, even when you are afraid. My mother was afraid, I know how afraid she was. She kept on going."

She could feel people waiting, expecting more, but she was done.

Astra walked down the steps, and her family folded her into their arms. When she had a chance to look down the aisle again, Nick was gone.

Chapter Twenty-Six

Her mother would have liked the reception, Astra thought. The hospital had turned out in force—Astra wondered if anyone was left at Columbia Presbyterian to take care of patients. When she was three, she had cracked her head open on a doorjamb, and her mother had put a bandage on it, told her to lie down, and then they waited three hours to go to the emergency room. "There's a plastic surgeon's conference, everyone's in Florida, so we have to wait until Ellen Wallach can drive in from New Jersey," her mother had told her.

Astra's mother always knew what times of the year it was best to get injured and what were the worst. Conference weeks were, of course, terrible, and then after that, certain holidays. Astra wondered if it had ever occurred to her mother if the day of her memorial service would also be a terrible time to have a heart attack in Manhattan.

A man approached her who she did not recognize. "Astra, I wanted to tell you how beautiful your words were at the service." He was about her height, a small, tidy man in an ill-fitting suit. She liked him immediately.

"I'm David Wanabo," he said. "I was at medical school with your mother."

Astra knew who he was. The man who was going to perform the operation she begged her mother not to have. She thought David Wanabo must know this, and she flushed as she shook his hand.

"I'm so sorry for your loss," Dr. Wanabo said. "We all admired your mother so much."

"Thank you for the kind words," she said, and then, quickly, as if she would lose her nerve, she added, "The idea of your surgery really gave her hope. I'm so sorry it wasn't able to happen."

"Well, she really appreciated the fact that you didn't want her to have it, Astra. She thought that took guts."

It broke up Astra that Thea had shared her daughter's concerns with her doctor, that it had meant something to her that Astra had spoken up. All that guilt she'd felt for not supporting the operation fired in her and then softened, changed.

"She said that?"

"She did." And then he squeezed her hands and folded back into the crowd.

Astra walked quickly through to the foyer—people would assume she was going to use the restroom—and just kept going, pushing though the heavy door, and when the cold hit her, it felt like a friend.

~

When Astra got home that night, she took off the black suit with silk piping. Her mother had gotten it for Astra to wear to her great-aunt's funeral a year ago, and it was the most beautiful thing she owned. Now, Astra wondered, as she thought about her mother walking through the large, cool chambers of Saks Fifth Avenue, if her mother had actually bought it for today.

She put on her pajamas. Reflected in the mirror were the aggressive sprays of lilies and prim white roses that Phoebe had started to bring into her room when there was no space left in the living room and front hall.

Astra padded quietly out into the hall, past her father's bedroom with the slit of light under the door, and into her mother's study. On her desk, right where it always was, she found the small red leather address book. Every year her mother would "do" her address book, rewriting it from A to Z, updating addresses, removing people who had died, adding in new parents from her and Phoebe's classes. Astra took it now and turned the little gilt-edged, blue pages to *R* for Rosenfeld.

It was 9:30 p.m. Too late to call someone's home—her parents had taught her and Phoebe that 8:30 p.m. was the absolute latest—but she thought that tonight, if Mrs. Rosenfeld answered, it would be okay.

It rang several times, and then there was a click, and her heart pressed against her ribs. If it was Nick, what would she even say? Then the answering machine recording started. No one was home. Astra felt such a queer blaze of disappointment, her desire to hear his voice had been so strong.

She hung up without leaving a message, and then she went back to her room and looked at herself in the mirror. Her face was flushed; she actually looked pretty, on this, the night of her mother's funeral. The thought made her feel strange again.

She brushed her hair, brushed her teeth, and then wandered into the hall outside of her room and opened the hall closet. All her mother's formal coats still hung there—her creamy camel floor-length trench with the belt, her green wool duster with the fur hood, a jewellike, quilted cape she had seen her mother wear only once, to a New Year Eve's party. Tucked to the side was the mink coat her mother used to wear to fancy parties—Astra remembered running down the hall and pressing her face against the fur, which still held the night chill.

She leaned into the closet and let herself be swallowed by the crush of wool and velvet, and then she grabbed her mother's duster and slipped it on. The coat pooled at her feet, and when she pulled the hood over her head, she could smell the faintest warm trace of her mother's perfume. Then she went outside for a walk in the frigid air.

Part III: The Pitch-Black Room

Chapter Twenty-Seven

Astra returned to school four days after the funeral. Some people hugged her and told her how sorry they were. Others, who she knew but not very well, spotted her and then glanced away, their eyes sliding off her when she looked over. She realized perhaps she'd come back too early. Not for herself—work and the routines of classes helped her—but for others. Amid the strange newness of her grief, she also held a sympathy for people who did not know what to say.

The first night, when she and Sonia walked into the dining hall, a girl named April from their year walked up to her and handed her a folded square of newsprint. It was her mother's obituary. "I'm so sorry Astra," she said, and hugged her quickly. "I wasn't sure if you had it." And though Astra did have it—had several copies, in fact, and had spoken to *The New York Times* reporter—she took it from her with gratitude. "That's really thoughtful of you, April, thank you." And later, when Sonia asked, "What, did she think you wouldn't have a copy?" and made a face, Astra stopped her. "No one knows what to do," she said. "April tried, and that means something to me."

On Friday night, Sonia convinced her to go to a party. "It might be totally stupid, and you only have to stay five minutes if you want," she said.

"And what should I do after five minutes? Should we have a signal?" Astra said, and smiled. "Like I hold my hand to my head and make a trigger pulling motion?"

"That's my signal," said Sonia. "You have to pick another."

"Deal."

Astra and Sonia walked together around 10 p.m. to the shabby off campus house where a group of seniors on the swim team lived, a lease that was passed down, year after year, to an interchangeable group of tall and friendly men. There was a uniform, at Longfellow, to going out at night in the winter, when the New England cold was still like a living thing, and both Astra and Sonia wore jeans and black ankle boots and heavy pea coats. Of course, there were always girls who showed up in tiny dresses and heels, blue lipped and beautiful, their legs pinpricked with goosebumps. Her mother would have thought they were ridiculous, but Astra felt a flicker of admiration for them.

They could hear the music playing from a block away—"Modern Love" by David Bowie—and smell the cigarette smoke from the few brave people standing outside on the steps, hands huddled around their lighters. Astra grabbed Sonia's hand right before they entered the house, and Sonia gave her five squeezes in rapid succession.

"Even if we have a terrible time, I'm glad you came," Sonia said.

Inside, the party was hot and loud and dark. She and Sonia pushed into the crowd by the bar, which was a long folding table set up under the staircase. A man wearing a tuxedo shirt and bow tie and only his swim team speedo down below was ladling drinks out of a silver punch bowl into red solo cups.

Sonia took a sip and winced. "It tastes like Kool-Aid and motor oil," she said, and then took another long gulp. Astra did the same. The punch burned, and she liked that, standing against the wall in the warm anonymity of the room.

"Hey, Astra!"

She turned and Jordan, Farris's son, was standing next to her. He wrapped his arms around her and picked her up clean off the floor. The last time she had seen him was at the funeral, when he was in a suit, giving her a different kind of hug.

He set her down and her drink sloshed, spilling on her. "Oh, god, I'm so sorry," Jordan said. "That punch is going to burn a hole in your jeans."

"Don't worry about it all," she said, and she meant it. "No one can see anything in here anyway. God, I'm glad to see you."

"Well, I'm glad to see *you*," he said. "Proof of life! I was worried about you coming back so early, but my mom told me routines are good for processing grief. You know, all the usual shrink stuff." He stood back and smiled, and it moved her, the way he had come to her in front of all these people. Jordan had a way of speaking directly about things that reminded her of Farris.

"I would feel useless rattling around the city, with all the Ericksons back at work," Astra said, and it was true, but as she spoke the thought aloud, she wondered at it, how quickly they had all returned to their jobs and classes, and whether this was worthy of praise or not. Should they feel proud of their ability to go on, or was burying themselves in work a weakness? Astra didn't know.

"Well, you guys are a tough bunch," said Jordan. He hugged her again, put his arm on Sonia's shoulder, and said, "I have to run but let's all get brunch tomorrow at Books Café?" They nodded and he smiled. "Okay, be good!" Jordan said, and then threaded his way to the door.

Sonia leaned into her and rested her head lightly on Astra's shoulder. "See? This party is awesome."

~

Later, when they were waiting in line for the bathroom, Sonia said, "Don't look now, but Cynthia Wolf is staring at you."

Astra did look, and Sonia was right—from across the room she could feel Cynthia's interested, appraising stare.

Cynthia was a senior, impossibly cool, with a dark curtain of hair that gleamed like a Pantene commercial. When Astra and Sonia were freshmen, Cynthia had been carried into the main dining hall on a sofa, dressed as Cleopatra, as a stunt to advertise an improv show. The impression had never faded.

"Cynthia has no idea who I am," said Astra. They were in the same Literature of the Gilded Age seminar, but Astra had only attended one class before she'd left for home.

"Okay, but she's been staring at you on and off for a while now. I'm only noticing it because we've been in two psych labs together and she still walks by me like I'm a ghost," Sonia said. "Oh wait, now she's coming over."

Cynthia was indeed making her way across the room, wearing a white T-shirt with safety pins with a sort of sailor jacket slung over it—an outfit Astra would never have thought to put together. Cynthia looked amazing in it.

"Hey, it's Astra, right?" Cynthia said. Then Cynthia nodded and smiled at Sonia, who gave a surprised smile back.

"Yes," Astra said. "Hi, Cynthia." She noted how Cynthia just assumed they would know her name, and how she was, of course, right.

"You haven't been in Professor Huynh's class for a few weeks," she said. "Did you drop it?"

"No, I had to go home to New York for some family stuff," Astra said. "I'll be there this week."

"Ah, okay," Cynthia said. "I was just wondering if you knew something I didn't."

"Oh no, I love Professor Huynh," Astra said. "Two thumbs up."

"I've heard she's a notorious hard-ass. Do you know what she did to Jeremy Tate?"

Astra did know. Last semester Jeremy had lost his laptop and most of his clothes in a fire at the Theta Fraternity House, and Professor

Huynh had refused to give him an extension on his final paper. Astra had felt terrible for Jeremy, but something about Professor Huynh's immovability had awed her. She felt she understood her, that she could see her mother doing something like that, in another life.

"That was brutal," she said. "But Professor Huynh is an amazing teacher. Tough but fair, as they say."

"Well, see what you think when she doesn't excuse you for missing the last three weeks," Cynthia said and laughed. It was supposed to be a laugh of camaraderie, but Astra felt a small, sour feeling in her stomach. This would have been the time to tell Cynthia, to explain to her why she went home, but she did not. Not just because it would have been awkward, but she could feel, in the other girl's tone, a false note that put her on alert.

Then Cynthia lay her hand on Astra's arm and smiled her lovely smile, leaning in as if they were having a just-us-girls moment.

"Hey, I saw you talking to Jordan Price earlier—how do you guys know each other? He's such a great guy. Are you dating?"

"Oh no, I've known Jordan all my life," Astra said. "Our mothers went to college and med school together and kind of became soul mates. It was just the cherry on top for them that their children went to college together too."

Cynthia laughed. "Oh, so your parents are friends? That makes sense," she said. Cynthia looked relieved, folding away the idea that Astra could date someone as popular as Jordan.

"Why?" Sonia said, and Astra froze. "Why does that make more sense, Cynthia?"

Cynthia's expression changed; it was like a small crack appeared and then closed, and then she smiled.

"Oh, I didn't mean anything by it, Sonia," she said. "I was just wondering. Jordan's a good friend, so I was surprised he didn't mention anything."

"Funny, he never mentioned he knew you either," Sonia said.

Cynthia tilted her head to the side and smiled. "What are you, Sonia, Astra's mother?" Cynthia's voice was low and smooth, with a tiny paper cut of an edge. "I don't think she needs two."

Both girls were silent. Astra could feel Sonia's churning anger, her own paralysis. She thought of all the worry from her lovely friends, all the fluttering concern she hated whenever the idea of someone's mother came up, because she was fine, nothing they could say could hurt her. But these words, tossed out of the mouth of this girl, they did hurt.

She could feel Sonia's consternation and knew she was about to say something else, and Astra couldn't bear it. She forced herself to speak evenly, in a voice designed to please.

"There's no problem, Cynthia," she said. "I totally get it."

Then Cynthia was gone, flashing her movie-star smile before turning on her heel and walking out of their sight.

"I shouldn't have pushed you to come," Sonia said quietly.

"Stop it now, Sones," Astra said. "I'm fine. This party is great. Let's get more disgusting punch."

Sonia smiled. "Well, we were clearly wrong about one thing," she said, as she reached for Astra's hand and squeezed it. "Cynthia does know our names."

Chapter Twenty-Eight

The Eat Your Books Café & Novel Emporium occupied a prime slot of real estate between Longfellow's chapel and art gallery. The university had long tried to pry the bookstore loose from its lease so it could buy the lot, but through a combination of savvy campaigning and genuine student fondness, Eat Your Books remained.

The sandwiches all had cheeky names like David & Goliath, the Independence, and Easy A, and Jordan had taken Astra and Sonia here for the first time when they were freshman. It was busy when they showed up, but the three of them crammed into a two-top right next to the espresso machine, which made astonishingly loud whooshing and whistling noises while they looked over the brunch menu.

"So how was the rest of the party?" Jordan asked, after they ordered.

"We didn't stay that long," Sonia said. "I think Cynthia Wolf has a thing for you."

Jordan laughed. "No, she doesn't. She's always dating some rowing or tennis guy. Why, did she say something?"

"Actually, she did," Sonia said. "She hustled over to make sure Astra wasn't your girlfriend, after your big bear hug."

"Huh," said Jordan.

"Are you friends with her?" Astra said. "She made this big to-do about what *good* friends you are."

"Friendly with everyone, that's my brand," said Jordan.

A server brought over an enormous slab of French toast, and Sonia plunged her fork into the eggy middle and tore off a piece. "She acted like there's some secret enforcement panel," Sonia said. "Only super popular people are allowed to date other super popular people. And clearly Astra and I did not qualify."

"Well, you laugh but I heard she blackballed someone from Papyrus just because they dated her ex-boyfriend," said Jordan.

Papyrus was one of the oldest secret societies at Longfellow, and it was known for producing an extraordinary number of successful politicians, even a vice president or two.

"How do you know that?" Astra asked.

"Well, I know because I'm in it with her, and she told me. Like it was a badge of honor."

"You're in Papyrus?"

"Yes."

Only three of the societies, Papyrus, Cross & Key, and Leviathan, were over 150 years old, and Papyrus was considered the most powerful. Its members met in a windowless building at the edge of campus, with a scrolled marble facade that stuck out amid the cheery brick. While the societies were supposed to be secret, everyone could recognize these nameless, formidable buildings sprinkled across campus, where you almost never saw anyone enter or leave. Astra even knew a few people who had been in Cross & Key, which had a literary bent. It was rumored it even possessed an original Shakespeare folio down in its basement, though this had never been verified.

"Wow. I can't believe I didn't know," Astra said. "Though I guess that's the point. I mean, what's it like? Do you wear robes or drink wine out of a skull or something like that?"

For some reason, she'd never assumed Jordan would be in one, but of course it made sense. Jordan wore his popularity lightly, but he was liked by everyone, and a star on the lacrosse team.

"Oh, come on. Honestly, it's like a drinking club with fancier digs," said Jordan. "There's so much mumbo jumbo out there about the societies, but most of the people in Papyrus are pretty cool."

"Just a drinking club?" said Sonia, with a smile. "Don't you get, like a bag of a cash and a bunch of senators' home phone numbers when you're tapped?"

Jordan laughed. "No," he said. "And they don't make us drink ox blood or do naked rituals either, okay? Mainly it's people presenting their biographies—some are ridiculous, like training for the Olympics or, you know, discovering some new molecule, but most are the usual stuff—parents being too hard on them, achievement anxiety, what's the meaning of life. You get the idea."

"Is that what Cynthia talked about?" Sonia said in a deadpan.

Jordan didn't answer.

Instead, he said to Sonia, "All right missy, what about you? I heard you were being interviewed by Artemis."

Something passed over Sonia's face—embarrassment, mixed with alarm.

"It's nothing. I'm not doing it," she said, and she saw Sonia shoot Jordan a warning glance.

Sonia hadn't told Astra she'd been approached by any of the societies. Hadn't told her on purpose. Was she worried Astra would feel left out? Did she feel left out? The thought that her friends were being tapped for societies and she wasn't had never occurred to her, but it did now.

"Well, that's great, Sonia," Astra said. "If I were going to be stuck in a windowless room with twelve people, I'd want one of them to be you too." She kept her voice light and easy, and she felt Sonia and Jordan relax.

In Astra's before life, before she knew her mother was going to die, a small part of her would have cared, quietly and with some consternation, that she had not been interviewed for any of the societies, even as she also thought the idea of a secret society was strange, maybe even a little cruel.

But since she'd gone home in January, she hadn't even thought about it. In fact, she'd forgotten that spring was the season when juniors were tapped.

And now, knowing Jordan was in one and Sonia was being courted—she felt something twist inside her, not envy, not exactly. She felt the rawness of being left out, but worse than that, the sense of not measuring up.

Astra thought her grief would be like a fire, sweeping away everything in its path. Instead, the feeling of loss over her mother and the feeling of not being picked existed side by side, the heartbreaking and the ridiculous.

Chapter Twenty-Nine

Astra arrived a few minutes early to her Literature in the Gilded Age seminar and sat down across from one of the big bay windows. Outside, the winter sun had already started to set, turning the sky the color of a wound.

Cynthia came in right after her and picked a chair a few seats away. "Hey Astra," she said easily as she unloaded her books, and Astra gave a little wave. It was strange, to be on Cynthia's radar now, and she thought back to the party, the hot tightness in her throat. *What, are you Astra's mother?*

Professor Huynh entered the room exactly at four o'clock, wearing the same thing she wore every week, a black belted tunic over leggings and loafers, with a rotating array of dangly earrings—tassels and jade drops and strings of tiny amethysts, as bright as a bird's plumage. On her way to her chair at the head of the table, she stopped to say hello to Astra and put a hand on her shoulder, an action that seemed to surprise everyone, including Professor Huynh herself.

"Astra, it's so good to have you back," she said. Astra thanked her, said she was glad to be here, and always, in every new room, she wondered. *Does everyone know?* She knew Professor Huynh would not have shared the news about Astra's mother, unless Astra asked her to, and she had not.

The class was small, just ten juniors and seniors. This week, they were discussing Edith Wharton's *The House of Mirth*. All Wharton's novels were fairly bleak, but *House of Mirth* was particularly so, Astra thought. It tracked the descent of its heroine, Lily Bart, from a beautiful woman established in society to an impoverished outcast who dies of an accidental morphine overdose. These kinds of stories always haunted Astra, the drip drip drip of small setbacks and societal injustices that gain speed until they exact the gravest price.

"Edith Wharton doesn't traffic in happy endings," Professor Huynh began. "But *House of Mirth* is different; it feels tragic in almost a classical way. Do we think there's anything Lily could have done to avoid her fate?"

Astra raised her hand and then put it down when Cynthia started talking.

"Well, she could have married Percy after chapter two," Cynthia said. "She has him in her sights, and then she doesn't seal the deal. She's always sabotaging herself. I know it's supposed to be her tragic flaw, but it just gets annoying."

"Actually, her tragic flaw is she must marry for wealth and position, because she's been brought up for nothing else," Astra said. "And then, when the moment comes, she can't bring herself to make the mercenary exchange. What must that be like, for her to know her only economic option is to marry, and yet she can't extinguish the last shred of herself that refuses to shackle herself to a person she can't respect?"

"That actually goes straight at the idea of fate," said Professor Huynh. "Do we think there was nothing Lily could have done? Or is it the fact that she holds onto her humanity that eventually dooms her? Did she make a choice?"

Cynthia spoke again. "That feels a bit dramatic," she said. "I think she keeps assuming something better will come along. When she finally decides to get her act together and settle for Percy, it's too late. I don't even think it's that tragic. She knows how to save herself, but she doesn't act. And then she stupidly overdoses on opium."

Astra looked down at the table. She thought of her mother, remembered her slow slipping away under the morphine, once they decided to stop treatment. Cynthia spoke in such an offhanded way, it stung, but of course she wasn't trying to be cruel. Yet once again, the words hurt. Astra thought of the way Cynthia had treated Sonia, her initial look of surprise and hot dislike when Sonia had questioned her. As if Sonia was stepping out of her sphere.

She felt something close to hatred for this girl, so strong it surprised her.

"I'm not sure why you're so hard on Lily," Astra said, looking straight at Cynthia. "She's a complicated character. She's not good all the time, or morally pure. She makes frustrating choices. But I think Wharton does this deliberately—she's not sacrificing some perfect little lamb. Wharton is interested in what happens when you go against the grain in a rule-bound society, especially as a woman."

"You're making her sound like some sort of feminist folk hero," Cynthia said. "I feel like we read different books."

"Funnily enough, I feel that way too," Astra said.

A weird silence followed. Atticus, a senior sitting next to Cynthia, who played number one on the squash team and always looked like he was waking up from a nap, suddenly stirred to life.

"So you don't think what happens to Lily is just bad luck," he said. "She understands the game, she knows how to play it, but in the end, she refuses. That's defiance, whether it's conscious or not."

Astra had been on one date with Atticus her freshman year, and then she'd had to break the second date to go to the city to see her family. It was the night her parents told her and Phoebe that her mother's cancer was terminal, and when she returned to Longfellow, Atticus had never called her back. Still, when they passed each other on the sidewalk or in a lecture hall, he always smiled.

"Yes, exactly," she said to him now. "If she were just a victim, that's a much less interesting story."

"I agree," he said. "I always think it's a cop-out when the protagonist is just this super virtuous, blameless paragon."

"Even though you were named after one," she said, and Atticus threw his head back and laughed so hard it was like a yelp.

"Ah, we've missed you, Astra," he said. "Welcome back." And then he winked at her.

Cynthia's face was narrow with anger. "I still don't think Lily is as special as everyone seems to think she is." She looked right at Astra as she said this.

Professor Huynh stepped in, starting to turn the subject, but Atticus said, in a low, easy voice that nonetheless carried through the room, "Don't worry, Cyn. We know you'd have locked Percy down in thirty seconds." Laughter broke out, and as Professor Huynh called the class to order, Cynthia turned on Astra with a look of slitted fury, as if it were her fault.

Then Astra saw Atticus lean over toward Cynthia and whisper something. Cynthia did not respond, but he leaned over and whispered again, and this time Cynthia gave a small smile. He laid his hand on hers and rubbed his thumb back and forth, until she drew her hand back with a smile and a little shake of her head.

They were together. Atticus and Cynthia. The knowledge crashed upon Astra all at once as she watched them, and she had realized she had wandered into something, something personal. When class was over, she gathered up her books and walked quickly out of the room, as if walking away from danger.

Chapter Thirty

Astra went straight back to her room, and when she unlocked the door, the phone was ringing. She picked up.

"Hello, Astra?" The voice on the other end of the phone was so warm and familiar sounding it startled her. "It's—it's Nick. Nick Rosenfeld. I'm sorry—I didn't expect you to actually be there. I was planning to leave a message."

"Nick?" she said. She felt disoriented and surprised, but also, a small jolt of excitement.

"I know it's so weird for me to be calling like this," Nick said. "I just wanted to make sure—well, the night of your mom's service, there was a missed call on my mom's phone. She thought it was your dad so she called back, but he said it wasn't him. And then I realized it must have been you."

"Yes, it was me," she said. "I saw you at the service, but you didn't come to the reception." It felt like a world could be contained in those short sentences.

He was quiet for a moment. "I didn't really think anyone wanted to see me there," he said.

"I would have liked to see you," she said, and then, when he didn't answer. "It was really kind of you to come to the funeral."

"Is that why you called, Astra, to thank me for coming?"

Why had she called? She didn't even know, except that she'd felt such a longing to speak to him.

"I really loved your eulogy," he continued. "I've been thinking about it so much, since your mother's death."

No one had actually said those words—*your mother's death*—since she'd returned to Longfellow.

"Thank you for saying that," she said. "I'm sorry I didn't leave a message and caused confusion for your mom. I wasn't really thinking straight—I realize you're not living there, you must be down by NYU."

"I'm not going to NYU," Nick said, in a tone she couldn't read.

"Oh, I—"

"I deferred for a year. I guess I didn't have it all figured out, after all."

He was referring to their conversation the night of the wedding, and the memory of it hung there, between them.

"I didn't know," she said. "Is it—when did you make that decision?" She found she was suddenly nervous about what he would say.

"We don't need to get into it now," Nick said. "But it's really wonderful to hear your voice, Astra."

"I'm glad you called," she said. "I have to head to dinner soon, but maybe we can talk again later?"

"I'd like that," he said.

She hung up and thought back to her instinct, the night of her mother's service, to reach out to him. She didn't regret it.

~

A few days later, Nick called again.

"You're actually there!" he said. "I'm going to start worrying you're sitting in your room all day, watching daytime TV."

She laughed.

"Are you hiding out?" he said, in a gentler voice. "Are people being weird?"

"Yes and no. My friends are amazing; my professors, the ones who know me, are kind. I just don't know who knows and who doesn't, and I feel like if I don't mention it, and someone finds out later, they'll feel terrible, but if I do mention it, I'm murdering the conversation. And if something comes up, like we're reading about a character who lost their mother or someone says something about mothers or whatever, everyone freezes. And I want to be like, 'It's okay! We all have mothers! It's not a taboo subject!'"

She did not tell this to Nick, but last night she had gone to an improv show with her friend Deirdre, and the group did a skit where they answered questions hurled from the crowd. After a couple of warm-ups—"Why can't I get laid?" "Who killed JFK?"—someone yelled out, "Why did my mother die?" It was supposed to be an edgy question, Astra understood that, and it did not even draw a scratch on her. She admired the performer who, after the slightest fraction of a second, answered, "Because she ate too many cigarettes." But then she saw the stricken expression on Deirdre's face, and she took her hand and said, "I'm okay, I'm okay really." It felt like danger was everywhere; not for her, but for others.

"Oh, Astra, that's hard," said Nick. "I'm sorry. I'm stealing this from the rabbi at my synagogue, but outside of the Jews, who literally have a handbook for death and what to do afterward, I think Americans are pretty terrible at dealing with it. In a way, it's very un-American to die, or even talk about it."

"Do you think I can get a copy of that book?"

"Yes, but only because you came to my bar mitzvah."

She laughed again.

"I want to know what's been happening with you," she said.

"Oh, there have been big doings here, Astra. I told my parents I'm not going to go to law school. I'm going to apply to medical school instead—I got into the postbacc program at Columbia."

For a moment, she didn't know what to say. She and Phoebe had, when they were little, dreamed of being doctors. Every child of a doctor thinks about it at some point. Phoebe had even started as a premed at Williams, before hitting the brick wall of organic chemistry.

"Oh, Nick!" Astra said finally. "I think that is wonderful. Did your parents freak out?"

"Not exactly. My dad took me out to lunch at the Post House and told me he would buy me an apartment next to NYU if I changed my mind."

"Wow."

"I know."

"I mean, have you seen the apartment? New York real estate is not a thing to take lightly." Nick laughed at this; he really laughed.

"Said like a true New Yorker. But the worst part is I felt anguished for him. I thought he would be mad, or spewing ultimatums, or saying how disappointed he was, but instead it was like he was begging me, and I hated that. My dad is many things, but he's not that." Nick paused, and she was quiet, listening. "It's like he was so desperately concerned I was throwing my life away he would do anything to stop me."

"I'm so sorry. But I also don't get it—he doesn't want you to be a doctor? That badly?"

"No, it's not that. He thinks I'll wash out, and then I'll have nothing going for me."

"Did he say that?"

"Not exactly. But it was the gist."

She paused. She imagined what it would be like, to have a parent who felt that way. "If you set your mind on something, I know you'll do it," she said. "What did your mother say?"

He hesitated. "She asked if I was doing this because of your mom," he said, and he sounded nervous.

"What do you mean?"

"If what happened this summer is why I was doing it."

Astra was surprised this had not occurred to her before.

"Is it why you are doing it?"

"Well, yes, a part."

Hearing Nick say it, she felt moved, and at the same time, jealous. She felt almost possessive of her mother, uneasy at the idea that she would have influenced him in this way and not her.

"She'd be happy for you," Astra said, and she meant it. Nick was quiet.

"Next time I'm in New York, we should celebrate," she said.

"Why don't you come down tomorrow?" Nick said lightly, though she knew if she wanted to, she could, she could see him tomorrow.

She laughed again. "I'll be home in March."

Chapter Thirty-One

March 1996
Longfellow College

It was a few weeks before spring break, and a surprisingly warm day, the kind of day that drove students out onto patchy lawns, showing bare limbs that looked frightened after months of layers and early dark. She'd waved to a few groups of friends sitting on blankets on the lawn.

When she got back to her dorm room, Astra found a note on her bed from Sonia. *A guy called for you twice. Not Nick. Wouldn't leave his name or number.*

While she was examining the note, the phone rang again.

"Is Astra there?" a male voice said.

"Yes, this is Astra," she said. The voice sounded so formal she almost added *May I ask who's calling?* but caught herself.

"Hi Astra," he said. "I'm glad I reached you. I've been trying you all morning."

"Yes, I've been in class. I'm sorry, who is this?" The man laughed softly.

"I know this is going to sound weird, but I can't tell you." There was a beat, where he clearly expected her to say something, but she did not. "Have you been contacted by any of the secret societies yet?"

"No," she said.

"Well, I wanted you to know you've come to the attention of Cross & Key, Astra. We'd like to interview you." Astra felt a bright, hot shock of surprise. At the small campus literary magazine she worked on, the editor had told her at least two Pulitzer Prize winners were among the society's alumni.

For several seconds she didn't speak, but the man waited, saying nothing. "Sorry, you caught me off guard," she said. "I wasn't expecting a call like this."

"Most people don't say that," he said. "It's interesting that you did."

"I'm—I'm very honored to be considered." It was true, and she was almost embarrassed at how excited she felt. After hearing from Jordan about Papyrus, a part of her had longed to be invited to join a society too. Now, the idea that Cross & Key saw something in her, maybe admired her smaller, quieter accomplishments—that meant something to her.

"I really appreciate you thinking of me," she said. "And I'd love to learn more." She tried to keep the eagerness out of her voice. How much she wanted to be wanted by a group of strangers.

"I'm glad to hear that," the man said. "Let me give you the details of where we will meet."

~

She called Jordan right after she hung up. Technically you weren't supposed to talk about getting tapped by the societies, but Jordan was basically family, and she knew he wouldn't say anything.

"So, he wouldn't even say who he was?" Jordan asked, after she'd relayed the conversation.

"No," she said.

"Wow, I guess they keep it pretty close to the vest there," Jordan said. "But Astra, this is a real feather in your cap. How are you feeling about it?"

"Well, I was surprised, but I also—well, I also feel really excited. Is that embarrassing? I feel a little embarrassed."

It felt so good to share with him, because he felt like home, and she thought how much she wished she could tell her mom and get her opinion. She said this to Jordan.

He was silent for a few seconds.

"You know that's how your mom and my mom met, right?"

"What!" Astra said, in genuine surprise. "I didn't know that! She never told me!"

"It obviously wasn't Cross & Key," Jordan said. "They didn't admit women until, like, the '80s. But yes, our moms were in a society, called Elsinore. It doesn't exist anymore, it eventually got folded into one of the other societies, but my mom says they still do a lunch for alumni, once a year or something. I know she sometimes goes."

This was the first new fact she had learned about her mother since her death. Astra wondered how many times this would happen in the years to come.

"Just let yourself feel good about this, Astra," Jordan said.

Chapter Thirty-Two

Astra stood outside the metal door, which was painted a listless grey. It was one of the basement seminar rooms in Sheffield, a residential college with Georgian architecture and an emerald rectangle of lawn, completely different from the run-down Gothic courtyard where her own dorm was.

She took a breath, turned the knob, and the door swung inward.

The room was pitch black. Not dim, not the gloom of shades pulled during the day, but so dark she could barely see her hand in front of her face. Even the line of small rectangular windows at the top of the wall above ground had been blacked out with what looked like construction paper. She could make out two figures, both wearing hoods, and though she couldn't see their faces, she could tell they were men.

"Come in, Astra," came a lovely sounding voice from the darkness. "Don't worry, you're in the right place."

It was a polished voice, friendly and correct, like the voices of the student guides who took groups of tidy-looking high schoolers around the campus. Not the person she had spoken to on the phone.

"Hi," she said. "I'm so sorry, I didn't realize I'd need a headlamp for this."

"Yes, sorry for all the cloak and dagger stuff," the friendly voice said. "I imagine it seems a little weird, but we don't reveal our identities during the candidate process."

"Of course," she said. "I understand."

"Only the most selective societies conduct their process in complete secrecy," the voice, clearly the leader, said, hovering silkily over the word *selective*. "There's a chair in the middle of the room, can you see it?"

"Yes," she said, and walked over and sat. She put her hands on her knees, the carefully selected jeans that didn't matter now. Jordan, when she had asked him about the process, had not mentioned anything about blacked-out rooms, and she wished he had, so she could have at least been prepared.

"Astra, we're so glad you've decided to come today. As you know, our society is interested in learning more about you, both as a student and as a person."

"That makes sense," she said. "Thanks so much for considering me." She could feel the raw edge of her eagerness to please. In the last few days, she had dwelled on the reason that maybe they thought she was special because she had tried to remain a thoughtful person, a good person, even through her mother's illness and death. That someone had noticed, and she was being rewarded for it.

"Why don't you start with telling us a bit about what you're studying?"

"Sure," she said. "Well, I'm an English major, you probably know that. I'm taking Emily Huynh's Gilded Age seminar, and I took Deacon Green's creative writing class. Everyone told me how amazing it was, and they were right, though during the first class I wasn't so sure. The guy sounded like some wild pirate."

A laugh came from the corner of the room—warmer, surprised. It was the other man, not the person conducting the interview.

"Did you also take his class?" she said, turning toward the direction of the laugh.

There was a short silence. "Yes," he answered; his voice was lower than the leader's. Deacon Green was a National Book Award winner who had been close friends with Bob Dylan; it was a point of pride that their buttoned-up university had gotten him.

"What did you think?" she said.

"I thought it was so good it blew my fucking mind," came the other voice, and she could tell, from the squeak of a plastic chair moving, that the leader was irritated by this off-script moment. But to Astra, it was the first thing said in the room that made her feel truly comfortable, and she laughed. She liked this person, whose mind was fucking blown, whoever he was. She hoped this was the kind of conversation they had in Cross & Key, and she thought about how to respond.

But before she could answer, the leader broke in. "We want to use this time to get to know *you* more, Astra. You were saying about your classes?"

"Of course, I'm sorry for going offtrack," she said. She had said *I'm sorry* twice now in ten minutes, she was aware of that. She remembered her mother, telling her once when she was in fourth or fifth grade, that it was okay for her to be more assertive. "It doesn't make you impolite, Astra, to be direct. You don't have to apologize for it."

She talked about her courses, how she wanted to be a writer, trying to sound charming and not ridiculous. "I know half of this school wants to be writers, so it sounds silly to say so, but it's true." The men laughed, though it sounded to Astra like polite laughter. They wandered into other predictable territory—her extracurriculars, her position on the small campus magazine.

"At Cross & Key, we're not just interested in your academic accomplishments; we want to understand the whole person. Were there any big challenges you've had to overcome at Longfellow?"

This was the *how have you failed?* question, and usually she was prepared for it.

"Well, like a lot of people, I struggled a little with going from a smaller pond to a much bigger pond."

"Mmm, hmm, yes," the voice said noncommittally. "Though you grew up in New York City, that's hardly a small pond."

"Sure, but I also graduated high school with a class of twenty-eight girls," she said. "That's like a goldfish bowl." Laughter came again from the corner, a real laugh, friendly.

"So that's the most challenging thing you've dealt with?" the speaker said.

"No, I didn't say that."

She thought they must know about her mother. Did they want her to talk about that? She felt hesitant to mention it, offering up her loss as some sort of example of character building. She felt like a student scrambling for the right answer on a test.

"Well, my mother was the first female chief of surgery at her hospital. It was both amazing, growing up with a mother like that, but also a little intimidating. I think I drive myself pretty hard, but I don't think I could take the same risks she did, do what she did. I struggle with measuring up."

"Well, I think lots of students here feel the pressure of having very accomplished parents," the man said. Underneath the politeness, he sounded a little bored.

Astra wished, in that moment, she were Phoebe. Phoebe would know what to say; Phoebe knew how to be daring without being overly confessional. She could walk that line in a way Astra couldn't. Because Phoebe wasn't a rule follower, like Astra. And in that moment, she knew what to say.

"My sister is the one you should be talking to," she said, in a stronger voice. "She's beautiful, impossibly popular, the one who everyone always wants to join their group. I'm five years younger, so in some ways it never occurred to me to be jealous. But then she got married last summer, to this wonderful guy, while I've never even really been in a relationship. You asked me about challenges, and I started to think—why haven't I met anyone here? Why does it come so easily to Phoebe, and not to me?"

She felt the interest in the room shift, and she knew it was because she was sharing something real, and uncomfortable for her, and that is what they wanted.

"And have you come up with any answers?" the leader said. "Do you think you avoid relationships?"

"I don't know," Astra said honestly. "Maybe it's because I don't think—" She trailed off. She thought of Nick kissing her at the wedding, and how for the first time in her life, she felt she could be truly desired, like Phoebe.

"I didn't really have a normal high school experience," she said. "My mother was sick. I wasn't necessarily going out and dating like a lot of my friends. There was something about physical intimacy that felt—like it would be too vulnerable." *Because there was something in me that was broken. Because there still is.*

When the leader spoke, his voice was sympathetic, and also careful, and she appreciated that tact. "I think we can all feel vulnerable in romantic relationships," he said. "But was there—did you have a bad experience with someone?"

If this were any other interview, Astra would have been startled by the question, even offended. But she thought for a small group like this, to be a part of it, there had to be trust. You had to be willing to open yourself up, and she wanted to show them she could. She could do this.

"No," she said. "Or at least, not in the way I think you mean. This summer, I did meet someone, and it felt really rare and special, and then this terrible thing happened. And the strangest thing was—I wasn't surprised. It felt like confirmation that I wasn't supposed to be with someone, that it wouldn't work out for me."

"Astra, thank you for sharing this," the leader said. "We know it takes a lot of courage, to open up. Do you feel comfortable telling us more about what happened?"

Astra hadn't meant to talk about the wedding, but as she began to tell the story, she could feel its currency. Was it wrong to use this story? In another setting, yes, but maybe here, in a place that promised trust and secrecy, it was okay.

She told them about Nick, the sense of a door opening, and then the cold horror of Allie lying on the dock, and how her mother had saved her. And then the fight with Nick that followed. She hadn't meant to tell them all this, but something sparked in the anonymous darkness of the room, as if she could say anything. She wondered whether that was why they conducted these interviews in pitch blackness.

When she was done, there was a pause, and then the leader said, "God, that must have been such an emotional night, Astra. I imagine it's hard to talk about."

"Yes."

"You shared a lot about regret, wishing things could have gone differently. Are there other things you haven't had a chance to do, that you wish you had?"

Maybe it was the fact that she had just been telling them about Nick. Or the fact that she and Nick had been talking regularly on the phone, one of the bright spots in her life since she'd been back. But her mind leaped to the answer, and she spoke it before she had time to reconsider.

"I've never slept with anyone before," she said, in a quiet voice. "I'd like to feel close enough to someone to do that. Sometimes I feel like the only person in college who hasn't."

The room was silent. She felt stunned at what she'd said, even frightened. This was a true secret, something she only discussed with people like Phoebe and Sonia. How could she have spoken it here?

As if he could sense how she felt, when the leader finally spoke, it was also in a soft voice, filled with compassion. "Astra, we really appreciate you allowing yourself to be so vulnerable here," he said. "This is the kind of honest discussion we value."

"We have just a few more questions, is that okay?" he continued.

"Yes, of course."

"And to be clear, there are no wrong answers. We're looking more for *how* you answer."

"I understand."

"The first question is, what's the hardest thing that's ever happened to you?"

She hesitated. There was only one answer to this question, and they must know that. She did not want to parade her grief, but it was part of her. She swallowed.

"We know it can be a tough question, so take your time," the leader said.

"I know the answer," she said. "I'm just trying to figure out how to say it." And then she took a breath, as if she were about to plunge underwater.

"The hardest thing that's ever happened to me is my mother dying," she said. "When she was really sick, I tried to be there for her as much as I could, and care for her. There were days when she was throwing up in the sink, or couldn't get out of bed, and I hated that, not just because she was in pain but because she had been so strong and powerful, all my life, and it was so agonizing, so devastating, to see her diminished like that. I know she hated it too."

There was a different flavored silence in the room now; no one said anything.

"And now, I'm still trying to figure out what it means to be in the world without her. She's always the person I want to call, to tell things to, that muscle memory is always there. I wish I could tell her about today. I miss her. I miss her like a limb, always. She's part of me and you can't just turn that off."

She was close to tears now. She heard the man in the corner shift in his chair again, and cough.

"Astra, I'm so sorry," came the leader's voice, after a brief silence. "When—when did you lose your mother? I didn't know she had died."

"In January," she said. "I just thought—I don't know the candidate process, but I thought that's something you would know."

"Yes, I would have thought that too," said the man in the corner, and he sounded upset. "Astra, we can finish this interview later, if you want. I know this is really emotional to talk about. You don't have to answer any more questions." A long silence followed these words, as if some sort of invisible struggle was playing out between this man and the leader of the interview.

"Actually, my friend is mistaken," the leader finally said in his velvety, kind voice. "We won't have time to reschedule before we have to make our final decisions. But I only have one last question. Would that be all right?"

Later, she would wonder if she'd just walked out then, what would have happened.

"Yes, that's all right," she said.

"I understand these questions can feel really personal, but everything you tell us is completely confidential."

"Okay," she said. "Thank you." It made her feel relieved to hear him say it.

"What's the worst thing you've ever done?"

Something pinged in Astra's mind, a tiny hint of unease. It's not that the question surprised her—it felt like the kind of question these societies asked—but coming so closely on the heels of the last, it felt almost like too much. Was she really being asked to dig around again in the most painful parts of herself?

She felt this unease mingle with her desire to please, to be liked, and wanted, by this group. She longed to be part of something that her mother had been part of, of finding a new community that could wrap around her in her grief. She longed to be seen as worthy. She felt all these feelings existing side by side. But the desire to be wanted was strongest.

What's the worst thing you've ever done?

Astra was not interesting in this way, she knew that. Doing bad things took a kind of courage. When Phoebe snuck out one night in high school to go to CBGBs with Allison, Astra told on her, because the idea of even being an accessory to breaking a rule was too uncomfortable. Afterward, she remembered her sister giving her a look of such disdain, it cut into Astra's soul. "You know Astra, people would actually like you more if you'd just let yourself fuck up once in a while."

And then the answer came to her. It wasn't fun or sexy, it wasn't about a prank gone wrong, or shoplifting, because she'd never done that. It wasn't even an everyday, unremarkable adolescent cruelty. The worst thing she'd ever done brought up a pain so lacerating it felt untouchable in its darkness. But she would try to speak it aloud, here.

"In January, when my mother was hospitalized for an infection, we met with her doctor," Astra said, describing the discussion with Dr. Bass in the sherbert-colored chairs. "And I told them not to give her the antibiotics. I wasn't the person in charge, but I changed the conversation."

No one moved, no one said anything.

"And what's so hard, and confusing, is that in some ways, this was actually the best thing I ever did. I was trying to stand up for her, so she didn't have to suffer anymore. I was trying to say the thing we were all too afraid to say." She thought of what was coming next, a thought she had never spoken aloud.

"But also, I couldn't bear it any longer," Astra said, in a voice so soft it was as if she were only speaking to herself. "And you can say, of course, that makes sense, that's human. It is. But what if she really wanted those weeks? I didn't give her the choice, and that was because of my love for her, but also, a tiny piece of it was I just couldn't do it anymore. I couldn't watch her be so sick." Her voice faltered. "Part of me wanted the person I love most in the world to die."

It was as if it severed her from a piece of herself to speak those words aloud.

The silence was total. There were no more words to wrap around this, and Astra wondered if they regretted asking the question.

And then she heard, from the back of the room the most chilling sound. She heard someone laugh.

The person tried to cover as if it was a cough, but what she heard was unmistakable—a high, nervous laugh. And it was not coming from the man who had been asking the questions, or the one sitting in the corner, occasionally chiming it. There was a third person in the room. Someone she didn't know was there.

She stood up, so quickly that her chair clanged against the floor.

"I'd like to leave now," she said.

"If you can just wait a second, Astra," the leader said. "We're not quite done. I know this must be very emotional, but at Cross & Key, this is the kind of thing we aren't afraid to talk about—"

She felt panic tighten inside her, a cold coil of fear.

"And then you laugh at it?" she said. "Is that what you do, in this society? I don't know who you are, but I know you're not Cross & Key."

As she spoke the words she felt their truth, a truth she had known from the moment she heard the laugh. This was not an interview with Cross & Key. She had no idea who these people she'd bared her soul to were. She felt like she was going to be ill, or start crying, but she held herself together.

And then the third person in the room spoke.

"What an interesting observation, Astra," came the voice from the back of the room, and it was a woman's voice, a low, rich alto. "One of so many you've shared with us today."

Anger bloomed insider her, an anger so great it could blot out the sun. In a ghost story, this would be the moment her mother would brush up against her, her body possessing Astra's for an instant. Her mother, her mother, a commander of men, who brought people back from the dead. She felt, in this moment, her mother's rage, and it filled her with such fierceness that if she had to kill one of them to escape this room, she felt she could.

She was about to speak, and then the other man, the one who had taken Deacon Green's class, shouted, "Astra, just leave, just get out of here! It's a prank!"

Adrenaline surged through her. She could make out the dim shape of the door in the darkness, and she sprinted toward it.

With one swift yank she had it open, and as the light poured in, she could see three figures, hovering back in the darkness. It was still so black in the room that she couldn't find the light switch at first.

She felt along the wall.

"Don't even fucking think about it," the leader said in a voice with all friendliness sanded away. Now it was just a beautiful low voice that vibrated with danger. And then he stomped his foot at her, hard, like he was scattering a flock of pigeons.

She ran. It was like something else in her body took over, propelling her out of the room. She slammed the door behind her, and then she was sprinting, arms churning by her sides, as she raced across the courtyard. She leaned into the turn as she rounded the corner and ran until she could see her own residential college in the distance. She didn't stop until she was outside the gate of her dorm, and her hands shook as she reached for her key card.

"Jesus, Astra, are you all right?" It was Jordan. She shook her head, she couldn't speak, and he put his arms around her. She was shaking so hard from the adrenaline that he started shaking too, but he just stood there, and held her, as people walked by, some staring, others about to open their mouths to speak, but no one did. There is a certain kind of wordless pain that is like a rock people break against, and as Jordan held her, the wave of students flowed around them, not making a sound.

Chapter Thirty-Three

March 1996
New Jersey

Tom thought it must be heartbreak. He could not understand why else Astra would come home in the middle of the night, and yet heartbreak did not really make sense either. There had been the business this summer, with Nick Rosenfeld—a business he and Thea had discussed deeply. But as for his daughter, she had told him nothing, had locked that summer night away in her deep unspoken place, where she stored so many things.

It was interesting to Tom—interesting being a benign-enough word to keep the bitterness he sometimes felt at bay—that stories were his livelihood and yet his girls always held theirs back, auditioning them with their mother before he ever got to hear them. He knew it surprised some of their friends, the ones from Phoebe and Astra's schools, that he worked in publishing and edited novels while Thea was the big deal surgeon. It was the '90s, so no one acted surprised—that would have smelled of regression—but he saw it, the small readjustment. People also assumed it was Thea's job that paid for the New York City private schools, but the truth was Thea's mother wrote the checks, a fact he was grateful for and that also chafed at him, like a tiny cut that wouldn't heal over.

And now Astra was coming home, to him. Even as he worried over her, he felt relief. His daughter had sought him out as a refuge.

Sonia had called him just before he was planning to turn off the light and go to sleep, telling him, in the politest voice, that Astra was driving home to the farm in New Jersey, late on a Friday night, even though it was two weeks until spring break.

"Did something happen?" Tom had barked, in the same voice he'd used when it was the hospital calling. He had to remind himself, sometimes, that there was nothing else to happen, and he could put that part of himself away.

"She'll tell you yourself, Mr. Erickson," she'd said. "She'll be okay." And then, after a dreadful silence, Sonia had started to cry. Tom had frozen in terror, but forced himself to find words, the words he owed this young person who had been so good to his daughter. "Sonia, you are such a good friend to Astra, I've never asked you how this has been for you. How are you holding up?"

"I'm okay, Mr. Erickson. I just miss her, too, I think."

He was confused for a moment; he thought she meant Astra, and then he understood. "You miss Astra's mother?" he said.

"Yes."

He was silent, digesting this.

"Well, she thought you were the bee's knees, Sonia. She was so relieved Astra didn't get some ninny for a roommate, and she said that. 'Thank god Sonia isn't some ninny.'"

They laughed.

"Okay, well, goodnight, Mr. Erickson. Can you ask Astra to call me, just to let me know she got in all right?"

"Of course."

He hung up. He thought he'd done okay, that Thea would have been proud of him. Her absence was an energetic pain that never left, and he'd been shocked that after years of illness, he felt no more prepared for the cold plain fact of her death than if she'd been hit by a bus. But he would think no more about that right now. His daughter was coming home to him, and he needed to be ready.

~

Astra woke up at 11 a.m. She'd slept for twelve hours. Her jacket hung on the back of a chair, neatly folded, and her shoes had been set on the seat with the toes pointed inward, conversationally. She could not remember doing these things.

She was in her old room, in the house in New Jersey where Phoebe was married. Last night, she had been walking back from dinner with Jordan and Sonia—who had not left her side since what happened in the black room two days ago, the thing Astra struggled to even find a name for or describe—and instead of turning toward her dorm, she had started walking in the opposite direction, toward the garage on Chapel Street, where she parked her car, an ancient Saab that was a hand-me-down from Grandy.

"I'm going home," she told them, and when they looked at her, distraught, she realized they thought she was leaving for good. Such a thing had never occurred to her, but the fact that it occurred to them made her feel even worse. "Just for a few days," she'd said, and they hugged her, told her to drive safe. They were good friends, truly good people. Even amid the wreckage of the past forty-eight hours, she had wondered at how these two people cared for her so much.

The drive and the Friday-night traffic had given her time to think. While Jordan had been so furious he'd wanted to do everything—talk to the dean, look at the code of conduct, write an op-ed for the student paper—Astra had stopped him. "We don't even know who they are," she said. "What are we going to do—charge them with impersonating members of Cross & Key and asking me personal questions?" Nothing the university could do, nothing that might happen to these people if they were discovered, could change what had happened, the wound she had inflicted on herself. No one had forced her to speak. That was the truth, dark and plain. She had done it all herself.

Someone had lured her to a dark room to humiliate her in this very specific way that required so much *planning*. I mean, Jesus Christ. She kept thinking about how they could have stopped, after she talked about her mother's death. But they had gone on. They *pressed*. The horror of it registered as a physical pain in her stomach.

And yet, what she could not explain to her friends was that finding these people, confronting them—it didn't really matter to her. It was not the central thing. She had told things to these people, who had brought her there in bad faith, yes. But still, they had not made her speak—she had told them private things about her family. She had traded stories of grief and pain as some sort of price of admission. The shame she felt about what she had chosen to reveal was total, immovable.

Since her mother's death, she'd believed her anguish gave her a kind of invincibility, a protection from anything else that could cause pain. It felt fair, in a way, that in return for such atomic grief she got this small, hard gift. What, after all, could hurt her now? But the shame of what she'd done burned even hotter right now than her grief.

There was very little traffic this time of night, as she drove from the Merritt Parkway to I-80 to the tiny dark roads that led to her father's house. Just her father's house, now. Her tires crunched on the driveway as she pulled up; she saw the light on in the kitchen. Sonia had reached him; he had waited up. She knew she would have to tell him why she had come home, but the idea of inflicting this on him felt impossible. What was she even going to say?

Astra tried to imagine why someone would want to go to such elaborate lengths to humiliate her in this way—the kind of cruelty you only read about in childhood books, like Jane Eyre locked in the red room. And it was that thought, like a bell of recognition, that finally allowed her to guess who had done this.

Chapter Thirty-Four

It was new for Tom, this strange and unfamiliar worry for his daughter. Astra had always been so responsible as a child, and even now, the habit of not worrying about her had stuck. Physical danger like the bobcat, or the bear, or the time a bookcase had fallen on her because she was trying to climb to the top, that of course terrified him. But the other, darker fears he'd left to Thea. God help him, he had. Of course, his wife had told him that after her death, this would change, that he would be called upon at some point to render service to their daughters.

"They won't do that with me," he'd said, and she'd smiled.

"They don't do it with you now because they get to be their best selves with you, and they love that," Thea had said. "But they won't keep that up after I'm gone." She had been right. She was almost always right, in these things.

The ache of missing her mixed with his worry over his daughter.

Perhaps it was grief that was bringing Astra home, but again, Tom doubted it. For all the ways she was like her mother, he sensed that Astra grieved like him—confronting a hole so planet-size it did not make sense to take time, because what did that even mean? This was not a flu to be gotten over. Tom understood the stubborn, obsidian nature of this kind of loss. And what he and Astra had in common is that they both liked their work and had an ability to go on. Grief wouldn't send Astra away from school. It was something else.

This is what he feared. Something strange and sharp and awful, something he would be called upon to help with and where he might be found wanting.

When Tom heard the crunch of the wheels on the gravel, he stood up, balled up his hands into fists, and said, "Tom Erickson, get your shit together now!" And then he walked out the front door, smiling and waving.

"Sweetheart, it's so good to see you," he said, in a voice that sounded heartier than he'd intended, and he saw something flicker over his daughter's face.

She got out of the car. He noticed she didn't have any luggage.

"Did Sonia reach you?" she said. "I'm sorry to show up like this; I didn't want to worry you."

"You know you can show up whenever you want," Tom said. "I'm just so happy to see you, and yes, Sonia called." He looked in the backseat, "Nothing else to bring in?"

"No," she said, almost fiercely. "I have some things here."

"Of course, sweetheart," he said. "Let's get you to bed, and we can have breakfast and talk in the morning. Do you need anything to eat?" She shook her head. He wanted to offer her a cup of hot chocolate or a glass of milk, the way he did when she was a child.

"No, I'm good, Dad," she said. "You're right, I just need to sleep."

He followed her inside, trailing her to her room, wishing she had a suitcase so he could feel useful. Instead, he went to the closet in the hall where Thea kept all the household stuff—extra toothpaste and toilet paper and Band-Aids and shampoo; the closet smelled like a pharmacy in a way he found comforting—and found a new toothbrush in its packaging and a fresh bar of soap. He pressed these small things into Astra's hands and hugged her goodnight. At all costs, he wanted to show her that he could think of these things, too, that he was competent and reliable.

"Lots of love, honeybunch," he said.

She smiled and said, "Love you, Dad. Thanks for taking care of me." And she shut the door. He stood there until he heard the sound of running water, and then he turned and walked back down the hall, carefully turning out the lights. *Thanks for taking care of me.* He wondered for a moment if Thea had told their daughters to say this to him, to buck him up during the fragile early stretches. But he didn't think so. His daughter, his daughter who had washed up here in distress, had sensed his own anguish, and worked to put him at ease. He put his face in his hands and cried.

Chapter Thirty-Five

Astra had been asleep all morning. He kept a pot of coffee on, hoping that when she came down they could have their breakfast together, but at 11 a.m. he put the eggs and milk back in the refrigerator and went outside.

It was one of those early March mornings where the air still smells cold, like an apple that's been cut. It reminded him of football weather. Tom had been the second-string quarterback at Lehigh the year they won the Patriot League, and he had taught his daughters how to play. Astra could still throw a perfect spiral.

"Hey, Dad! I'm alive."

Astra stood a few yards away, smiling. She was bareheaded and wearing her mother's maroon quilted bathrobe with white piping.

"Good morning, sweetheart," he said. Her face was flushed from the long sleep, and she looked like herself again.

"Aren't you cold?" Tom said. "Your mom would call this hat weather." Astra laughed.

"Mom would call this hat weather while never actually wearing a hat."

"Well, of course."

She fell in companionably beside him as they walked back to the house.

"I'm sorry I missed breakfast."

"There is no missing breakfast at this house. I'll get it ready right now." When they got inside, he was grateful for things to do with his hands—making a fresh pot of coffee, frying the eggs, and steaming the yolks with a spoonful of water, until they were pink. Astra unloaded the dishwasher and set the table.

Tom carried over the platter of eggs and toast, and Astra took the coffeepot off the hob and put it between them on a cork mat.

"I know I need to tell you why I'm here, Dad," she said. "But to be honest, trying to string together words to describe what happened feels a bit beyond me now."

"Is it something to do with Mom?" he said. Once, before the funeral, when he had said *your mother* to Astra, she had leveled him with a look whose meaning he understood instantly. It was a bloodless phrase, and he never used it again.

She shook her head. "No. Well, no and yes," she said, and she started to sob, her hands flat against the table. Tom knocked over his coffee as he pushed back his chair and put his arms around her, around the bathrobe that still smelled like his dead wife.

"Leave it, just leave it," he said as he felt Astra tense up as the coffee pooled on the table. "It doesn't matter at all."

She shook in his arms, and he held on. He held on.

~

When she had finally gotten through the story—in the middle, he had yelled, "Jesus Christ!" But that had been his only outburst—he saw his hands had gone numb from gripping the arms of his chair. He thought if he ever found out who these people were, he would drive up to campus and he would confront them, with his greying quarterback height and his wide strong hands, and he would not lay a finger on them, but he would want to. He wanted to kill them, in fact, and they would know this, and this feeling ran through him like an electric current. He took a breath.

"Well, who do we call at Longfellow? What do I talk to? This is completely unacceptable."

"Oh, Dad," his daughter said. "We're not calling anyone at Longfellow."

"Well, it happened on university property."

"Yes, I know. Jordan already looked at the handbook—there's nothing about holding unofficial meetings in a college seminar room. I told him not to bother."

"Well, we can't just let them win, Astra!"

She looked at him, a long steady gaze. He knew this was not the tack he was supposed to take; he could sense that, but he wanted to extract consequences for this horror visited upon his child. He wanted, quite simply, for someone to pay.

"Dad, it's not about what they did," Astra said. "Yes, what they did was cruel and humiliating, but it's about what *I* did. Don't you see?" Her voice was quiet, and she looked so small in the chair.

He'd had a hard time, at first, understanding what she was trying to tell him as she'd poured out the story between sobs. The fake interview with a society—that alone made him vibrate with anger, and for a moment he was terrified she was going to tell him they'd lured her there to assault her in some physical way, his most obvious, awful, and unremarkable fear as a father. But that is not where her story went at all. Instead, she was telling him things she'd said about the wedding and Thea's death. Things she had never told him, but she'd told these strangers.

He remembered Astra, pale and thin as a blade, sitting in the plastic chairs of the hospital waiting room, asking the doctor, "What's the point of the antibiotics?" It had taken him a second to even understand what she was saying. His twenty-year-old daughter, having the conversation with the doctor he should be having. And then the doctor turning to him, and saying with a gentleness that startled him, "Are these your wishes too?"

And then, what she'd said about a part of her wishing Thea would die!

"You didn't do anything wrong, Astra," he said.

"But what about what I told them, Dad?" she said, and it was as if the words mangled in her throat, just speaking them was painful to her. It made him feel furious and tender at the same time. "They have my stories now. Private things I told them about *our* family. They'll always have them."

"Astra, these people took advantage of you—of your openness, your inability to imagine anyone could act in the way they did. You didn't do anything wrong, do you understand that? It's not your fault."

As he looked at his daughter, crumpled up in front of him, her arms wrapped around herself, he'd realized her pain was so deep and physical that she had experienced Thea's illness and death differently, not just as an endless loss but as a wound on her body.

"You told them those stories because you couldn't see who you were speaking to and you aren't trained to answer the kind of questions they were asking, okay? Listen to me, Astra—" It was here, it was here Tom felt he actually had something to offer, a wisdom of experience that was his own.

"I read manuscripts all the time," he said. "A lot of these books are based on conversations with people. And here is what is always unfathomable to me. Unless they are a politician, a CEO, a member of the CIA—someone with actual media training or who is used to working with sensitive information—you cannot believe what these people will say. You cannot believe what they will reveal to someone who is not a friend or a family member. The writer knows this; they count on it. We are human. That man in that room asked you questions in every possible way in order to get you to say something that would hurt you. Someday—not now, when they're patting themselves on the back thinking what . . . what *pranksters* they are, but someday—they will realize what they actually did and have to live with it."

She was quiet for so long that he thought somehow he had made another terrible error, and then she spoke.

"You know what's funny, Dad," she said. "I always wanted to want to be a doctor, but all I ever did was read books. I got that from you, and I'm grateful. I don't know if I've ever said that before."

Tom looked down at the table, then back at his daughter. "Astra, I won't go on the warpath, I won't call the school. I respect your wishes here. But can you tell me who you think put these assholes up to this?"

She almost smiled.

"Yes. Her name is Cynthia Wolf."

"What happened with her?"

"I was, I was sort of hostile to her in a seminar. She'd been mean to Sonia, and our conversation on Edith Wharton got weirdly confrontational. Which is not, by the way, a sentence I ever expected to utter," his daughter said, and they smiled at each other. "And then her boyfriend—I didn't know they were dating—jumped in and cracked a joke at her expense. I don't think she planned for me to pour out my soul in the darkest possible way. I think she just wanted to get something on me—take me down a peg. I don't know."

"Are you going to say anything to Cynthia?" he asked.

"No. I'll tell Jordan, and he knows her, and he may want to confront her, but she could just deny everything. It's not like I have any proof; I just know in my bones it was her. But don't worry, Dad. When I see her, I'll hold my head high."

"I know you will, sweetheart."

Chapter Thirty-Six

The next morning Astra walked into her mother's dressing room to look for waders. They were hanging next to a grey cashmere sweater with maroon cuffs, and she fingered the light wool, then carefully took it off the hanger and put it on. She thought wearing her mother's sweater would make her feel sad, but it didn't, and she wrapped her arms around herself. Today was cold, the sky stuttering between drizzle and damp, caught in the strange pause between seasons.

She had always loved her mother's dressing room, the plain wooden walls covered with photographs and framed Mother's Day cards from her and Phoebe; the collection of slender bottles and brushes and wooden boxes of hairpins arranged on top of the old pine dresser. She opened the top drawer. It was filled with jewelry and scarves and small woven baskets heaped with shells and wooden beads she had never seen her mother wear. She put on a necklace with a small carved elephant.

Next to it was a square, fabric-covered box embroidered with foxes. She thought there would be jewelry inside, but when she opened it, she found a small notebook, with *TLL, 1965–66* written on the front. Astra hesitated. Should she ask her father first? In the weeks after her mother's death, they had all understood that the papers and things and clothes could not be faced yet, not until the summer at least. But her mother's handwriting was intoxicating. She opened the notebook.

> Cutter is back in Boston. He gave me a key chain from Paris with a lady who in a certain light is fully clothed and in a different light is stark naked. I left it by mistake on the table at the St. Regis last Saturday night and haven't had the courage or the vocabulary to write and ask them to send it up. I'm afraid he may ask me to marry him again, but I've told him my focus is on medical school, that it's hard enough being one of the only women and no one will take me seriously if I'm married. (Also, I don't want to marry him.)

She flipped forward a few more pages.

> Huge, awful fight with Cutter. I know he's upset with me, and I am very aware of what I did, but it also didn't feel like there were a lot of options. It's like he wouldn't accept things ending unless I told him to drop dead, which I never would. I care about him, I just don't want to be with him. Something nasty comes out in him in these fights, which surprises me. I hope that's an end to it. I do feel for him, though.

Cutter. It was the name on the flowers at her mother's service.

This must be the college boyfriend her mother told her about, the person who she had felt, with absolute and immovable force, she couldn't marry. That conversation about the past had surprised Astra so much, but this was different—it was a window into the person her mother had been then. Her other life, before Phoebe and Astra. She sounded both exactly like herself and like a stranger.

Astra left the room and walked downstairs. Her father was at the kitchen table, a jumble of trout reels, fly boxes, and fishing leaders in front of him.

"Good morning, sweetheart!" Her father looked at her for a long time. She had forgotten she was wearing her mother's sweater. Yesterday, after she had choked out the story, they had gone for a walk, cooked dinner together, and shared an entire bottle of wine. Her father had suggested they go fishing the next morning, and while it had been years since they'd gone out together, she'd agreed.

They drove her father's truck and parked alongside the road and walked in through the gate. There was no one on the river. They had come here all the time when she and Phoebe were kids, and the sound of the water, the cold, mossy smell of the river, was familiar in some deep, soothing way. She appreciated this suggestion by her father, who worked in silence the way her mother had worked in words. She thought of how almost all her memories of her father were side by side—walking, standing next to each other at the stove, building a fort, fishing, reading next to each other.

"Don't work over the same water twice," her father said. "The fish spook easily here." Astra tied on a silver rat and started casting out behind a log where the current broke. The big browns liked to rest there.

She hooked one on her third cast, an eight-inch brown trout. Then she moved upstream, downstream, throwing out more line. The second fish she hooked was a small brook trout.

"What flies are you using?" her dad called out.

"Silver rats."

"Do you have any more?"

Astra unhooked one from her vest and waded up to her father. She watched while he tied it on and then hooked another brown on his second cast. He removed the hook with pliers, holding it in the water for a moment to let it get oxygen back through its gills, and then it flickered away, a shadow on the water. She found it immensely comforting, more comforting than any words her father could say to her, that he could do these things—his hands steady, his body strong and spry.

"Dad, did you know Cutter Nesbit?"

Her father was examining the hook after releasing the fish, making sure the barb was fully sanded off.

"I only knew what your mother told me. We never met. He was in love with her. I mean, I don't blame him," her father said.

Her father flicked out a few false casts to dry the line and then threw out a good, tight drift.

"Mom said he asked her to marry him."

"She told you that?" her father said, surprised.

"Yes, right before she died. And then I found—I found some writing of hers, in her dressing room."

He really looked at her now.

"He sent that wreath, at Mommy's service," Astra said.

"Yes. He must have seen a notice—maybe it was in the alumni bulletin, I don't know."

A man, a young-looking father, in waders and a worn felt hat came around the bend, dragging two small boys. The children made no effort to walk, but rather hung from the father's hands like shopping bags, twisting and screaming.

"We want to go home, we want to go," they screamed. The man said nothing but kept walking at a steady pace, his face set.

"We want to *go home*." The words swelled to a howl.

The man picked up a boy under each arm and walked up the bank, to the road, out of sight. One of the boys' boots had come off, a bright-blue rubber blue with loops, and the dad just left it, lying there on the bank.

Her father looked at her and smiled.

"I miss that," he said.

"Really?"

"Really."

"You know you can have whatever of your mom's things you want," he said. "You and Phoebe. They're for you."

"I know."

Chapter Thirty-Seven

Astra helped Tom break down the rods and put away the gear. "I do think I'd like to go through some of Mom's stuff," she said. "Were there—were there things she wanted us to see?"

Tom paused. "I don't know. I thought she would go through it all, let me know what to do with it, but in the end, she didn't. Most of it is in storage in the apartment. But I don't know if there were things she didn't want to see. You'll have to decide whether that's a door you want to walk through."

"I understand, Dad," she said. "I'm not going to put this on you if I read something I wish I hadn't."

He looked at her. "Sweetheart, you can put things on me. You can put everything you need to on me. You know that, right?"

His daughter said nothing.

"Do you remember that weird part of Longfellow's application, where the parents had to write a letter about who their child was?"

"Yes, and Mom wrote about me running into the springhouse with the raccoon, to save Phoebe."

"I wrote that, Astra."

He was not saying it defensively. He was giving it to her, an offering.

"And I'm not saying that to try to pretend I can be what your mother was to you. We've always had something different, you and me, and I've loved that. But I'm here. I can handle the hard stuff. You don't have to be okay for me."

She looked at him, and her face looked so much like her mother's it was a new pain he had no idea how to categorize. "But I do have to be okay for you, Dad," she said. "I do."

He shook his head, and spread his hands out, palms up. "You don't, Astra. Please hear me say this. I don't love you because you always try to be good. That's not the reason I love you at all, but I worry sometimes you think it is."

He watched her face. They were very far out on a limb, further than they had ever traveled as father and daughter.

"Did Mom tell you to say that?"

"No."

"Sometimes I'm scared, if I really fall apart, I won't have anyone left," Astra said quietly. "Sonia and Jordan, they're amazing, but when I get back to school, I need to be myself again. I don't want them to feel like they have to be so careful around me, as if I were something that might break. And I don't want to be some burden on you and Phoebe."

"You are never a burden, Astra."

She nodded, and a tear slid down her face and hung on her jawline, she didn't bother to wipe it away. "Well, okay, I'm glad to know that," she said, and she smiled, and he could tell she was taking a step back, signaling that this moment of truth telling was over. It was all right. What he'd said could not be unsaid, and that was a good thing. He wanted her to know there was nothing conditional, ever, about his love.

Chapter Thirty-Eight

The next morning Astra called Sonia from her bedroom.

"How are you, Sones?" she asked. "I promise I'm coming back, probably tomorrow, so don't get too into the single life."

"I won't. I have no one to do late-night runs to Wawa with, after all," she said with a laugh. Then there was a pause. "Nick called. I told him you'd gone home for a couple of days. He sounded surprised."

Astra was sitting on her bed, and out of her window she could see the corner of the pond, where a dogwood tree grew by the spring that fed into the water. It was always the first tree to bloom in spring, opening itself to the sky like a fan. Her father would call her every year to tell her it was out, a tiny ritual between them. On this March morning the buds were still closed and there was just a faint shiver of green along the branches, and she thought how this year, her father would watch the tree bloom alone.

"Sonia, I can't talk to Nick right now," Astra said. "If he calls again, tell him I'm going to write him and explain."

"Why? Did something happen?"

"No, it has nothing to do with him."

There were a few seconds of silence on the phone.

"Astra, I've seen you talk to Nick—he makes you happy."

Talking to Nick did make her happy. He felt like this one thread of connection that somehow wound up the pain of her mother and the pain of the summer in a way that didn't require an exhausting explanation.

"I know," Astra said. "It's just—things feel a little too raw right now. Like I get so excited when I talk to him, I think we're going to get together, and I'm not sure I can handle something else going wrong."

There was another pause on the phone. It was as if Astra could hear Sonia trying to figure out what to say.

"Please don't let those assholes get to you," she said finally. "What they did to you doesn't mean Nick is going to do something to you."

"No, it's not that," she said quickly. "Nick just represents something I can't do right now. It's not—it's not the part of my life where good things happen."

There was another silence, and then Sonia spoke, slowly and carefully.

"I'm sorry, I love you, Astra, but what you're saying is dumb," she said. "I get that it feels scary to be back in touch with Nick, to see what might happen with him, and if you were sharing concerns about him, that would be different. But you're not."

"I just can't do it, Sonia," Astra said, her voice rising. "I don't have it in me. And yes, I'm sure if I open myself up to him again, it will end badly, because it always does. And I said all those things about him to those strangers! I feel awful enough already; I can't bear to be reminded of it, over and over."

"Astra—" Sonia said, and stopped. "Okay, I get that this is how you feel right now. Okay? I respect that. So just don't make this decision now. Give yourself some space. Don't cut him off now, when all you want is to be hard on yourself because you feel guilty about what you said to those fake Cross & Key monsters."

Out the window, Astra saw her father walking alone to the little kitchen garden, carrying a split wooden basket. He lifted the latch and let himself in, and from the upstairs window, she thought his figure looked lonely and small.

"Okay, Sonia," she said. "I'll try."

They said their goodbyes; Astra hung up. She thought of the guts it must have taken for Sonia to speak so directly, to be honest with Astra even when she knew her friend was in pain. Sonia was probably right, too, that it would be stupid for Astra to cut off Nick now. But it didn't matter. She knew she only had enough strength to keep putting one foot in front of the other, in the world where her mother was not, the world where she had betrayed her family to strangers in the dark. She was too tired for anything else.

~

Her father had moved things around so he could stay with her on Monday, and the plan was she would drive back to Longfellow on Tuesday morning, before her classes. They went for a walk, read the paper, watched a movie. It was a quiet, almost absurdly normal day.

After dinner, her father insisted on doing the dishes while she got ready for bed. But instead of going to her own room, Astra walked back to her parents' bedroom. She was not exactly trespassing—she had been in her mother's closet, and her father knew that. She even walked into the closet now, as if she was pretending that's what she was there for. She ran her hand along the tidy row of jackets and shirts so that they swung gently on their padded hangers.

But then she walked out, past the wide tigerwood maple bed and the windows looking out over the pond, and into her father's closet. It always surprised her, the few times she had been in there, that there was one tiny corner of the house she was so unfamiliar with. There was the rack of his country clothes, flannel and poplin button-downs and a few weathered wool blazers, none of the herringbone or windowpane suits he wore to the office, and the small oak dresser crowded with photographs. These were not the photographs displayed around the house or in the albums, not the Christmas card snapshots, but more intimate, mostly of her mother before she or Phoebe was born, and this was what drew her in here. The photographs of her mother as a person, a woman, with her own desires and longings.

She picked up a framed photo of her mother and father at their engagement party, her mother's dark-chestnut hair curled into waves, wearing a long multicolor skirt of braided silk. Such a bohemian outfit for her mother, who'd always had a sharp career woman's style. Then there was a photo of her mother on the beach, lying down with her long legs bent in front of her, looking toward the camera.

This photo, it still had heat, and Astra felt embarrassed looking at it, as if she were a child trespassing. Phoebe, in her cool, aloof way, could be seductive, she knew that, but she did not think of the Erickson women as sexy. Had her mother folded up that part of herself and put it away, or had it always been there, and Astra had not noticed, because she did not have it in herself? And then, she remembered those minutes with Nick by the pond, how he lifted her up to face him in the darkness and she moved against him. It was like thinking back to the memories of another person, but it was also her, she knew. She was also that person.

She turned to a photo of her mother looking at someone while she nursed Phoebe. There was such young joy in her face, Astra could understand why her father kept it here, hidden away. Phoebe had just been born, and her mother was just becoming a mother. That private, secret happiness—it was as if she was sharing a look with their father in that final liminal space.

She opened the top drawer of the dresser. There, above the carefully folded socks and belts, lay another notebook, and the unmistakable slant of her mother's handwriting. *TLE, 1995–1996.*

But this was something else.

She reached for the book and opened it to a random page.

> I can't stop thinking about Astra begging me not to have the surgery in Rhode Island, and I didn't listen to her. Not because I wasn't so grateful to her for sticking up for me in a different way—if she had

been a doctor Astra would have been a quality of life doctor—but because I couldn't feel like I hadn't tried everything I could. I tried to make her see that, but I don't think I succeeded. And in the end, all that fuss and it never happened.

She flipped feverishly through the journal, stopping near the end.

I feel a strange, almost girlish excitement for the wedding. Phoebe and I went together for her final fitting last week. The bridal salon was on the second floor, and there was some consternation, when I showed up in a wheelchair. But they were very kind, and I could manage up the stairs with my cane. Phoebe looked so beautiful I did weep. And when the French woman who was helping us, with dark bobbed hair as tidy as a seal's, smiled at me, it was like she was saying, "I know you are not feeling your best, but look, you have this beautiful daughter, and there must have been a time you were beautiful too." And I felt such pride. Is that superficial? Oh well, so what. Off to bed.

Astra remembered Phoebe calling her at Longfellow to tell her about the dress, and how happy their mother had seemed. She'd felt a small twist of disappointment she'd not been able to come.

I keep dreaming about Phoebe's wedding. Maybe because I'm scared I'm going to conk out and die before it. In the dreams I only see Phoebe and Astra, not Eli. It's like he's a minor player, even though he's the groom, which is ridiculous. He will be good for Phoebe, I think.

> Last night I dreamed the tent was going up, the scaffolding like a carcass of a massive beast. It was not white, but rather these wild carnival colors, and it was huge, several stories high. And then, just when it was fully erect, a gust of wind came and blew it over, and the sound it made when it struck the ground was terrifying.
>
> I ran outside to check on it, but the tent had vanished, it was suddenly just a field of early alfalfa, that bright, almost sick shade of green you only get at the beginning of spring. And in this empty field I realized suddenly that I was a child, no more than six or seven, and I was alone. I could hear my mother's voice, calling for me, and she sounded so worried I ran as fast as I could back to the house. "There you are, sweetheart," she said, "where have you been?" and I could not answer. The words would not come out of my throat, it was that horrifying dream silence, where you cannot speak. And she kept saying, "why won't you tell me?" in this sweet, loving voice that was totally unlike her.

To feel her mother close again, to hear her voice, even in this strange way, caused Astra's heart to jerk queerly.

> I wish my dreams weren't so obvious. When Tom tries to tell me about his dreams, I have to force myself to pay attention, they are so boring. But I never tell him that. I'm surprised, sometimes, by the things I don't tell him.

Astra turned the page, but there was nothing else

Part IV: The Letter Box

Chapter Thirty-Nine

January 1999
New York City

Phoebe took off her hat, unwound her long tartan scarf, shrugged out of the dark wool duster that she wore on the coldest days of the year. There was no snow—snow usually made the city feel warmer—it was just bare, freezing sidewalks and ice. The winter, to Phoebe, had felt endless.

She hung her jacket in the coat closet that all the employees who didn't have offices used and sat down at her desk. Phoebe worked as a junior analyst covering telecom companies at the securities firm Kemper, and she was good at what she did. But while her parents had been nothing but proud of her when she got a job in finance, she felt a throbbing suspicion that she looked like a sellout to her friends. And that maybe even her family, deep down, expected her to do something else.

Then there was the fact that she was married, and no one else in the office her age was. "It's just all so conventional," Allison had told her, as the fissure that opened around her wedding became a chasm in their friendship, a fact that caused her such distress that sometimes she lay in bed, unable to sleep, while Eli lay like a stone beside her. It was not just the loss of Allison—Allison who was Phoebe's wild friend, the first concert they'd gone to together was Liz Phair at CBGBs during her Exile in Guyville tour—but the fear that she was right. Allison, more than anyone, represented the sense of intoxicating, youthful rebellion of her teenage years, that stretch of time when she was horrible to her mother because her mother was not yet dying. When anything was in her grasp.

Phoebe had thrown open doors and then closed them, one by one. She had chosen to live in the city of her birth; she had chosen to spend her life with one person; she had chosen to work on spreadsheets and make airtight models of telecom companies for her boss.

And for the last six months, Phoebe had been trying to get pregnant. She told no one—not Astra, not her father, certainly not her friends—it would be one more untouchable topic lying between them. Even Eli told her there was no rush, she was only twenty-nine, and Phoebe could not explain to him the desperate need she felt to have a child now, when she was healthy and strong, so she could run up the chances of living until her son or daughter was at least as old as Phoebe had been when her mother had died. How do you explain this to someone whose family is intact? It had been three years now since her mother had died. How did she explain to Eli that her biggest fear was dying on her kids, kids who did not even exist yet, and this lived, alongside and in opposition to, her horror at the idea of living beyond her mother. That too felt impossible, and like a betrayal.

That morning, when she got her period, she had sat on the toilet and cried. Eli found her like that when he came in to brush his teeth, in his pajamas, and he threw his arms around her, laid his head against hers. Where did this fathomless well of kindness come from? Was it inexhaustible? Should it be? Phoebe didn't know.

Later, at work, she was about to go get some coffee from the office kitchen when the phone rang, and she saw her sister's number on the caller ID. "Hey Astra," she said, trying to sound cheerful.

"Hey Phoebs! I was checking on dinner with you and Eli next week. With me and Adrian? I made a reservation at Malatesta at eight p.m."

"Oh right, I forgot," she said. "That sounds great."

There was a short pause. "Is everything okay?"

Phoebe considered the question. Since Allie's accident at the wedding, and what happened with Nick, Phoebe had worried about her sister, joining her worry to her mother's. "She didn't get as much time with me as you did, before I got sick," her mother told Phoebe once, and Phoebe remembered feeling a fierce relief that she was the oldest and then wondering if she should feel ashamed. But Phoebe didn't feel ashamed; she was grateful she'd had more time. She had always liked being the older sister, the one who did everything first.

And now, suddenly, with a sort of vertigo, it felt like Astra was all accounted for, in a job she liked, dating a wonderful man, and Phoebe was the one struggling with uncertainty.

The everyday parts of life had always fallen into place more easily for Phoebe than Astra, and now she felt confused, disoriented. All she ever wanted was happiness for her sister, but not, perhaps, without the griefs and disappointments that made Phoebe feel needed.

"I'm a little blue today, that's all," she said.

"Did something happen?" Astra asked. "Or is it just normal mulligrubs?" That was their mother's word, one they used only with each other.

"No, nothing happened," Phoebe lied.

"Is Eli okay?"

"Yes, he's perfect, maybe that's the problem. It gets sort of annoying." There was truth in this, but she found herself with the unfamiliar feeling of wanting to throw her sister off the scent.

"I had the dream about Mom again last night," Astra said, suddenly changing the topic. "The one where I'm trying to tell her Dad is getting remarried, but I can't speak?"

Phoebe was quiet. "Why do you think you're having this dream when Dad isn't, in fact, getting married?" she said finally.

"I don't know. But I keep having it, over and over." There was a pause on the line, and then her sister said, "Hey, why don't we meet for lunch today, just you and me? We could do the Palace?"

"I'd love that. You sure you can get away?"

"Yes, I'm not on deadline today," she said. "I'll see you at what—twelve thirty?"

"Done."

Phoebe hung up and felt her spirits lift. She went and got a coffee, then sat down and opened her work email.

At the top of her inbox was a name she did not recognize. C. Nesbit. The subject said, I knew your mother and have been trying—the rest was cut off. *Nesbit.* A bell rang in Phoebe's mind. The man who sent her the wedding gift, and that big funeral wreath at their mother's service? She tried to recall something Astra had told her a few years ago, when they had gone through their mother's papers. Then she remembered. Cutter Nesbit. The man who had proposed to her mother when she was in medical school. She clicked on the email. I knew your mother and have been trying to reach you.

Phoebe looked around the office, as if to make sure no one was watching her, and then she started reading.

Chapter Forty

Astra was sitting in their booth, her hands circling a mug of coffee, when Phoebe arrived fifteen minutes late.

"I'm so sorry, Astra, but I do have an excuse. You're not going to believe the email I got."

Her sister leaned in.

"It was from this man named Cutter Nesbit."

Astra, unlike her, instantly recognized the name.

"Oh my god," Astra said. "Mom's old boyfriend? What did he say?"

"He said—well, I printed it out. He said he has some letters of hers and wanted to get our address so he can send them to us."

Phoebe was holding the typed pages, but Astra held up her hand. "Wait, I can't—I need a minute."

The waiter came, and they ordered their usual—a grilled cheese for Astra, a BLT for Phoebe, plus fries and a salad that was just a wedge of faded iceberg lettuce they would not actually eat.

"Okay, let's have it," Astra said, and Phoebe handed over the pages. She had stood next to the laser printer in the office as the text inched out, to make sure no one else saw it.

She watched as her sister read it twice.

"Jesus," said Astra.

"I know."

Phoebe watched as she took a sip of coffee, then put the mug down carefully.

"It's like—do you think he's been in love with Mom, all this time? The way he talks about her, it's her but also not her—not Dad's version of Mom."

"The story he tells about Mommy steering that sailboat away from the rocks, because she was the only one who actually looked at the charts? I didn't even know she could sail," Phoebe said.

"Well, Dad doesn't like the water," Astra said, and they both paused, mulling this over. The idea that their mother could have been a different version of herself, without their dad, had never occurred to Phoebe, and she doubted it had occurred to Astra either. She'd loved her mother infinitely, but she'd had very little imagination about her.

"Have you responded to him yet?" Astra asked.

"Of course not! I was waiting to talk to you first."

Astra nodded. "I think we should ask him to send the letters. But maybe we don't—maybe we don't tell Dad until after we get them?"

Phoebe looked down at her hands, her unpolished nails.

"I agree," she said. "And I know this is going to sound weird, but could we also not mention this to Adrian and Eli when we're out to dinner next week?"

"You're not going to tell Eli?" Again, Phoebe had surprised her sister. In most of her life, Eli was her first call, the person she talked things through with. She was still just as close with Astra and her father, but there was a natural reordering. But when she opened Cutter's note, that gravity reversed itself, and she felt the bond between her and her sister pull tighter.

"I'm going to tell him, just not right away."

"Okay."

"Thanks, Astra."

Her sister nodded, then smiled. "A family secret!" she said. "Remember the time we got chased by Mrs. Newsom's dog, after Mom and Dad warned us not to go over there, and we never told them?"

Phoebe remembered. Mrs. Newsom had a German shepherd named Tiny, and the girls, playing in the woods one day, crossed the fence line, exploring deeper into the forest. Phoebe remembered her parents' warning, but ignored it—it wasn't like Tiny was going to come bursting out of the bushes. But then he literally did; they heard the galloping jingle of his collar before they saw him, hurtling toward them through the leaves. "The fort!" Phoebe had yelled as they ran, arms knifing the air. They were in actual danger, Phoebe knew that, but sprinting next to her sister, scrambling up into the branches of the ancient oak tree where they had a tree house, laughing and panting until Tiny lost interest—well, that was living.

"Of course," said Phoebe. "It was an adventure."

"An adventure," Astra said. "We haven't had one of those in a long time."

Chapter Forty-One

Astra had met Adrian during the spring of her senior year at Longfellow. He was a first-year law student, so they didn't have any classes together, but he was a regular at a café off the beaten path where she went every week to work on her thesis. It was a sunny, run-down coffeehouse that smelled like old paperbacks and espresso grinds. Adrian would work there, too, and for weeks they came at the same time, recognizing each other though they never spoke.

Sometimes she would find herself looking at his slim wrists emerging from his threadbare cardigan as he read with a hand against his head, a book propped up in front of him. He wore soft button-downs with frayed collars and flip-flops when it was below freezing. A classic prep school look, but it seemed natural on him. She often got the feeling, when she looked over at him, that he had just looked away from her.

He came to a party her friend was having before Easter, arriving with another graduate school student who was dating a senior. She gave him a little wave—it seemed ridiculous not to, they saw each other at least twice a week—and he walked over, drink in hand.

"Hello, Astra," he said. She did not realize he knew her name, and he seemed suddenly embarrassed, a faint blush creeping up his neck, above his collared shirt. "Sorry for the familiarity, my friend knows you—" He vaguely gestured to the other grad student, who Astra had never seen in her life. "I'm Adrian."

She shook his hand, and he smiled, a dazzling smile with a touch of goofiness. He put his hand in his hair and ruffled it, the way she'd seen him do in the coffee shop. "I should have said hi before, but I think it's kind of creepy for random guys to start chatting with girls in cafés."

"I can see that," she said.

"Of course, nothing was stopping you from saying hi."

"That's true," she said. "And yet, I didn't." She smiled, and there was both a challenge in her voice, but also a playful note, so he wouldn't just think she was unbearably rude. She was more guarded now with strangers, after what had happened with Cross & Key.

When he realized she wasn't going to say anything else, he laughed.

"Do you want to go out for a drink with me sometime?" he asked.

She hesitated, she was actually considering it, and he saw this, and smiled that goofy smile again. "Or, you know, just get coffee and talk about *Middlemarch*?" She had carried it with her to the coffee shop for weeks, since her thesis was on George Eliot, and to realize he had watched her closely enough to know this made her feel both excited and strange.

"All right," she said. "But only because you've made me an offer I can't refuse."

Adrian clapped his hands together like a little boy. "Yes!" he said. "Tremendous."

The first four or five times they hung out, she wasn't even sure if they were dates; he barely touched her. She felt grateful for this—ever since the horror of the pitch-black room, she found she couldn't bear to open herself up to someone new in that way. She could only let someone get to know her in friendship, even that felt hard at times. And yet, each time they had finished coffee, and he had walked her back to her street, and then said goodnight and walked away, she always felt a tug of disappointment. This surprised her.

Adrian had, indeed, read *Middlemarch*. His mother was a high school English teacher, at the boarding school where his father was the headmaster. "My mom has a PhD, she could've been a professor," Adrian said. "She came here to study from Taiwan, and then she met my father and ended up staying."

"Why didn't she want to teach in college?" Astra asked. She was not sure if the question was too direct, but she was always fascinated by other people's mothers.

"She says she didn't want to deal with college politics, but honestly I think it's because she didn't want to outshine my dad. That always bummed me out."

"Do you think your dad sees it that way?"

"Oh no," he said. "I mean, my dad thinks she hung the moon, he always jokes about how much smarter she is than him. But I don't know if he would do that if she was actually a bigger deal than him. He's not a small person, though."

"My mom had the bigger-deal job when I was growing up too," Astra said. "She was the first woman to be head of surgery at her hospital."

"Wow," Adrian said. "Does she still practice medicine?"

"She died, about a year and a half ago," Astra said. This moment had come earlier than she expected, but she found she didn't regret it.

"Oh, Astra," he said. "God, I'm so sorry. I'm sorry for asking that."

"No, please don't worry," she said. "I wouldn't have brought her up if I wasn't comfortable discussing her. The truth is, I don't talk about her as much now, and that makes me sad."

"Well, whenever you want to, I'm here," he said carefully. She felt he was trying so hard to say the right thing, and it endeared him to her.

~

Adrian grew up as a classic FacBrat—faculty brat, as he explained to her—running around campus when the students were away on vacation, finding bottles of Absolut vodka and loose cigarettes hidden in people's rooms and throwing a little party for himself. "I was a terror, but I also loved school, I loved studying," he said. "I looked up to my parents as educators. It wasn't until high school that I realized no one thought being a teacher was cool."

"Do you want to be a teacher?"

"You know I'm in law school, right?" he said, and smiled. "I think my mom wanted me to be one, but she's let it go."

"I mean, I can think of some girls' schools where you would be very popular," she said. It was the first time she'd referred to his looks, and he smiled and took it easily.

When the check came, Adrian grabbed it before she could. He paid, always.

"You know, this is starting to feel prehistoric," she said. "Why don't you let me treat today?"

"The last thing I want is for you to feel unliberated," he said. "How about this? My roommate really loves those little Splenda packets, but they're hard to find," he said, pointing at the small ramekin filled with sugar and yellow sweetener packets. "You have such an innocent face—why don't you just grab an inappropriately large handful and shove them in your purse?"

He smiled like a little boy, which threw into relief how tall and wide in the shoulders and not-a-boy he was physically, and Astra felt her face growing warm.

"I'm sorry, are you asking me to steal these sweetener packets for you because you bought me breakfast?"

"Well, they're for my roommate, but yes," he said, and then he picked up the dish and dumped the entire thing in her purse. "See how easy it is?" he said.

"Adrian!" she cried, but what struck her was how happy this tiny transgression made her. Adrian didn't care about being embarrassed, he didn't care about nudging a toe over the line, and she knew that a large part of this was because of his beauty, and the fact that people instinctively liked him, but still. It was thrilling.

When they were outside—she did not put the packets back—he grabbed her hand and swung it wildly. "See? The perfect getaway."

"Adrian, I had no idea you were so weird," she said.

"Isn't that why you like me?" he said, looking right at her. "I mean, if I were you, that's why I'd like me."

She thought he was going to kiss her, but he just said, "You know I'm going to be a bad influence on you, right?" and smiled.

~

The next time he suggested they go out for breakfast, she said, "Let's go to a bar tonight instead. I can't drink any more coffee."

It was their first time getting a drink together, and as they settled into a booth at the Anchor, near campus, she thought he seemed uncomfortable. Astra saw another senior who she knew a little from one of their history sections glance at them and quickly look away.

She started to ask him a question, and he shook his head. "No, I want to talk about you tonight. I'd like to hear more about your mom, but only if you want to talk about it."

She didn't say anything right away, and a look of worry crossed his face. "I know I like to joke around, to have fun. But I can talk about serious things. I'm not, you know, the court jester."

"I know that," she said.

"It's just . . . you said you were sad you didn't talk about her much—I don't want you to feel like you have to hold back with me."

What Astra liked most about Adrian was how easy he was to talk to. She knew how overused that phrase was—when she'd told him he'd made a face and said, "I just hope that's not what they put on my gravestone"—but what she couldn't fully explain to him is what easy to talk to meant to her. With Adrian, she could be a different version of herself, not a lie, but less raw. She had grown more comfortable sharing with him. Adrian listened. He listened and he remembered the things she said, down to the smallest detail. She felt it was a chance to retell her story, on her own terms.

"What would you like to know about her?" she asked.

"I don't know," he said, and he laughed. "I didn't think you were going to ask me that. I guess—I can tell your mother is a big part of how you see the world. So that interests me. It's clear she had a really demanding job, that she was—well, she was a big deal. That must have been amazing, but were there were ways it was also hard? Did she have to be away a lot?"

"I didn't find it hard," Astra said. "There were some nights when she was on call, and had to go back into the hospital, but I also thought that was exciting. She was important. I mean, that sounds weird how I put it. But I liked having a mother who was really good at something, and other people saw that. But now that I've said that out loud, it sounds sort of grandiose."

"You were proud of what she did. Some people go through their whole lives without feeling that way about their parents. That was like, half the kids at boarding school."

"But I don't want you to think about her as some sort of saint. She had a really salty sense of humor. She swore a lot when she was driving. She could be really strict, but I liked that, actually. Her sense of right and wrong—it wasn't inflexible, but she had clarity. I remember once trying to wriggle out of going to a dance with this guy, Evan Stubbs, when I was fifteen. She was having none of it," Astra said. "I can still remember her, standing there in her bathrobe—'You said you would go to the dance with Evan and that's who you are going with.'"

She imitated her mother's voice as she said this, the note of authority that came so easily to her mother, and Adrian smiled.

"But in the end," she said. "I was relieved."

"Why?"

"Because I knew it was wrong to stand up Evan, and I needed someone to tell me that. Now I don't have her anymore to do that."

"I think you have that part of her inside you, Astra," he said.

"You don't know me well enough to say that."

She saw something flicker across his face, as if he was afraid she was upset with him, and then he said, "I know, but I can tell anyway." And even though he couldn't, not really, it still made her feel good.

That night, when he walked her home to the tiny off campus apartment she and Sonia shared, he said, "Thank you so much for telling me about her, Astra. Your mom, I mean." And then he put his arms around her, and pulled her into him, and she could feel his heart like a piston in his chest, almost as if he was afraid.

She looked up at him and said, "It's okay, Adrian." And he smiled, and then he brushed her hair behind her ear and kissed her, very slowly and gently at first, just with his lips, and then harder, when she kissed him back.

When they finally broke apart, he smiled at her, and said, "Goodnight Astra." He did not ask to come up, and she did not invite him.

She thought, as she climbed the stairs, that it was the most lovely kiss she'd ever experienced, except for one.

~

When she was alone in her room, she thought she would lie in bed and turn over Adrian's kiss in her head, but instead, she found herself thinking of Nick.

She'd called him, after she drove back to college from her father's, and told him what happened with the Cross & Key interview. She remembered the sound of his voice, his anger. He'd said he wanted to come see her, and she'd said no.

It would be too risky to open herself up to Nick again. It was too risky to open herself up to anyone. She had her friends and her work and her family, and that would need to be enough.

What she was able to understand now, as she lay in bed after the kiss with Adrian, was that she had been wrong. She could open herself up again. She had not let herself do it with Nick, but now she had a second chance.

~

Adrian also understood her fear. The first time she went up to his room, they were lying in bed, kissing, and then he started to lift her shirt over her head, and stopped. He smoothed it down and put his arms around her.

"Is this the part of our relationship when you want to tell me you've never slept with anyone before?" he said, in the gentlest voice.

"Wait, are we in a relationship?" she said. She hated it, this defensive lightness that wasn't her, but had become like her.

He was quiet for a moment, and then he said, "It's okay, Astra. We don't have to talk about it, we can just lie here and I can hold you, if that's all right."

She turned her face into his neck, and then she said, "Yes, I haven't, but that's not even it. I feel like a total fraud, acting like I can be with someone in this way."

He didn't push her to say anything more, and then after a few minutes, he said, "The first time I kissed you, I was terrified. We can take this as slow as you want. But you saying you feel like a fraud—I don't understand that. But if you're willing to talk about it, I would like to try."

"There's something broken inside me," she said, quickly, as if she would lose her nerve. "You haven't noticed yet, but there is. Relationships don't work out for me."

Adrian was silent, she felt his chest rise and fall, and it was okay, this silence. The words were outside her now.

He turned his face toward her. "My beautiful girl, there is nothing wrong with you. We all have our broken things, yours have just been harder than most," he said. "And I know"—and his voice changed, for a stunned moment she thought he might cry—"that maybe I can't help at all, but I want to. I want to so much."

She kissed him then, and he could tell from the kiss that something had changed, and he let out a small sigh. Inside, she felt a realization settle upon her. She'd told Adrian the truth. He could understand her, fully, and still want to be with her. She hadn't been sure that was possible, until now.

~

A few days before Astra's college graduation, when they were out to dinner together, Adrian looked up from the menu and said, "What if I just stayed in New York, after the summer?" He had an internship at a law firm in the city.

"Well, how does that work if you're going back to law school?"

"What if I tried to transfer to NYU or Fordham?"

She put down the menu and looked at him.

"I was thinking about it before we started dating," he said, without defensiveness. "I think it was a mistake to go straight to law school after undergrad, in the same school. I should have taken some time off, but then I wouldn't have met you," he said, and grinned, making a little flourish with his hands. "So, the next best thing seems to be to move to New York."

She felt a churn of fear in her stomach, a panic she didn't understand. As the silence stretched on, she saw a shadow cross his face.

"You're scaring me a little," Adrian said.

"I just don't want you to make such a big decision because we are dating," she said, which was true, but also felt like a stall. "It's only been a few months. What if we bust up and you've left a top three law school for a top ten law school? How could I forgive myself?" She was smiling, and he was smiling, but she could feel her heart as if she was sprinting uphill.

"Wow," said Adrian. "You actually want to take things slower than I do. It's pretty hot."

Since meeting Adrian, she'd let herself feel happy, truly happy. It was like a bargain she'd made with herself, that at first she'd told herself she would allow until graduation, and now she was extending through the summer. But Adrian wanted to be with her in New York. He didn't just want end-of-senior-year, Longfellow Astra. He wanted all of her, and while she was trying so hard to be that person with him, the idea of living together with him in New York made her falter.

"Adrian, thank you for being so understanding," she said. "That sounds like a good plan."

He leaned back, took a sip of his drink, and smiled. "Well, this is new for me," he said. "I kind of like it."

She smiled at him, relieved he wasn't upset or angry. "You are just the loveliest human, you know that?" she said.

For a long moment, he was silent, as if he was thinking of what he wanted to say.

"Astra, I—" he said, and then he stopped. He reached across the table to take her hand. "Don't worry, I love running after you."

His words thrilled her, and she also wondered what it was he'd wanted to tell her, and then at the last moment changed his mind.

~

Adrian met her family for the first time at graduation. He joined her at a dinner with her family, Farris, and Elizabeth and Allie.

While it was the first time he was with the people she loved most, she found that she did not worry about him. Someone like Adrian was made for this dinner. He had perfect manners when he wanted to use them.

He was a warm listener, asking specific questions that disarmed them. When Phoebe left for the hotel, early because she had to catch a flight in the morning for work, she squeezed Astra and said, "What a gem. It's like all your relationship karma has been stored up for this person." And Astra had glowed. She had glowed.

And then Farris had said, as Astra waited with her for her cab to come, "Well, he certainly put on the charm offensive."

Astra had in fact told Adrian, before dinner, how important it was to make an effort with Farris. But now, she felt the tiniest bit let down. Charm was not particularly high on Farris's list of important qualities.

"But what else?" she said, and she could hear an almost plaintive quality in her voice she didn't like.

"I mean, he's certainly eager to please," Farris said.

"Farris!"

"That's not a bad thing. You're a reason to try hard, that's obvious."

"What do you think my mother would have thought of him?"

"Well, she would have liked that fact that he loves you so much."

Astra was taken aback. "It's only been a few months."

"What, have the words not been spoken yet?" She smiled. "It's so funny, that word, you young people act like it's crossing the Rubicon. It's obvious he loves you."

Farris looked at her intently, as if she was considering saying something else, and then she kissed Astra and got into the cab.

~

After dinner, Allie insisted on walking Astra back to her apartment. "I need the air," she said, and as soon as they were around the corner from the restaurant, she took out a pack of Parliaments and started tapping them against the palm of her hand.

Astra watched her cousin draw out a slender cigarette and hunch over, lighting it.

"Want one?" she asked.

"You know my mother was a cardiac surgeon, right?"

"I sure do," Allie said, and grinned. "Don't worry, I'm going to quit this summer."

Astra thought Allie would start talking about Adrian, but she didn't. It still touched her that Allie was here, that she had specifically said she wanted to come to Astra's graduation. She and her aunt had flown in from Chicago together.

Allie took a long drag and blew the smoke out, away from Astra. "There's something I've been meaning to tell you," she said. "But I keep chickening out."

Astra felt a little ping, like fear, but she reached over and put her hand on Allie's shoulder. She wanted to be reassuring. Maybe it was because she idolized her own sister so much, but Astra liked to try on the older-sibling role with Allie, to be there for her. She remembered visiting Allie after the accident, holding her in the jackknifed hospital bed. But now, the way Allie was telling her she had something to say—it made her nervous.

"I didn't tell the truth the night of Phoebe's wedding," Allie said now, holding Astra's gaze. "I do remember what happened."

She dropped ash onto the sidewalk. They were walking next to the Art History building, where a few lights were still on.

"What are you saying, Allie?"

"You shouldn't blame Nick for what happened," Allie said. "He kept trying to find you, to get me to come inside. What I feel most shitty about"—she took another drag, and Astra waited—"is that I wanted to put him in that position." She blew smoke out of the side of her mouth, like a '40s film star, and glanced sideways at Astra. "I wanted to see what I could get away with. I could have talked to anyone else there, but I talked with him. Because I knew he liked you."

It surprised Astra, how plainly Allie spoke.

"You never told me exactly what happened, between the two of you, after I almost drowned, and I was too chickenshit to ask," Allie continued. "But I know from Phoebe you got into a fight about what happened to me. And I've always felt bad about that. Like it was my fault."

Astra felt her stomach churn. She did not want to talk about this, did not want to know this.

"Allie, he knew you were headed to the water," Astra said. "He didn't do anything to stop you."

"What was he going to do? Physically drag me away? Run in and tell you? Sure, that would have been noble, but I don't think he believed I meant it. I didn't even believe I meant it. Think about it, Astra. As soon as I started talking to him and then made my mind up to go to the pond, he was screwed. I was a mess that night, and I—it's like I had to make everyone else as miserable as I was."

Astra stopped walking. She thought of that night, when Nick told her the only person he wanted to be with was her. She had been so hard on him, but he had deserved that, hadn't he? She had stood up for Allie, for her family. That's what she had thought, at least.

"He still shouldn't have given you the drinks," Astra said, as if she was speaking to herself more than Allie. "You were underage—"

"Jesus Christ, Astra, *you* were underage then! God, your whole family, it's like you have this overdeveloped sense of righteousness. And sure, I get it, I probably have an underdeveloped one. But it's like you think as long as you do the right thing, you can control everything. You can't."

Astra looked at her evenly. "I'm pretty sure I can't control everything, Allie," she said, in a different voice. "If I could, I hope I'd be doing a better fucking job."

Allie threw her cigarette down and crushed it with her heel, and then she smiled. "There she is," she said. "Secret Astra. I know you can get mad when you want to."

She slid another Parliament out of the box and lit it. "And obviously I know I am ruining another Big Erickson Moment," Allie said. "That's my specialty. And I am really sorry that I didn't bring this up before. It has been so nice being here for your graduation, and to meet Adrian. He's great." She paused, as if she expected Astra to say something, but she didn't.

"But I'm telling you this now because I love you, and even more than that I fucking admire you, and I wanted you to have this information about Nick. You can do whatever you want with it, but please don't blame him on my account."

Astra stood there. She felt the events of that night rearranging themselves in her mind. What if she and Nick had never gotten in that fight? What if Allie had told her right away, and she'd called him that summer? Had Nick truly done nothing wrong? No, that wasn't right—he himself had felt so guilty afterward. But had he done something irredeemable? No. Not even remotely. And she'd acted like he had. Of course, when they talked after her mother's funeral, she'd started to come around to him again, but always, what happened at the wedding hung between them. She felt her thoughts swooping around, circling and circling.

She could still call Nick. It had been over a year, but she could call him. And then the thought she kept coming back to was: She was happy now. She was actually happy, and for once, she wanted to just let that be.

~

Adrian transferred to Columbia in the middle of his second year at law school, after the holiday break. They had agreed that Astra would keep living with her roommates, and he found a small studio near campus. A week after he got there, he asked her to move in with him. "Adrian, your apartment is the size of a bathtub, and I can't leave my roommates high and dry," she said. A week later, when he asked again, she said yes.

She never called Nick.

Chapter Forty-Two

A few months before Astra and Phoebe met at the Palace Diner and discussed how they should respond to an email from their mother's old boyfriend, Astra started a new job as a reporter at the Associated Press.

She worked for the day supervisor, Carol Brodie, who kept a pair of Reeboks under her desk and had timed exactly how long it took for her to run from the office to the closest NYPD precinct, in case she needed news updates on anything. Carol worked for the news editor, but Astra could tell it was Carol who ran the show.

"Just do everything exactly like Carol, and you'll be fine," an old hand named Ed Sobel told her on her first day, and she had taken the advice seriously.

Every day, Astra arrived at the office at 7:30 a.m. to relieve the overnight editor. She'd learned that even being a minute or two late got you talked about. At the AP, you could never leave the news desk unmanned, so if you were late, that forced someone else to cover for you, which was decidedly uncool.

Her ability to write quickly and clearly under a deadline surprised her. She remembered, with a painful yank, that this coolness under pressure was part of what had made her mother so good as a surgeon. Always, always, her mother's absence exerted a force of its own, and she imagined how they would have talked about this, what her mother's perspective would have been. These ghost conversations, she had them all the time.

What Astra loved most was that people always knew what to do at the AP. Carol had recorded the numbers of pay phones at Times Square, Grand Central Station, Penn Station, City Hall, the concourses of the major New York airports. They were all stored on a file called **EYEWITNESS** on the server. That way, if something happened—a protest, a parade, an arrest, an accident, whatever—you could call the phone and see if you could reach a person who'd seen it. Astra looked at this woman, and tried to imagine how she would become the kind of person who thought to do that.

~

From the time of Phoebe's wedding to her mother's death to the fake interview in that dark room, Astra had believed, with a deep, unshakable certainty, that a normal life wasn't meant for her. But then, brick by brick, this life she did not expect had started to come back—she was with a man she loved; she had a career she enjoyed; she even got to live in the same city as her family. The steadiness of this life had comforted her.

And then Phoebe had burst into the Palace Diner, flushed and breathless, and Astra had felt another feeling, one so familiar it was like an old friend. Something was about to change.

Chapter Forty-Three

February 1999
New York City

Astra got home, threw her keys in the tray by the door, and started unwinding her various layers, tossing them in a heap on the kitchen table. Adrian would not be home from work for hours—he was a second-year associate at a white-shoe law firm, and the hours were as ridiculous as everyone said they were. She thought she could order in sushi and watch an episode of *The Sopranos* on demand. She coveted the idea of this small evening alone.

She was just about to call the restaurant when the phone started ringing. It was Phoebe. Her sister's voice sounded strange.

"What's going on, Phoebe," she asked. "Is everything okay?"

"Yes, it's just—I got another email, from Cutter. I need to talk about it with you. Do you think you could come over? I can order Arturo's."

"I'll be there in twenty minutes."

She wrapped herself back up in the clothes she'd discarded only minutes before, slotted her feet into clogs instead of heels, and ran out the door. When she got to the street, she saw a cab with its light on, rolling along the cobblestones toward her. Sometimes, the city appreciated a sense of urgency.

As the cab slingshotted up the West Side Highway to her sister's apartment, she thought about the correspondence they'd had with the man who had wanted their mother to marry him. It had taken Astra and Phoebe a solid hour at the diner to craft a response, and Astra knew it by heart:

> Dear Mr. Nesbit (not Cutter, they'd decided it was too familiar)
>
> Thank you for reaching out, and for your kind words about my mother. I can tell her death is a loss to you as well. Thank you also for offering to send her letters. You can send them to the below address.

They had agonized over how to sign off. Yours or Sincerely? Phoebe or Ms. Erickson? It all sounded so formal, but there was no handbook for this sort of thing. In the end that had compromised with, "Sincerely, Phoebe."

They'd sent the note on Friday, and on the same day Mr. Nesbit had sent a nice reply, telling Phoebe he appreciated the note and would put the letters in the mail. Then, for the next three weeks, they'd heard nothing, and no package arrived. The sisters talked about it every time they were together, and they brought Eli and Adrian into the conversation as well.

The idea of the letters gave the girls something they had not had in years. It gave them an ability to talk about their mother with urgency, as if her story was still unfolding. When Astra said this to Phoebe, her sister burst into tears. "I know," she said. "We're talking about her, for the first time in such a long time, as if she's still alive." They did not say anything to their father yet. What was the point of telling him they had agreed to receive their mother's old love letters, written to another man, if they never arrived?

But why had they not arrived? Cutter had seemed so eager to contact them, and now, nothing. He'd even said, in his first email, that he'd wanted to get in touch earlier but did not have their address, until he'd recently found Phoebe's email online.

This is what Astra thought about, as her cab pulled up outside Phoebe's lovely, unfashionable prewar building on the Upper West Side. The doorman waved her up, and when she got to her sister's floor, she saw that Phoebe had left the door ajar. Astra walked in and closed it behind her. Her sister was sitting on the couch, her legs drawn up against her stomach. She was wearing sweatpants and a long grey cardigan sweater.

"I'm here, Phoebs!" she said. "I got the Bat-Signal."

"Oh, Astra," Phoebe said, and she stood and threw her arms around her. Astra thought she looked different, as if all her features had been slightly rearranged, but she couldn't pinpoint what it was.

"What's going on? What did he say?"

Phoebe shook her head. "I'm having trouble even getting my mind around it," she said. "I'm sort of glad Eli is traveling. I can't deal with his rational, let's-walk-through-this-step-by-step shtick right now."

Astra smiled. "That's why I'm here, Phoebs. Let the irrational enabling begin!"

Phoebe laughed so hard she snorted. "Oh, Astra, it's just—sometimes you want to talk to someone who grew up in your family—you know what I mean? Eli is family, but it's different."

"I totally get it," Astra said. "Now please, for god's sake, don't keep me waiting anymore."

"He emailed this evening, right as I was getting ready to leave work. He apologized for not sending the letters; he says he actually has a big box of Mom's things to show us. Some keepsakes and things she wrote. And it would be better for us to look at it all at once."

Astra was silent. She knew her sister well enough to know that this was not the most important thing she had to say.

"But here's the thing," Phoebe said. "We have to go to him in Malibu to see it; he says he can't risk shipping it. He says these are all things she wanted us to have."

"She wanted us to have? Didn't he last see Mom when she was, like, in her twenties?"

"Yeah, I think so? Do you think they stayed in touch?"

"When Mom mentioned him to me—that last Thanksgiving—" Astra's voice hitched a little. "It sounded like she hadn't even thought about him in years. So, I don't think they did, but I don't know."

Astra's face felt hot, her heart was pounding, but her sister looked as if she was pulling into herself, getting smaller and quieter in front of Astra's eyes.

"He asked her to marry him," Phoebe said softly. "What if he actually does have something important of hers?"

"We'll figure it out, Phoebs. We can make a trip of it over the summer—"

"He has her journals, Astra," Phoebe said.

"What?"

"He said he has her journals. We have to go as soon as possible."

"But why would he have them? Why would Mom give them to him?"

Phoebe looked down at her feet. Her toenails were painted a pale pink. Even in winter, her sister's feet always looked tidy and neat, like all the parts of her, Astra thought.

"They're from back when she was in college. And as to why he has them . . . I didn't want to tell you. You can be so—well, you have a very highly developed sense of right and wrong," her sister said.

"Phoebe!"

"Okay, so, apparently Mom left them at his house. He said that she asked for them back, but he lied and said he didn't have them. I'll show you the email. He says he's ashamed he kept them, but he loved her and wanted to hold on to this piece of her. He wants to do the right thing now and give them back to us."

"Oh my god," Astra said.

"I know."

"I can't believe he kept them," Astra said.

"I can," Phoebe said. "But please don't dislike him because of it! I really think he wants to do right by us now."

Astra swallowed. Was her sister really so worried that she couldn't understand someone making a mistake, or a bad decision? Hadn't she made her own terrible decisions, and had to live with those?

"I don't dislike him at all," she said. "I understand. And I want to see these journals, just as desperately as you do. But I just started a new job; I can't take vacation yet. Can we just take a beat?"

"No," Phoebe said. "I have to go now."

"Why are you acting like I care less about this than you do?"

"It's different for you," Phoebe said, and she sounded almost anguished. "You were there, every little step of the way."

"What does that mean?" Astra asked, more sharply than she intended. And then Phoebe started crying, and after a moment of frozen silence, Astra rushed to her and put her arms around her.

"Astra, sometimes I feel jealous—god, I don't even know how to say this—I feel jealous that you were the good daughter."

Astra drew in her breath, said nothing. It had never occurred to her that Phoebe could think such a thing.

"You were home when Mom first got sick, and then when you went to college, you still did more, you know you did. What did I do? I was a beast to her when I was a teenager at home because she was healthy, so healthy and strong, and I thought I could scream at her about curfew and rules and whatever and it didn't matter, because she would always be there to love me. And then she got sick." Phoebe's sobs were shaking them both. Astra could feel the silk of her blouse become wet.

"And then I went ahead and got engaged at the ridiculous age of twenty-four," Phoebe cried. "And my wedding became the focus of her last year, when it should have been her, it should have been her!"

Astra thought of the time when she was twelve, and her mother and Phoebe had a terrible fight, with Phoebe screaming that she was the only girl in her class who wasn't allowed to go to a party at Chris Zertoss's house. "First of all, I don't think that's true," her mother said, in a voice that only got calmer and quieter as Phoebe's rose. "And second of all, I think it's amusing you think that would matter to me."

"Phoebe, don't torture yourself with this stuff," Astra said. "Mom was so glad to know Eli before she died, to know you were with such a good person. She got to see so many people at the wedding she never got to see again. And it gave her something happy to focus on. You were a wonderful daughter, and she was proud of you." It felt strange, to say these things to her older sister.

Phoebe sat back, her face blotchy and tight.

"Oh, Astra," she said. "It doesn't matter what you say. You'd say something nice even if I murdered someone."

Astra could tell her sister was so wound up in her own anguish that nothing would reach her. She knew she should just shake off what Phoebe had said; she was clearly upset. But her words burned Astra.

"I know that's what you all think, but it's not true," Astra said. "I didn't, for instance, contradict you that you were horrible to Mom in high school. That part is true."

The fight between Phoebe and her mother had ended when Phoebe screamed, "I wish I had any mom but you!" Words that frightened Phoebe so badly she started to cry, and her mother had stepped forward and held her in her arms like a child.

"Astra—" Phoebe said.

"I hate how everyone thinks I'm just this goody-goody who never gets mad at anyone. There are some things I am mad at, furious at, but what would be the point of screaming at you and Dad about them?"

Phoebe had stopped crying. She was regarding her sister with both fear and interest.

"What are some of those things, Astra?" she said softly. "That you're still mad about?"

"It doesn't matter now," Astra said.

"No, I want to know."

They were facing each other, their hands clenched

"You got the good time slot with Mom—at the end!" Astra said, her voice rising, feeling the bright prick of tears under the words. "You and Dad didn't call me right when Mom had her embolism in the hospital! Why did you do that to me? You waited a whole day because, what, you didn't want to worry me at college after I'd spent the last four years watching her die?"

Phoebe stared at her.

"I could have made it to the hospital before she disappeared under the morphine and hardly even recognized me. I could have made it! And I've never said anything to you and dad because I knew you were just trying your best. I never held it against you. But if you want to be punished for something, if you insist upon it, then feel guilty for that. You got the good time slot and you're exactly the same now, insisting we see this guy and what he has to show us on your timetable. It's always about you."

"Jesus, Astra," Phoebe said, pale and still and quiet. "I didn't know you felt that way."

This was the time when Astra should have stepped forward and hugged Phoebe, when the sisters could have cried together, and Astra could have told Phoebe she forgave her, because honestly she did. She had forgiven her long ago for what happened in the hospital.

Instead, she said, "Well, that wouldn't be a fucking first in this family."

Phoebe started, like she had been hit. Then she began speaking in a quiet, even voice.

"Do you know, when I was around fifteen or sixteen, I overheard Mom talking on the phone to someone," Phoebe said. "It must have been someone she was close to—Dr. Wilson or maybe Farris—and she was laughing. I don't know what the other person said, but I remember Mom's answer. She said, 'Oh no, Astra's not my wild one.' I've never forgotten that. It stung. *Not my wild one.*"

As her sister spoke, Astra felt all her anger drain away, as if she had tapped into some ancient, slumbering vein, and now it was spent.

"Being the way you are takes guts," said Phoebe. "Mom saw that, and I always felt jealous of it. You're not a Pollyanna, you're the strongest person I know." Phoebe went to the sink, took a glass from a cabinet, and filled it with water from the tap. She did not offer Astra any. "And I'm really, really sorry we didn't call you soon enough, with Mommy. It was wrong, and I'm sorry."

Phoebe drank the glass, then refilled it. "The reason I want to go to LA as soon as we can, the reason I feel like I have to understand what this man wants to show us now, is that I don't know how to be a mother without Mom. And I'm terrified, Astra."

Astra stood there, immobile. "Phoebe, are you—"

"I'm pregnant," Phoebe said.

Chapter Forty-Four

Most of the people who worked at the AP were hungry, but there were a handful who were just running out the clock until retirement, and Ed Sobel was one of these people. Every morning, he would come in, wearing a plaid shirt tucked into khaki pants, and go to the pantry and make coffee. "There's a pot of fresh and hot in there," he would say to Astra, passing by her desk, and she would go get some. Astra loved Ed Sobel.

Ed was a veteran sports reporter, but in his early days, at the Atlanta Bureau, he had covered the most state executions of any member of the AP. "It definitely made the wardens squirrelly, having a Black man witness those executions," he'd told Astra, when they went out to lunch soon after she started and she'd asked about his early career. She wondered at the fact that Ed—who left cookies on Carol's desk and quietly checked the lottery numbers the first time it was Astra's turn to enter them on the state wire—had sat in a room and watched strangers die.

The day after she learned Phoebe was pregnant, she stopped by his desk to chat, the way she usually did in the morning.

"What's the news, little miss?" Ed asked her.

"I've got the lottery numbers today," she said. "So that's a bit of a white-knuckle affair, but other than that, all good." One of the jobs for junior editors was to put the lottery numbers up on the wire, and you could not get them wrong. The first time she'd had to do it, Ed had checked behind her. The second time she asked him to, he'd told her she could do it herself, and he was right.

"Well, good is good," he said, and smiled. This was usually the time she headed back to her desk—you didn't dawdle at the AP—but something kept her standing there.

"Okay, out with it," Ed said, looking at her.

"What do you mean?"

"I mean you're dancing in front of my desk like a hot potato. What is it?"

She hesitated. "Well, my sister and I got some surprising news last night. I'm just trying to process it."

Ed reached into a paper bag on his desk and took out a raw jalapeño and bit into it like you might bite into an apple. "I'm listening," he said.

"My mother's ex-boyfriend, from college, contacted us to say that he has some of our mother's journals. But the catch is, we have to fly to LA to collect them."

"That is a catch," Ed said. "And this person has a reason for not contacting your mother directly?"

Astra hesitated. It was a strange thing, that Ed did not know her mother was dead, but it had not come up in conversation before, and she refused to just offer this information up as if it was an essential part of her, even though it was.

"She died of cancer, when I was in college."

Ed nodded slowly, then reached into the bag for another jalapeño. "I'm so sorry to hear that, Astra," he said. "It's awful, losing a parent that young."

"Thank you," she said simply. "That's very kind of you." She meant it. Most people froze when she told them; she still seemed so young to be half orphaned. But Ed was a seasoned reporter, and he took it in stride and didn't fuss.

"So, what are you and your sister going to do?" Ed asked.

"We're definitely going," Astra said quickly. "We're just figuring out when—" She paused. There was something about Ed, about his matter-of-fact experience of the world, that made her comfortable opening up.

"I mean, we didn't know she kept journals in college," Astra said. "We didn't know there was this window into what she was like when she was younger, closer to our age. It feels like—well, it feels really exciting. Maybe too exciting? Does that make sense?"

"Yes," Ed said. He leaned back and templed his fingers, waiting for her to go on.

"It's like—it's like when you stumble upon a great source for a story, but so much more."

He nodded. "I get it," he said. "And I really appreciate you telling me. Is it okay if I ask a question?"

"Of course," Astra said.

"Do you want any advice on this situation, or are you just here to share?"

Ed was the only person she knew who asked if she wanted feedback, rather than just giving it.

"I always want to know what you think," she said.

"Well, I think it's wonderful you have this chance to learn about your mother," he said. "But I also know that whenever I go into an interview expecting it to go a certain way, I'm usually wrong. So first and foremost, you're going there as her daughter. That's as it should be. But wear your tiny reporter's hat too. Because you're a good reporter."

"You think I'm a good reporter?" she said, and smiled.

"Okay, get out of here, Astra," he said, smiling back.

Chapter Forty-Five

April 1999
New York City

Phoebe burst into the restaurant, breathless, the colorful scarf she had thrown around her shoulders almost dragging on the ground. Astra had assumed her sister would be one of those women who grew even more luminous in pregnancy, but in fact it had been the opposite. There was a light scattering of acne across Phoebe's forehead, and her hair hung listlessly at the sides of her face. It made Astra feel more tender toward her.

She was back from her thirteen-week ultrasound. "It went okay," Phoebe said, smiling almost shyly at Astra. "Everything looked good."

"Oh, Phoebe, that's wonderful!" Astra said. "I'm so happy to hear that." Astra had been surprised, at first, that her sister was so worried something would be wrong with the baby. Phoebe was young—"you're like a teen mom," she'd joked, trying to make Phoebe feel better when she first shared her fears. But she also understood, in a deep, primordial way, Phoebe's fear.

"Will you start telling people now?" Astra asked.

"I'd like to wait just a little while longer," her sister said.

"Okay, but at some point you'll need to let me plan the shower."

"Yes," Phoebe said, with a smile. "It's all I can do to hold Sarah back, as it is." Sarah was Eli's mom, whose kindness extended to sending even

Astra a birthday present, every year, something that had first surprised Astra but now moved her. But Astra felt, acutely, the need to take the lead with Phoebe's shower, and not surrender it into Mrs. Friedman's willing hands. An Erickson woman needed to organize it; this was an article of faith to her.

"How is Adrian?" Phoebe said. "Is he okay with not going to LA with you?"

"Not really. But I told him I'd rather have him save his vacation days for, you know, an actual vacation."

Over the last two months, since Cutter's email had arrived, a plan had started to take shape. After she learned Phoebe was pregnant, Astra had offered to fly to LA on a weekend and take the red eye home, but Phoebe had demurred. "Let's wait and make it a girls' trip," she said. "Like a babymoon, but with siblings, and our dead mother's journals." She'd kept a straight face while Astra cracked up.

The sisters would go in late May, when Astra had some vacation saved up and Phoebe could still safely fly. The timing coincided with Sonia graduating from her master's program at Stanford, so Astra decided she would leave a day or two early to see her, and then meet Phoebe in LA.

When they'd shared the plan with their father, he was encouraging.

"I think it's important to talk to people outside of our family circle who knew your mother," he said. "And who knew her from a different time in her life, before she was your mom." He paused here, touched his temple. "We used to joke, sometimes, about what it would be like when you girls were older, the horror of you seeing us as real people."

"If it helps, Dad," Phoebe said. "I've never been under any illusions that you aren't a real person."

"You know what I mean. Your mom was always so amazing, so patient with you when she was helping you with your homework in middle school, and then she'd come into our bedroom all worked up and say, 'Jesus Christ, I don't remember anything about the fucking Krebs cycle!'"

They all laughed. It was a nice moment.

"And I'm glad you're going to get her journals," their father said. "We should keep all her papers together, at the farm."

"That sounds lovely," Phoebe said. "If this is 'real person' Dad, he's pretty with-it."

Chapter Forty-Six

May 1999
New York City

Despite Astra saying again and again that she could take a cab, Adrian insisted on driving her to the airport. "You know no one in New York actually drives people to the airport, right?" Astra said as they muscled her roller bag into the apartment's tiny elevator.

"Well, I live to upend all your expectations," Adrian said, and then he pushed her against the wall and kissed her, and her arm hit four of the elevator buttons. They continued to kiss as the door yawned open on each floor, then shuddered closed, as if disappointed.

Adrian had offered, again last week, to come with her, and it had started faintly to annoy her. "I just think it's going to be really emotional," he said. "I want to be there for you. The trip might be harder than you think."

"Adrian, I so appreciate it, but this is kind of like Phoebe's and my last hurrah before the baby comes," she'd said. "Plus, I want you to save up your vacation days for a romantic trip. As excited as I am to go to LA and talk to my mother's ex-boyfriend, I don't think this qualifies."

What she wanted to say was, *Don't ever tell me I don't know how hard something is going to be.*

He was quiet for most of the drive, and they listened to Astra's music—The Pretenders and P. J. Harvey and Tori Amos—on the CD player. "I hate how good your chick music is," Adrian said.

"You are powerless to resist," she said. "Also, this is not chick music."

When they got to the departure curb, Adrian pulled her bag out of the trunk, and then stood there, holding the handle. "Astra, I really hope you have a good trip. Call me if you need anything, and I'm on a plane."

"I know, Adrian," she said. She did. "I'll let you know when I get in safely."

"Okay."

"Okay."

They stood there, neither of them moving. "One of us has to go now," Adrian said, smiling.

She started wheeling her bag toward the revolving door, and then she turned, ran back, and hugged him. "Adrian, I wish you'd met her. Even just once. I want you to know that."

He'd kissed her then, with an urgency that surprised her, and then she was through the doors, heading toward the gate. She felt a small electric jolt in her stomach as she walked; realized it was happiness, excitement.

She had a really good feeling about this trip.

Chapter Forty-Seven

To Astra, LA felt dazzling—so young feeling, filled with people gliding past her with their orange juice smiles. She found herself smiling, too, staring at palm trees and the hot, bright late-spring light. What kind of person would she be if she lived here, she wondered? She couldn't wait to tell Adrian what it felt like to be here; she narrated the conversation in her head as she would explain it to him later.

Phoebe had splurged and booked them two rooms at an inn in Santa Monica she'd read about. As Astra walked into the lobby, she wasn't sure where to check in at first—there didn't appear to be a front desk, and then she realized she was supposed to sit in a low chair covered with a sheepskin while someone in a Hawaiian shirt typed into a laptop next to her. It was weird. She liked that.

Phoebe would arrive that afternoon, so Astra had the morning to herself. She planned to walk everywhere, though it quickly became clear that no one did that here. She spent the day exploring long, deserted blocks that were clearly not meant for pedestrians, then stumbling upon little enclaves, each with a café and a juice shop and a boutique with frayed jeans and shirts with writing on them in the windows. Los Angeles was like a series of little villages connected by highways, and she was surprised how charmed she was by it. It was funny to her, the wariness between New York and LA, when it was like comparing a peacock to an elephant.

She got back to the hotel after lunch to meet Phoebe. While she was walking to the elevator, someone from reception waved at her eagerly. "Ms. Erickson? I'm glad you're back. You have several messages, from your sister, I believe?"

He handed Astra a stack of missed call slips, with the times—11 a.m., 1 p.m. If Phoebe was calling then, she had not gotten on her flight. Astra ran up the stairs two at a time.

She called Phoebe from her room, and her sister picked up on the first ring. "Oh, thank god it's you," she said. "You know I think people with cell phones are ridiculous, but I really wished you had one today."

"Phoebe, what's going on? Did you miss your flight?"

"It's worse actually," her sister said in the same hard, bright tone, and then she burst into tears.

Astra's mind immediately started cycling through the scariest possible explanations—their father was in the hospital; something happened to the baby; their father was dead.

"The baby is fine, he's doing really well," Phoebe said, as if reading her mind. "It's actually me; I have a complication. It's something called a placenta previa. I had my twenty-week scan today. That was so dumb of me, why did I schedule it right before my flight, it was like I was tempting fate. They told me I can't travel."

"What is a placenta previa?" Astra said. Her voice sounded high and scratchy.

"It means the placenta is partly or fully covering the cervix—for me it's fully covering it—and while it usually resolves on its own before your due date, if it doesn't, they have to put you under general anesthesia and do surgery. The risk is the placenta can tear—" Phoebe broke out again into wordless sobbing; it was as if Astra could hear her shaking over the phone.

"But the doctors said it will most likely resolve, right?" said Astra, searching desperately for the right words she could string together to make her sister feel better. "I know it feels so scary, but this is probably something women didn't even worry about before we had all these tests. Have you called Farris? Or Ted Wilson to see if he could connect you with a specialist at Columbia Presbyterian?"

As Astra spoke these names, she felt something thick and hot in the back of her throat.

Phoebe took a jagged breath, and then she said, "Astra, I know. You are saying all the right things, everything the doctors and Eli are saying. But I still feel that I will be the one person where it all goes wrong. I can't explain it—it was awful, but it was also as if I've been expecting this, waiting for it, all during the pregnancy. Does that make any sense?"

Astra didn't answer right away. She wanted to say something upbeat, to dismiss Phoebe's fears as ridiculous, but she could not, not when she understood in her bones exactly how her sister felt.

"That makes sense, Phoebe," she said quietly.

Phoebe didn't say anything back, she just cried and cried into the phone, and then she said, in a choked voice, "It's just one of those moments where I think, where is she? Where is she, we need her!"

They cried together on the phone, a sort of mutual soundless wail that to Astra felt was so much more of a release than when they'd gathered around her mother's bed at the end, or after the memorial service. She was crying for her sister, crying for herself, but also crying for her mother, for how unfair it was, that she couldn't be here in Phoebe's hour of need.

"Sometimes I wake up, and it's the same feeling, as if a day hasn't passed," said Phoebe. "I feel like if I open my mouth in front of anyone else but you, I'll scream. What am I going to do when I have a baby? Eli said—he said he thought I hadn't done the full work of grieving, and we should wait to have a kid, and I got so angry at him. As if that was something I could just cross off the to-do list. But what if he was right?"

"I love Eli, but that is fucking ridiculous," Astra said. She felt a fierce clarity now that she had an idea to push against. "Maybe it's because he's from an intact family, so he can have this tidy notion of life. Maybe it's because he loves you so much, he worries about you too much. But losing our mom isn't the kind of grief that gets tied up in a neat bow, clearing the space for the next chapter. You're going to be a better mother for what you have gone through, Phoebe, I know that."

"Do you really think so, Astra?"

"I do."

Phoebe took a deep breath. "I think—I feel closer to you now than I did when we were kids. Is that okay to say?"

"It is."

"Okay. That's the other line. It's probably Dad, so I should go. I'll call you again before bed."

The line clicked and went dead. Astra sat down on the bed, and drew her knees up against her chest and lay there as the afternoon drifted into dusk.

~

She woke up to the phone ringing. It was almost dark outside, and she was aware of being very hungry. For a startled moment she thought she had slept through the night, but when she looked at the clock it said 8 p.m.

She picked up. It was Phoebe.

"I'm sorry it took me so long to call you back," she said. "I'm feeling better now. Talking with you and Dad helped me off the ledge."

"I'm so glad, Phoebe," she said. "But it's late—you should be in bed!"

"I can't sleep. I keep worrying about me and the baby, but also you, out there alone. I can't believe I am missing this trip. Our trip!"

"It's okay, Phoebe. I'll go see Cutter tomorrow, I'll get the journals, and I'll bring them home. You won't miss out on that."

Her sister was quiet.

"Phoebe?" Astra said.

"Sorry, yes, I'm here," she said slowly. "I just really wanted us to do this together. Whatever you learn about Mom tomorrow—maybe it will be something big, and I won't even be there with you."

"I know, Phoebe," Astra said. "I shouldn't have delayed us—we should have gone right away, as soon as we got Cutter's email."

"Stop it," she said. "You're doing that thing, that thing you always do, where if you blame yourself, it's like you feel better, because it feels like you have some control versus having to accept the universe just totally sucks sometimes."

Astra opened her mouth to speak, then closed it.

"Don't be mad I said that, Astra," Phoebe said. "It's all part of what a—what a lovely soul you are. But you don't have to feel responsible for everything. This is just bad luck. Oh, and shit—I just realized another thing."

"What?"

"I was supposed to get the rental car; it's in my name. And he's way up in the hills. Maybe you can ask him to come to the hotel instead?"

"I'll ask him," Astra said. "But I'm sure I can manage."

"Okay. I love you to the moon," Phoebe said.

"I love you to the moon and back."

"Call me as soon as you get back tomorrow!"

"I will."

Astra hung up the phone.

Chapter Forty-Eight

In the morning, she called the number Phoebe had given her. A man's voice answered after two rings.

"Oh, hello, is this Mr. Nesbit? This is Astra Erickson."

"Hello, Astra! Did you get into LA all right?" The voice sounded completely at ease, as if she had been talking to her mother's former boyfriend regularly for years. Astra tried to picture him, this man from her mother's past, and all she could see was someone tall in a tweed jacket, and she realized she was picturing her grandfather, a man with the voice of a PBS broadcaster who used to let her drink ginger ale and eat stale Ritz crackers out of a glass canister from the pantry.

"I did, thank you. But unfortunately, my sister had to cancel her trip. A family issue has come up."

He did not press for anything further, and Astra noted this tact.

"I'm truly sorry to hear that," Mr. Nesbit said. "I feel like I got to know your sister a little, through our correspondence. I am of course still happy to meet, but let me know if you would prefer to reschedule?"

Astra hesitated. She could try to catch an earlier flight, get home to Phoebe. Maybe they could even raincheck for early next year, after the baby was born, though even Astra, who had very little experience with babies, knew this was wishful thinking. No. She was already here; she had taken time off work. She could do this alone.

"Thank you for being so understanding," she said. "I would still love to see you, but would it be possible to meet at my hotel instead? My sister rented the car; I don't have one."

There was the slightest pause, and then his voice came, warm and assured. "Of course," he said. "But I wouldn't be able to transport all your mother's things. We can always do that another time, though, if it's easier for me to come to you."

Astra and Phoebe had had months to think about what Cutter Nesbit might have wanted to show them, what, in addition to the journals, was too bulky or too precious to put in the mail. They'd thought of all sorts of things. Perhaps he wanted to give them the wedding ring that he had proposed to their mother with. Maybe it was something crazy, like a portrait he'd commissioned. Maybe she'd written him letters that felt too sentimental for him to part with, but he wanted the girls to see in person. Who knows, maybe he had her old medical school textbooks or exams? Or maybe he was embarrassed to show her the journals in front of other people? In any event, it made no sense to move the meeting to her hotel if he couldn't bring all her mother's things.

She told Cutter she would be at his house in an hour.

~

Astra's cab snaked up the long gravel driveway. Cutter's house looked worn and beautiful, the stucco faded to a quiet blue, almost European-feeling. It was not like the other houses she'd passed on the way, blazing with their fresh paint and porticos, muscling close to the drives, as if to make an entrance. This house did not want to be seen.

It sat up on a hill, on top of a long flight of stone steps. She paid the driver and got out. As the car pulled away, she started to climb the stairs. About halfway up was a small landing, with a pair of stone benches, cracked and stained. A bush with roses as large as grapefruits grew next to the bench, alongside another that was just a tangle of empty thorns. For a second she felt like she was in a place much older than Los Angeles, but then the feeling passed, the bright sunshine reasserted itself, and Astra resumed her climb.

The door had both a bell and a heavy metal knocker in the shape of a pineapple, and Astra decided to ring the bell first. After about ten seconds she was contemplating using the knocker, when she heard the sound of a lock being turned. The door swung in, and a man stood in front of her, younger looking than she was expecting, wearing a light-blue blazer over a polo shirt and dark pants. His hair was still jet black, with no grey.

"Astra?" he said, and he smiled and took both her hands in his as if it was the most natural, expected thing to do. "Come in, my dear. It's so nice to meet you."

She found she liked him immediately.

"Thank you for all your patience as our plans changed, Mr. Nesbit. It's nice to meet you too."

"Please, call me Cutter," he said.

"I'll try, but it will be hard," she said with a smile, and he laughed.

He led her into the front hall. A collection of photographs in a mix of leather and enamel frames stood on a small wooden table—a woman in a green sweater with dark hair, laughing, a dog and a small child, a wedding photo taken outside on a lake. The photos were not in tidy rows, but in a cheerful jumble. As she studied them, she felt a prick of apprehension that she would spot her mother, but she did not.

Cutter spread his hands and smiled. "Do you need something to eat? A glass of water? Or do you want the grand tour of the house first?"

He was nervous, and she found this made her like him more. Astra was beginning to realize that she hadn't thought through this visit at all. It had all been focused on the *thing*—the journals, the papers, whatever else he'd been planning to show them. Not actually on Cutter Nesbit, a human being who had loved her mother, who she was now engaging in small talk with. She'd imagined they'd march right to the matter of hand, and then she would leave. Now she could see how preposterous that was, because Cutter Nesbit was an actual person.

"I'd love a tour," Astra said. "I'm not in a rush."

"Wonderful," Cutter said. As he led her through the house, gesturing to this or that, she found she liked the overstuffed way the house was decorated—carpets layered over each other, sandalwood boxes and letter openers and small statues of animals cluttering the surfaces of antique wooden tables. Everything in her short visit to LA seemed shiny, minimalist, new, but nothing in this house was new.

"How long have you lived here?" Astra asked.

"I moved to LA in 1972, though we didn't buy this house until 1985," he said. "I needed a fresh start. Leaving my family in New York, I felt like a pioneer. You're from there, so you understand what I mean."

"I do," Astra said automatically, but her mind was turning over his phrase *fresh start*. Was he referring to her mother? She felt a tinge of embarrassment. Cutter had also mentioned a *we*? Phoebe had not said anything about a wife or girlfriend. But then again, maybe that would have been strange, since he was emailing about their mother.

"Does it surprise you that you never moved back east?" she asked.

He barked out a laugh. "Said like a true New Yorker," he said. "It does surprise me, if you want to know. A lot of things about my life do. LA's a city for the young, but I don't particularly mind being old here. There was always something stifling about living in the Northeast for me."

"I think it shows a lot of imagination, when people decide to move far away from home," she said.

"And do you plan to move far away from home?" he said.

"Oh, never!" she said, and he laughed again. She was surprised at how much she was enjoying herself.

Astra had pictured someone so different from this vital, energetic person. She had thought he would seem old, formal, awkward, but he was none of these things. She could see, for the first time, the man her mother might have loved in college, the life her mother could have chosen where Astra and Phoebe did not exist.

"My wife's family has a business in LA, so that was part of the reason we stayed here," Cutter said. "She died last year, so if I wanted to move, that would have been the time."

He said it casually, as if he thought she knew. "Oh, Cutter—" Astra said, it was the first time she had used his first name, and it felt strange in her mouth. "I'm so sorry to hear that. I didn't know."

They were still walking through the house, and Astra thought he might stop and invite her to sit down, but he did not. After a brief pause, he said, "I'm really sorry for assuming you knew. I thought your sister would have mentioned it."

Astra knew, the way you know the earth orbits the sun, that Phoebe would have told her about a dead wife. She wondered if an email had gone astray, or if Cutter was not remembering correctly. She felt a surge of compassion for this man, and this also surprised her. "Compassion," Ed Sobel had told her once, "is often the enemy of a news story, but not always."

"I know it must be very hard," she said. "That first year was really tough for my dad—" she said, and then she stopped. There was no roadmap for this kind of conversation.

"Astra, it's okay. I don't need to share my tale of woe. I know you understand."

It was their first moment of intimacy, traveling beyond the polite phrases of two people meeting each other for the first time, and the strangeness of this encounter settled upon her anew.

"Would you like to see the garden?" Cutter asked, smiling and turning the subject with ease. She smiled back. Cutter may not have liked her mother's New York, she thought, but he has its manners.

He led her through a small hallway, to a covered porch that looked out over a stone pool with a long white diving board. The water looked black and freezing.

The garden was scraggly and overshot, and as they walked past overgrown flower beds and small vines struggling over wire, she wondered why he wanted to show it to her.

"Do you like to garden?" she said.

"No, as you can probably tell," he said. "That was more my wife's department."

"My mother loved to garden too," Astra said. "She used to say it was cathartic because if the plants died, she didn't have to tell their family members."

Cutter threw his head back and laughed like a pirate.

"I didn't mean—she obviously cared so much about her patients," Astra said.

"Oh, Astra, I know how much your mom cared—she used to tell me about how she sometimes kept up a correspondence with the family after a patient died."

"She told you that? I didn't know you two were in touch."

"Oh, yes. We used to talk, maybe once a year or so." Astra didn't say anything. *We haven't been in touch for a long time.* Those had been her mother's words. But she and Phoebe had speculated, from almost the first moments of Cutter's email, that perhaps their mother had been nostalgic and gotten in touch with him in the final months of her life. She wanted to ask him if this was so, but she felt suddenly shy.

They circled back around the house, in silence. Then, when they were standing in front of the screened porch, Cutter said, in a voice that startled her with its gentleness, "I know it must feel odd to talk about your mother with me. She was a remarkable person." He looked at Astra closely. "How about we go sit down and I can get you something to drink."

The large, wraparound porch reminded her of her grandparents' sleeping porch in Maine, where her grandfather used to keep little cans of ginger ale and club soda on a small cart. When they arrived, after the ten-hour drive from the city, she and Phoebe would always run and pour themselves cold, fizzing glasses, plunking in ice cubes from a wooden bucket. She could remember it so clearly, the sweet cold smell of the ice, the sharpness of the ginger. Those tiny rituals of childhood.

She sat down in a white wicker chair, the navy fabric faded to a robin's egg blue, while Cutter went to a small sideboard and poured two tall glasses of iced tea. She imagined him setting all this up before her arrival, carrying out the sweating pitcher and glasses on a tray, slicing the lemons.

"Thank you so much," she said, taking the glass from him. She thought this would be the natural time to discuss whatever Cutter wanted to show her, but he seemed in no hurry to bring it up. Instead, he leaned forward and said with a smile, "Phoebe told me you're in journalism? I imagine it's not an easy profession."

"I love it," she said. "There's a way of doing it and a way of not doing it, and I like that."

"So not surgery, but sort of like surgery," he said, and Astra laughed.

"Yes, a bit like that."

"Where do you work?" he said.

"I started a new job at the Associated Press in January," she said.

"Wow, good for you," Cutter said. "That must be a pressure cooker."

"It can be," she said. "The first time I filed a story I must have checked it twenty-five times, until an editor reminded me that speed was also part of the job."

"That editor sounds like a piece of work." *Piece of work.* It was a phrase her mother always used.

"No, she's great, actually. I sort of aspire to be her one day."

"That's one of the things I admired so much about your mother," Cutter said. "Her drive. I mean, she was born with a silver spoon in her mouth, but it was almost as if that drove her more fiercely."

Astra had been leaning forward while they talked, but now she sat back. The woman he described was different from the one she knew, not a false note, exactly, but an unfamiliar one. She could feel Cutter's eagerness to demonstrate how well he knew her mother, to bring up details from when they were together. She realized it was the first thing she didn't like about him.

"How long was your mother sick?" he asked.

"Four years," Astra said. "She was first diagnosed when I was in high school." He had such a look of sadness on his face that she reached out and took his hand, and he seemed surprised by this, and moved. He squeezed her hand, and she returned the pressure.

"She didn't tell you, when you spoke with her, about being sick?" Astra asked.

"We weren't in touch as much in the end," he said easily.

"I see," Astra said, and she sat back, drawing her hand back into her lap.

"Four years—that's so hard," Cutter said, in a voice filled with kindness. "My wife had breast cancer, and it was awful too. My sons—I have two, they're out of college—I was almost surprised at how hard it was for them. But then for Hillary—she was so determined to get to these milestones like graduation, and then she would, and she'd still say, 'I'm never going to meet my grandchildren.' It would break my heart."

Astra flushed. She had failed again to have any imagination about Cutter. She had thought of him only in relation to her mother, but of course he had his own life, he hadn't just been holding a candle for her for thirty years.

"Oh, Cutter, I'm so sorry to hear that. With my mother it was the same—she wanted to get to Phoebe's wedding, and she did, but she never saw me graduate," Astra said, and her voice faltered, he was looking at her so intently. "How are your sons doing now?"

"We've become closer in some ways, though more distant in others," he said. "My wife, she was the one who planned the dinners, the holidays. They don't call as regularly now."

"I think it takes a while for a family to figure out who they are after you lose someone," she said. "I see that in my own family. It's not just going forward with a person missing; it's new, and strange."

"In what way?" he said. "How has it been for Phoebe and your dad?"

Cutter was looking at her with such kindness, but there was something else too. A sense of longing was practically smoking off him, which hadn't been there before.

"It's been really hard," she said carefully. "But we were really lucky to have the time with her that we did."

"Of course," Cutter said, after a moment's pause. "We felt that way about Hillary as well. But my boys—I just don't know. I miss being able to talk about them with her. I mean, it's lucky we have a family business or I'd really despair for them. I don't mean to sound harsh—they are good kids—but there's no ambition."

"I'm sure they'll find their way," she said reflexively, though of course she had no idea, she wasn't an expert on motherless children, or these recently half-orphaned sons.

Cutter smiled. "They're just so passive. I would wave my hands and say this whole generation is, but you and your sister clearly aren't."

Astra didn't know why he was saying these things about his children to a person he barely knew. "I would give them some time. A loss like that takes a long time to unfold," she said.

Then she stood, smoothed her dress, and politely asked where the restroom was.

"I'll show you," Cutter said. And then, as if taking the hint, he said, "And then we can go over your mother's things."

He led her back down the hallway where they had come. As she walked in from the bright sunlight, she realized how dark it was inside. The shades were all partly pulled down, and the house felt stuffy in the midday sun.

He gestured to a door off the hallway and told her he'd meet her in the living room next to the foyer where she'd first come in. Astra carefully closed the door. It was an elegant powder room, with green-and-cream-striped paper and vintage-looking pictures of botanicals on the walls in slender gilt frames. A framed newspaper clipping that was only visible when you closed the door showed Cutter with his arms around several other grinning young men—"Cutter Nesbit graduates,

Police Alerted!" the headline splashed. It was the kind of joke gift you presented at a birthday celebration or graduation party, but she found herself studying it closely. The exuberant confidence of each person looked like it came from a mold.

She turned to the mirror, looked at her face. She was acutely aware that this was the first time she had been alone since entering Cutter's house, and she felt suddenly exhausted.

She took her time walking back to the living room. The house struck her differently now. Other than the collection of photographs she'd seen when she first walked in, there were no others—no shots of his sons as little boys on the wall, no silver frames of his wife on the bookshelves. For a house so crowded with personal objects, it struck her.

There was another corridor branching off to the right, papered in a faded coral, with darker squares on the wall where pictures used to hang. She could see the frames stacked on the ground, facing the wall. She wondered why he had taken them down.

And then she was in the living room, and Cutter stood and gave a little wave, smiling his lovely, warm smile. He was sitting on a small ottoman, next to French doors that opened onto the garden. The curtains here were open, letting in the clear bright sunlight.

"Come have a seat, Astra," he said, gesturing at a small sofa upholstered in a delicate pattern of birds.

Cutter went to a chinoiserie cabinet in the corner, opened it, and took out a large leather box. The way he carried it, she could tell it was heavy, but not too heavy, certainly not something that was too bulky to transport to a hotel. And for a man in his sixties, he seemed in very good shape.

He laid the box down on the coffee table in front of her. "Should I just open it?" she asked, looking up at him. "Yes, I think that's better than me giving a long preamble," he said, and smiled. His expression had changed, and Astra searched for the right word to describe it. It was not excitement, not quite. As he stepped back from the box and folded his hands in front of him, the word came to her. Cutter Nesbit looked exhilarated.

Chapter Forty-Nine

Astra stared at the box. It was made of soft saddle leather, no clasp. When she removed the lid, it was lighter than she had expected, and she laid it carefully beside her on the sofa. Inside was a jumble of papers that smelled old, like the stacks in her college library.

Resting atop a pile of papers was a postcard, with a picture of the ocean at dusk, the palm trees dark and dramatic. In black script across the water was scrawled *Miami, Florida*. She turned it over and read.

> Dear Cutter,
> We arrived at Eden Roc last night. Elizabeth doesn't arrive until tomorrow, so it was just me and my parents—I drank too much champagne and could sense my mother's disapproval, though of course she said nothing. Whenever I'm alone with them I still feel about seven years old. In the morning, when I woke up, there was a storm—the wind was so strong the trees were bent double, and all the pool umbrellas had been blown inside out, showing their spindly insides.

> They looked almost embarrassed. I rolled over and went back to sleep for two hours.
>
> How are you, rattling around in New York?
>
> T

It was her mother's handwriting. She would recognize it anywhere, but it was a different, earlier version. The handwriting of a younger woman. She thought about the person in the postcard, how young she sounded, how funny and nimble.

Astra laid the postcard aside. She could feel Cutter looking at her from his seat across the coffee table. In her mind, when she had imagined this meeting with Phoebe, it had always been the two of them alone, while Cutter stood discreetly outside, like a banker allowing his clients to open a safety deposit box. It felt strange to have him watching her so closely.

Under the postcard was a photo of her mother, wearing a fisherman's sweater and a yellow rain slicker, laughing. She must have still been in college, Astra thought, even younger than Astra was now, and yet the woman in the photo seemed more grown-up than her. She laid the photo down on the table carefully.

She picked up the next envelope and opened it. It was the bill from a hotel in Boston, dated 1966. There was nothing handwritten on it, but she assumed he must have kept it because he stayed there with her mother. She almost looked up at him. The next piece of paper was a handwritten note, in her mother's script. *3 p.m. at the library—bring application!*

She started going through things more quickly. Another handful of envelopes contained more receipts—restaurants in Manhattan and Boston, an old train schedule and Metro North tickets, a receipt for a scarf from Gimbels. Then one more note: *Dear Cutter, Didn't want to wake you, out for a walk, then we can get breakfast and Explore! I know you are probably still recovering from last night—I'm sorry, I'm sorry is all I can say, since I had no answer when you asked.*

This was the last thing she would read from the box that was in her mother's handwriting.

She wanted to ask Cutter what her mother had been sorry about, but she did not. She kept her eyes on the clutter of papers in her lap. A feeling was still taking shape inside her.

This visit was supposed to be a portal back to their mother's past. Maybe they'd even discover a secret, she and Phoebe had thought, but not a bad one, nothing shameful. Their mother didn't lie to them, so whatever Cutter might have was a part of her they just hadn't had time to plumb, to ask about or understand. As children they hadn't had any curiosity about their mother's past, they'd just loved her with an almost-boring ferocity. And then, when it was clear she was dying, there was not enough time to ask all the questions.

She turned back to the box. There was a random slosh of newspaper clippings—old sports games, a dispatch from Wimbledon. There were receipts from CVS and Duane Reade and Fedex, jumbled among old utility bills. She carefully unfolded leases from apartment buildings in LA, filled out with the names of people she'd never heard of. At the very bottom was a stack of crisply folded travel brochures, secured with a rubber band. And then, a crisp clipping of her mother's obituary from *The Times*, the details of the service circled. It's how Cutter must have known to send the flowers.

That was all, the entire contents of the box. This is what she'd been brought across the country to see.

She turned back to the photo, turned it over. There was writing on it in light pencil—*Thea, Maine, 1964.*

Astra had seen a hundred photos like this—clustered on her father's dresser, hung up in the tiny hallway off the kitchen, on her own bedside table. They were in the photo albums her mother meticulously updated every December, pasting in a year's worth of snapshots into the thick, creamy pages, using an orange pot of rubber cement. The sweet, solvent smell of it would fill the house.

There was nothing extraordinary about this beautiful photo of her mother, except that it was here, lodged in this box of nothings, and so she looked at it. She really looked at it. How healthy and radiant her mother was, with her hair long before she cut it short. Astra had never thought of herself as having a beautiful mother. Growing up, she'd loved the way her mother looked, but it wasn't like the mothers of some of her friends, who were younger and more stylish and wore makeup.

But here, now, her mother's youth was transfixing. She held the photograph at its edges. How much she'd hated the way her mother had looked when she was dying. A parent is a physical thing—she remembered her mother's hands, how strong they were. She could open any jar, lift heavy boxes down from the top of the linen closet. When Astra was ten and sprained her ankle a mile from the house, her mother had carried her the entire way home, Astra's arms around her neck, her legs swinging at her sides. When her mother's strength had started to fail, Astra had lost part of her, a part she counted on, and it had felt like a betrayal.

Her mother, her mother, her mother. She would not be found in this box, or in anything Cutter had to show her, that had become coldly clear. She was left with the same person she'd known before this visit—the mother of her heart.

And Astra knew her. She knew her laugh, headlong and unembarrassed. She could hear the crisp snap of irritation in her mother's voice when they were running late, and the same voice, softened into comfort, when Astra had nightmares as a child. She could feel her mother laying her hand on her forehand to check for fever.

This visit to Cutter was supposed to be a loophole, a gift. A window into her mother before she became a parent, as if the universe, after yanking her mother away with such indifference, had repented. But she would not get that here, she realized that now. The hopes she and Phoebe had pinned on this visit felt heartbreaking to her, because they represented such longing. But what she understood is that even if this box had contained Thea's journals and letters, filled with her innermost thoughts, that still could not have done the work of a lifetime, the attempt of a child to understand her mother not as a parent but as a person, separate from her.

She sat in silence for so long, it startled her when Cutter spoke.

"Would you like to keep that picture of your mother? It's beautiful, isn't it?"

"Yes, it is," she said, laying the photo down atop the pile of papers. "That's very kind of you, but you should have it." Her voice sounded high to her.

"I showed it to Helen once, but I think that was a mistake."

"Who is Helen?"

"My wife."

Astra's heart started beating like an animal in a cage.

"Oh, I thought you said her name was Hillary."

For the briefest moment, he looked at her, as if he were reevaluating her. Then he laughed. "I'm pretty sure I know my wife's name."

"Of course," she said. "I'm so sorry."

On the porch, he'd said Hillary. Her reporter's brain knew it. She knew it. He was lying to her.

She thought back over her conversations with Cutter. He had told her he had been in touch with her mother, but he had not known when she got sick. He'd said he told Phoebe he lost his wife, but Phoebe had said nothing to her. She and Phoebe had speculated that their mother must have reached out to Cutter, but Astra didn't think so anymore.

She could hear Cutter shifting in his chair, growing impatient. Some instinct told her that he would not speak again until she did, and that gave her time to think.

Why had he brought her here? Why was he showing her his box of paltry keepsakes? Could he possibly believe that anything in this box was a revelation to Astra, something worth flying across the country for? She tried to think of a simple explanation—he had recently lost his wife, he was lonely. His sons didn't visit. Maybe he just wanted to get a look at her and Phoebe. She felt a cold, sharp pain in her stomach as she thought of her sister, her pregnant sister. For the first time, she felt a fierce relief Phoebe wasn't here, in this house.

Her head cleared, as if a hunger lifted off her. There was no one else in the house, not even a dog—its emptiness had struck her at first, then receded.

Had Cutter deliberately invented it all—the journals, the idea that their mother wanted them to have them—in order to bring her and Phoebe to his home? And if so, why?

Sometimes it's hard to know a thing is happening when it's happening. Maybe he was just a sad, sweet man who carried a torch for her dead mother. Maybe this was something else. But a part of her went cold and clear, and she listened to it, just as she had listened to it in the woods when she saw the bear; just as she had listened to it sitting in the pitch-black room, after telling her story to strangers. It was the part of her that was alert to danger.

She tightened her hands on the box and looked up to meet his gaze.

Chapter Fifty

"How thoughtful of you to put all this together for me and Phoebe," she said as she started to put everything back in the box, laying the photo on top. Her mother looked back at her, young and blazing with health, and Astra took a breath. Then she fit the lid on top.

Cutter stared at her for a moment, and then he smiled.

She stood up and smiled at him. "Thank you so much for your hospitality, Cutter. I know Phoebe is so sad to have missed this."

Cutter continued to look at her as she spoke to him in a voice as calm and bland as a twelve-year-old thanking a friend's mother for having her to dinner. "I should head back to the hotel now—Phoebe is expecting me to call—but thank you for the iced tea. Thank you for all your kind words about my mom."

People are subdued by politeness, Astra knew this. Whatever confusion or consternation or uneasiness he expected her to show after flying across the country for a box of CVS receipts, she wouldn't give it to him.

"Do you have to go so soon?" he said, finally. "There's more I want to show you, downstairs. The door is just over there," he said, pointing to a small door off the hall.

"That is so thoughtful of you," she said. "But I should go back to the hotel so I can pack. My flight is this evening."

"Don't you need to call a cab?" Cutter said.

"I scheduled one to pick me up. It's probably outside now."

He smiled, and then he walked in front of her, blocking her path.

"Your mother told me a lot about you, you know," he said. "She sent me letters, after you were born. I can show them to you."

She never sent you any fucking letters. That is what Astra wanted to say. Something hot and defiant starting to burn inside her, but she pushed it down—she needed to stay calm, be polite, so she could get out of this house. Now.

"Oh, what did she say about me?" Astra said.

Cutter smiled; she felt him relax. "She talked about how much she loved you and your sister, and how surprised she was, at how happy being a mother made her. She didn't expect it. She thought, in fact, it might get in the way of her medical career. When we were together, she always said she had ambivalence about having a family. I wanted one, but she wasn't sure. It's why I didn't propose, why I waited even though I wanted to, and then she met your father. I've always regretted it."

How good he was at this, Astra thought. He was lying to her, straight to her face, and yet his voice was so pleasant, so warm and refined. When she spoke, her voice was soft; she forced it to sound compassionate.

"Cutter, I can tell how much you cared about her, how much you still do. I understand," she said. "Losing someone doesn't—doesn't turn that off. That love stays with you. I'm still trying to figure out what it means to love my mom after she's gone."

She paused, took a breath. "And I know my mother thought well of you," Astra continued. "She told me that, right before she died. She mentioned you. She said—" Cutter was watching her with such an eagerness that Astra thought, *it's working.* "She told me we all have roads not taken in our lives, that there isn't one right choice. I want you to know she thought about that." Cutter's face had softened, and there was a look of such pain on it that Astra thought maybe it was the first real thing he had showed her all day.

"When I'm back home, with my family, we'll talk about it more," she said. "But right now, I have to go so I don't miss my flight." She started walking toward him, smiling, her plan was to shake his hand, thank him again, and leave. Cutter was staring at her.

"Astra," he said.

"Yes?"

"What if I don't want you to go?" His expression had changed. There was still a mask of politeness, but it was slipping; his hands curled at his sides. Astra thought they looked like talons. She felt a fear like the hot thickness of a nightmare, knowing she was alone in this house with this man.

"I'm sorry, Cutter, I have to leave," she said, keeping her voice steady, and then she started walking quickly to the door, but then Cutter was beside her, grabbing her arm with enough strength to hurt.

"No!" he said, spinning her around. "No!"

"Let go of me!" she cried, raising her voice. She thought it might shock him into releasing her, but he didn't. He pulled her back toward the sofa, and she found herself stumbling next to him, too shocked to try to break free. He pushed her back down on the couch and then stood there, looking at her.

"Did your mother really say those things to you, about me?"

Her arm still hurt from where he'd grabbed it, but he made no move toward her now. She thought, perhaps, if she could keep him talking, let him say his piece, she could leave. Her breathing was short and shallow, as if the air had been forced out of her lungs.

"No," Astra said. "She told me you proposed, and she said no."

"And you always believe what your mother says?"

"I do, actually."

"You know what I thought, when you first arrived?" he said. "I thought, 'This girl can't be Thea's daughter. She's so—she's so sweet and deferential.' Those are not words I'd ever use for your mother. She could be ruthless, did you know that? But I see some of her in you now. You're smart, you keep your cool. She did that. She was a cool customer, your mother."

He slowly lowered himself into the chair beside her. Astra didn't move, though every muscle in her body was tensed.

"And you're right, I did propose. And she said no. Forgive me for trying to smudge that a bit, all these years later. It still stings, you know."

He was talking now as if they were still having some facsimile of a normal conversation, as if he hadn't dragged her back from the door.

"I can see she hurt you," Astra said slowly. "But you still got to have those things. You have a family, Cutter." As she was saying the words, he smiled, a rotten smile, and she thought, *Maybe he doesn't.* Maybe it was all fiction, not just his wife, whatever her name was, but the sons, too, the real estate business, all of it. She felt a cold bubble of fear in her throat and pushed it down.

"Look at you, so *compassionate*," Cutter said. "You know your mom and I were still together when she started seeing your dad. That hurt, it hurt a lot. But it wasn't the worst thing she did."

There was such a raw longing in his voice now, that even Astra felt it. She found herself bracing for what he would say next.

"And then I learned—I learned she'd been pregnant. Pregnant with *my* child. And she never told me. She just went and had her abortion and never told me." His voice was ragged. "So, I thought—let me see these girls, this family, that I never got to have. That she *took* from me."

The words registered like a blow, but Astra didn't flinch. For all the lies Cutter had told to her today, this story might be true. Her brain circled it, the choice her mother may or may not have made, what it was supposed to mean. What Astra did know, is that her mother had refused a life with this man, and chosen another life, and that was powerful.

"Is that everything you wanted to tell me, Cutter?" Astra said. "Or is there more?"

"Well, Astra," he said slowly. "I'd like to hear what you think of this. I'd like to hear you apologize to me for what your mother did. I'd like you to face the fact that your mother wasn't the person you thought she was. I've waited a long time for this, and I would like my due. Though I'm surprised at how easy it was, to get you and your sister to say yes to coming here. Just dangling the idea of journals—" He laughed. "The idea of your mother keeping a diary in college."

Astra was quiet. Yes, it had been easy to lure her here. That was the truth. He had dangled the idea of their mother as a young woman, and she and Phoebe had jumped at it. They had jumped at it like children awaiting a gift.

She thought of the pitch-black room, of the horror and humiliation she'd felt, giving away her stories to strangers. And what had they dangled? Prestige, the idea of being wanted, of being part of something, like her mother had been. She had been different ever since that day—less open, less trusting.

"You knew my mother, Cutter," she said finally. "You're here, decades later, obsessing over a box of nothings, because of how much you loved her. Can you imagine what it was like for me, actually being loved by her? So yes, I'm here. I'm fucking here, because I loved her. I'm not ashamed of that."

Cutter had stopped laughing, but his face was tight and watchful.

"Maybe she did do those things you said, Cutter," she said. "If so, she would have her reasons. But honestly, I just don't care. You're angry at me and Phoebe because we belong to her, and she belongs to us. Not to you. I know the mother of my heart, and you can't touch her." It was the truth; Astra didn't care. She trusted her mother, she trusted in the force of her mother's love even when she was gone, and that took strength. Holding people at a distance—that was the opposite of strength. She refused to let Cutter shame her for coming here. She refused.

She knew now there were no words, no apologies, no lies she could tell Cutter that would ease the poisonous, broken thing inside of him. In this way, she actually understood him. She'd tried to subdue him with politeness, she'd tried to placate him with kind words, with lies, and here she was, sitting on a couch with a bruise forming on her arm while he savaged her mother in his silky, Ivy League voice. She was scared, but underneath that, she felt all her courage rally against him. *Fuck him,* she thought. *Fuck him.*

"Do you want to know what my mother told me, about when you proposed?" Astra said, and her voice grew stronger, fiercer. "She felt something immovable, telling her no. I guess she had your number."

Cutter's face darkened, and she could tell he was going to do something awful, but before he could, she grabbed the box and leaped to her feet.

"She loved us with everything she had!" Astra cried. "You want to add some poisonous asterisk to every memory I have of her, but you can't. You don't get to have her stories, Cutter. That's why there's nothing in this fucking box of yours!"

Cutter jumped up, too, now, his hands white fists, and she lunged forward and shoved the box into his chest. He grabbed it reflexively, and it almost gave her enough time to run, but then Cutter, moving faster than she could have imagined, threw the box aside and crashed into her with her shoulder. She stumbled, almost fell, and he grabbed her by both shoulders. She thought he was going to shake her, or hit her, but his face changed, and there was a sort of dark longing in it.

He pulled her toward him and crushed his lips into her, and a sound came out of her, not a scream but something else, a keening outrage. Using all her strength she wrenched her head to the side, feeling his lips and tongue against her cheek, the indescribable horror of their wetness, and then she kicked his shin, once, twice, ferociously, and when he took a step back, she drove her elbow into his torso.

Then she was free, sprinting past him into the foyer, yanking on the door handle.

The door was locked.

She turned the latch, felt it click, but still the door did not open. In a nightmare, this would be the point where she would wake herself up. And then she saw it. An old-fashioned dead bolt that slid into brackets at the very top of the doorframe. It had been pulled closed from the inside. When had he done that? She realized it must have been when she was in the bathroom.

Her fear roared back, so intense it was like a physical pain.

She pulled the bolt, and then she was through the door, running so fast she thought she might fall. At one point, she could see the ground coming up to meet her, but she caught herself and kept going.

She threw herself down the steps. She refused to look behind her.

Someone was shouting her name, and at first she thought it was Cutter, coming after her, and she ran even faster. But it was not. There was a man at the bottom of the steps, a younger man. Adrian. She felt relief flood through her like euphoria. And then the man called her name again, and she realized it was not Adrian, it was someone else, someone it could not possibly be. She wondered if the fear had made her hallucinate, or maybe Cutter had put something in her drink.

Any moment she expected the image to shift, to resolve into someone else, to disappear entirely. But it did not.

The person running toward her was Nick Rosenfeld.

Chapter Fifty-One

Nick learned he had been accepted to the UCLA School of Medicine three weeks after Astra told him not to call her anymore. He was a bit of a wild card as an applicant, but he interviewed well. Lawyer to doctor. People liked that, apparently.

The first year of medical school was the hardest, not because of the academic work, though that was almost comically difficult, but because he didn't fit in. All his classmates were there because their parents were doctors, or because they had always wanted to be a doctor, or because they loved science. His reasons were strange, discomfiting. How do you explain you want to be a doctor because a doctor saved you from a life that was irrecoverable, a life where you felt responsible for the death of a child? Dr. Erickson had not literally saved his life, but then again, she had.

During his first week at UCLA, he saw a tall man at one of the events for first years, older than him, wearing a light-blue linen blazer and jeans. He was looking at Nick with great interest. At first, Nick could not place him, and then, as the man raised his glass and started walking toward him, he knew him.

"Nick, right?" the man said. "You're a bit of a dark horse, aren't you?"

"I'm sorry, I can't remember your name."

"Charlie. The jerk at Eli and Phoebe's wedding."

"Right. It's coming back to me now."

Charlie spread his hands and smiled. "Hey, I was just pissed the younger sister wanted to dance with you. What was her name again?"

"Astra."

"That's it."

Charlie took a sip of his drink.

"So, did you have an interlude before starting med school?" Nick asked. "Banking? Maybe a stint in consulting?"

Charlie grinned. This guy could take a joke.

"This is my prodigal son moment, actually. My dad's head of orthopedics at the Hospital for Special Surgery in Manhattan"—Nick knew it of course, it's where all the professional athletes went with injuries. "Can't dodge my fate any longer. I tried the more creative thing, had some internships and actual jobs in film, and then my dad was like, 'Charlie, it's time.' While it was enraging, the funny thing is, he was right. I think if your parent is a doctor, part of you always thinks you'll be a doctor too."

"I get it," Nick said. "My dad is a partner at a law firm, and he thinks I'm having a nervous breakdown."

"Fathers and sons." Charlie nodded, and for a while he said nothing. He seemed totally comfortable in the silence. "Hey, I heard about what happened that night," he said finally. "After the wedding. The bus that was taking us all back to the city actually had to pull over when an ambulance came screaming up the road. We wondered where it was going. We found out the next day, but I didn't get the details from Eli until much later."

Nick was silent.

"You're certainly modest," said Charlie. "I heard it was you who pulled her out of the water."

"What do you mean?"

"You helped save her, the little cousin. That's what Eli told me."

Nick had always wondered how the Ericksons had discussed that night and his role in it, and now he knew.

"Did you see her again? The sister?"

"You know, for a dude, you ask a lot of fucking questions," Nick said.

Charlie laughed again. "I like you. It feels like there are no New Yorkers here—everyone's talking about some triathlon they're doing. There's no one to laugh with."

Charlie put out his hand and smiled such a disarming smile that Nick couldn't help shaking it.

"What a good sport you are," Charlie said, and then Nick did laugh, because he realized this guy he thought he hated was going to be his first friend in LA.

~

Nick didn't set out to stay single during med school, but that's what ended up happening. He did ask women out for drinks, and occasionally he had flings, but his heart slumbered on, flat and quiet. After a few weeks or months of occasional hookups with the same girl, they would have particularly wonderful sex, and then she would turn to him and tell him that she'd met someone else, and it was starting to get serious. This happened several times.

"You know what the lady doctors call you, right?" said Charlie, over beers one night.

"We're not doctors yet, Charlie," he said.

"Oh, don't be such a lawyer. It's good, though. They call you Hot Duckie."

"Excuse me?"

"Like Duckie from *Pretty in Pink*, except hot. You're like the good-looking version of the friend they spend time with before they meet Andrew McCarthy."

"Jon Cryer?" Nick didn't hate it, actually. "How do you think I should feel about it?" he said.

"I think it's a pretty good rep. It's obvious you're not interested in a relationship, even though you're a good dude, so it's kind of the perfect place to be. Of course, only I, who knew you in the before times, understand what's actually going on."

"And what's that?" Nick asked.

"You carry a torch, my friend."

"You know I hate it when you get dramatic," Nick said.

"Well, whatever—torch, flashlight. Your flame has got some battery life."

Nick shook his head. "I'm getting us another round before you mangle any more metaphors," he said.

This shared knowledge was always between him and Charlie, like a magnet that pulled you closer until it flipped and became repellent. Charlie was his only friend here who had even the slightest window into that night, who had seen Nick with Astra, and this made Nick feel close to him. But Charlie never pushed too far. He understood the boundaries.

Chapter Fifty-Two

In Nick's third year, after his clinical rotations, he chose the intensive care unit as his first elective. He had never seen so many people die, not even during his surgical rotation. But you also saw all of Western medicine rally in the ICU, and often, it made the difference. Nick found, to his surprise, that he felt more at home here than he did in an operating room.

A few weeks into his rotation, an elderly patient, Mrs. Tannenbaum, was admitted in the middle of the night from the emergency department. The senior resident, Dr. Green, asked him to start taking her health history while he supervised.

"My name is Nick Rosenfeld," he said.

"You're new here, doctor," she said. "You look younger than my grandson, practically."

He did look young. He knew it would hurt him, at least in the beginning.

"I'm not a doctor, actually. I'm a third-year medical student. Dr. Green will be supervising me."

"Ah, you've still got your training wheels, I see," she said.

Mrs. Tannenbaum had been admitted with a fever and painful breathing. She had a history of heart disease, and five years ago she'd had a valve replaced. They had taken this information when she came to the

ER, but Nick did it all over again, as he'd been taught. The emergency room doctor suspected endocarditis, which was an infection of the heart valves that can happen when bacteria or fungi enter the bloodstream. But they didn't know what was seeding the infection, which is why they referred her to the ICU.

In the middle of the intake, the code-blue alarm went off in the hall. Dr. Green ran for the door. "Nick, keep going, I'll be back as soon as I can," he yelled. Then the door swung shut, and it was just him and Mrs. Tannenbaum. It was the first time he'd been alone with a patient.

"Don't worry," he said. "Dr. Green will of course be reviewing everything."

"He seems like a cold fish," she said, her eyes following him out the door.

Establish rapport. Build trust. Be matter-of-fact but not indifferent. There had been nothing in the lectures about what to do if a patient bad-mouthed a much more senior colleague.

"Well, he doesn't like me either," Nick said, and Mrs. Tannenbaum smiled. "But he is an excellent doctor."

"What a diplomat you are," she said, amused.

They continued to go through her history. Nick knew he should be faster, that was the feedback all third years got, because a good doctor had to be efficient and deep at the same time. But he did not know how to do this yet, and he didn't want to miss anything. He asked her about her childhood illnesses.

"I had rheumatic fever when I was a child. My mother made a salve out of eucalyptus and would rub it on my chest, then she would heat flannels in the oven and wrap me in them," she said. "No one loves you like your mother, after all. She saved me, but I've always had a weak heart. Like Beth, in *Little Women*. But, of course, you haven't read it."

"I have read it," Nick said. "We all want to think we're Jos, but we're probably Amys."

Mrs. Tannenbaum laughed, a loud, frank laugh. “I get very few surprises these days, and I am enjoying this one,” she said.

When he was finished with the history and about to start the physical exam, one last question occurred to him. “When was the last time you went to the dentist?” he asked.

“Dentist? Oh, gosh, my dentist, Dr. Warner, died a year or two ago. I’m not sure I’ve been since then.”

“In that case, I think it best to do a dental exam,” Nick said, his voice rising slightly at the end of the sentence.

“I trust you, young man. Do what you need to do.”

He looked at the door to see if Dr. Green was coming. Time mattered with an infection, but he had never performed an unsupervised physical exam. Mrs. Tannenbaum was looking at him expectantly.

Nick got a tongue depressor from a metal drawer and a penlight and asked her to open her mouth. He could see angry red swelling of the gums over a back molar. Possibly a dental abscess. He felt his heart beat like he’d been running.

He withdrew the tongue depressor and switched off the light.

“Have you been having any pain in your mouth?” Nick asked.

“Yes, but I have pain everywhere,” Mrs. Tannenbaum said tartly.

The door swung inward, and Dr. Green came back into the room. Nick couldn’t tell from his expression whether the patient who had coded had lived or died.

“Jesus, are you still doing the H&P?” said Dr. Green.

“I was just finishing up,” he said. “There’s something I think might be relevant—I did a dental exam and—”

Dr. Green shook his head and took the clipboard from him, scanned it.

“Okay. I can take over now.”

“I think she might have a dental abscess.”

“You did a dental exam?”

“Yes.”

“First, before the rest of the physical exam?”

Nick stood there mutely.

Dr. Green turned away and removed a tongue depressor out of the drawer. "Could you open your mouth please?" he asked Mrs. Tannenbaum. He took his penlight from the pocket of his scrubs and shone it into her mouth. Then he sat back, clicked off the light.

"We need to get an oral surgeon in here immediately. Nick, can you ask the nurse's station to page Dr. Galloway, please?"

He left. When he came back, the attending physician, Dr. Cooper, was also in the room, reviewing Mrs. Tannenbaum's history. "This is a good history," he said, looking up at Nick. "It's also too long—with experience you'll learn what to focus on."

Nick nodded.

"The dental abscess is what's seeding the endocarditis," said Dr. Cooper. "Dr. Green says you are the one who found it."

"I wasn't sure. It was Dr. Green who confirmed it."

"That shows good instincts, to do a dental exam. Even experienced doctors can skip over that."

Nick nodded. "Thank you."

For him, the episode with Mrs. Tannenbaum was like the unclenching of a fist. He had helped save this woman's life. There was a relief, like water, in knowing it was not all for nothing.

Chapter Fifty-Three

On the last day of Nick's ICU rotation, he got a message from Dorothy at the nurse's station. "Nick!" she said, waving a pink slip in the air as he was heading to the break room. He thought, instantly, of his father, and could feel the cold, hard shape of it.

"Who is it from? My mom?"

"No. They left their name." She looked at it closely. "It's from Phoebe Erickson."

~

Nick dialed the number, a 212 number in New York, and Phoebe picked up immediately. "Phoebe?" he said. "It's Nick Rosenfeld. I saw you called?"

"Nick! Thank you so much for calling back."

"Of course."

There was a brief pause, and then they both started talking at once.

"Is everything okay?" Nick said.

"My dad had your number, he told me to call you," Phoebe said.

"Is it Astra?" Nick asked, and he felt his hand tightening on the cord of the phone. He could still remember, with perfect clarity, the look on Thea's face when he gave his promise.

"Well, yes, it is," she said. He heard the surprise in her voice. "I'm sorry, I know this is really strange, to be reaching out like this. We don't know many people in LA."

"Just tell me what's going on, Phoebe."

"It's a long story, but here's the short version," Phoebe said, and explained to him where Astra was and who she was meeting with. "She told me she'd call after the meeting, which I thought would have been hours ago, and she's not at her hotel."

"Do you think she's still with Cutter?"

"Yes. She's at his house. She told me she'd ask to meet him at her hotel, but then she left a message for me this morning, changing the plan."

"But do you actually have any reason to be worried? This was a person your mother knew well," Nick said. He was keeping his voice relaxed and polite, he wanted to seem calm for Phoebe, but inside a sense of dread was building. Was this the moment that Thea needed him for? After all these years, was it actually happening?

"I know," Phoebe said miserably. "I'm sure it's totally fine, but it's unlike Astra not to check in. My dad and I talked, and I thought he was going to tell me I was being worried about nothing, but he didn't." Phoebe paused. "He told me to call you."

"Give me the address," Nick said. "I can leave in five minutes."

There was another startled pause from Phoebe, and then she spoke slowly. "You're actually going to go?"

"Yes," he said.

"My dad knew you would, but I didn't believe him," she said. "You are—thank you."

He thought of how much he used to long for this chance, to repay the Ericksons, not just for the role he played in Allie's accident, but for Thea, for the different life her bravery had given him. *Promise me, Nick,* she had said. He had promised. He was here.

"I want to help, Phoebe," he said.

She gave him the address, and then she said, "Astra won't know you're coming, Nick, so it's going to be awkward—I know it's been a long time since you've seen her."

"It's okay, Phoebe. I'm on my way."

Chapter Fifty-Four

Nick almost never drove into Malibu, and now he was lost. He believed he was still on the right street, but the numbers were going in the wrong direction. He cursed, pulled a U-turn, and sped back down the road. There it was. Number 118, on a grey mailbox in tiny numbers. He could not see the house, just a narrow drive lined with a tall hedge that headed up a hill.

The driveway must be a mile long, he thought, and so narrow he could not imagine two cars passing each other. When the hedge ended, it revealed a splendid house up on a hill, with a narrow staircase leading up it like something out of the fantasy books he'd read as a child.

He parked in the gravel roundabout, got out of the car, and looked up at the house. Part of him dreaded walking up there, ringing the bell. But he would do it.

And then the door flung open, and he saw her. Astra was running toward him, a girl in a dress sprinting as fast as she could, just like that night years ago. Her hair flew behind her as she galloped down the steps as if she was running from a fire, but the house was silent and undisturbed.

Nick shouted her name and began running up the stairs toward her, hurtling himself two at a time. There was real fear on her face, and as he called her name, he could tell she didn't recognize him. Then, all at once, she did. "Nick," she cried out.

She reached him and grabbed his hand. "We've got to get out of here," she said.

"My car's right down there," he said. "It's unlocked." They sprinted to the doors, yanking them open, and then for a few cold seconds he thought he didn't know where the keys were, before finding them on the dashboard. Then they were driving down the long, narrow driveway. She sat pressed back against the seat, her head turned toward him. She did not speak. He had to get them out of there. He thought if a car came up the drive he would lay on the horn and force it to swerve into the bushes.

Nick turned right when the driveway met the road, because it was faster than turning left, and he didn't have any idea where they were going except away. After several miles of him driving at least twenty miles above the speed limit, Astra reached over and laid her hand on his hand, which was lightly grasping the gear shift. "It's okay, Nick. It's okay. You can pull over now."

He slowed down, carefully navigated off the road, and put his hazards on. Then he turned and looked at her. Her clothes and her hair were different, but in her essential parts she was the same.

"Astra, are you okay? What happened? Did he hurt you?" Nick asked carefully. He leaned toward her, but she shifted back slightly.

"I'm not hurt," Astra said in a quiet voice. "I will tell you everything that happened, I promise, I just need a minute—" Something passed over her face, like a look of physical pain. He noticed she was still shaking. "But first, Nick, can you just tell me how you are here? So I know I'm not going crazy?"

"Phoebe called me. She was worried you hadn't checked in with her, and asked me to come. I live in LA now—I go to med school here—and your dad has my number . . ." He trailed off. Everything he'd said was true, but it wasn't the reason he was here. Not the real reason.

Astra waited for him to go on. Her face was flushed in patches, deathly white in others.

"I know that must sound really strange," he concluded lamely.

"It's not the strangest thing I've heard today," Astra said. She did not smile, but there was warmth in her voice; it sounded more like her.

"Astra, I'll explain everything, just let me get—well, just let me get you wherever you want me to take you," Nick said. "I just want to make sure you're okay first."

She took a breath. "I need to call my family. As soon as possible. If you can drive me to the nearest place I can do that, then we can tell each other everything. Starting with why my dad has your number."

"My apartment isn't that far—you can call them from there and have some privacy."

"Okay," she said. She leaned forward and took his hand and squeezed it. "Thank you," she said. He thought she was going to say something else, but she didn't.

As he drove toward his apartment near the UCLA campus, he could feel his heart pounding. He'd had all these years to think about how he would tell Astra about his promise to her mother, and he still had no idea what to say.

Chapter Fifty-Five

They pulled into Nick's apartment, and he shut off the engine. For a few seconds, neither of them moved, and thick silence filled the car.

Then Astra turned to look at Nick. "Nicky Rosenfeld," she said, and gave him a small, slow smile. "It's actually you. I saw you and thought maybe I was having a brain aneurysm."

"I know it must have been such a shock to see me—after a day of crazy shocks," he said. "I'm really sorry about that."

"At least it was the first *good* shock I had today," she said, and then she opened the door, as if she wanted this part of the conversation to be over.

Nick rented a small in-law apartment on the second floor of a house that was painted a peeling lemonade yellow. As he climbed the stairs and he got out his keys, he could feel Astra behind him, and felt a tingle of self-consciousness, fumbling at the lock. Then they were inside, walking through his small, extremely tidy apartment. He was hardly ever here.

"This is lovely," Astra said. "I assume your father didn't buy this one for you?" He felt a tightness behind his eyes. She'd remembered their conversation from years ago.

He showed her the phone in his bedroom, so she could be alone while she talked to her family, and then he sat out in the kitchen. He could hear the rise and fall of Astra's voice, and then once, a different sound, that he thought was crying.

In the car, she had told him, in short, choked phrases, a brief version of what had happened at Cutter's house. Now his mind raced over the few threadbare facts he possessed—the man who had loved Thea; his creepy box of receipts; his hands and lips on Astra, an image that filled him with a blotting rage and made him tighten his hands into fists.

As he waited for her, Nick thought about what could have happened if Astra had not gotten out of Cutter's house. She was so brave, he thought, in the face of physical danger. He'd seen it the night of the wedding, and he'd seen it as she ran from Cutter's house. Physical courage was a quality people underestimated. He'd learned this as a medical student.

When she came out of the room, her face flushed and damp, he jumped up from his chair. "Oh, Nick, they were so scared," she said. "I think—I think they were just expecting me to say we'd spent hours talking, and when I actually told them what happened . . . In some ways, it felt worse, having to put words to what Cutter did. What he tried to do."

She dropped her head into her hands and started crying, and he crossed the room in three strides and put his arms around her. They stood like that for several seconds, and then she stepped back and said, "Well, at least that call is over. I was dreading it."

"Astra what can I do? Drive you to the airport? To the police station? What do you need?"

"What I really need right now is a drink," she said, and gave him a small smile. "And then I can think about that other stuff later."

He walked to the fridge and opened it. "I've got . . . two Heinekens and a lemon?" he said. "Half a bottle of Tito's?"

She shook her head. "Nick, let's go somewhere," she said. "Aren't we near the beach? Take me somewhere ridiculous, a tiki bar, I don't care. I just need a total change of scenery."

They drove to a restaurant with an outdoor patio near the Santa Monica Pier, which was popular with tourists. "I've never been here either," he said when they walked in. "But at least we won't run into anyone I know." They found a table outside, with a view of the water.

"All these palm trees, I can't get over them," Astra said. "It feels hard to process what happened in a place that's—well, a place that's so cheery." She gave him another small smile. He felt like she was trying so hard to fumble through the unspeakable events of the day as if they might, somehow, resolve into something rational, something that could be explained away.

"We can process or not process, Astra, however you want," Nick said. "We can just drink in silence too."

A waitress took their order.

Astra got a margarita, something Nick found strangely touching, as if this were a celebration. And then she started telling him the story, in full, going back to the first email Phoebe had received six months ago. She talked about her and Phoebe's speculation about what might be in the journals, their anticipation of the trip, and the slow, dawning horror of Cutter's real intentions.

"I think—" she said, and then she ran her hand quickly over her eyes. "It's strange, I've never been that scared. The only other time I felt that way was when I thought Allie was going to die." She looked at him then, with a softness in her expression he couldn't read.

"But then, the craziest thing is, as the adrenaline fades, it's not just how scared I felt, I also just feel so *disappointed*," Astra said.

"You mean because of the box? After all that buildup?" Nick said. He had thought this too. Even as she had told the story, he found himself wanting, wishing for the contents of the box to be anything else than what they were.

She nodded. "I wanted—I wanted those journals so much. Like there was going to be some kind of catharsis in that box, enough for me and Phoebe both."

"I think that's a really human feeling, Astra," he said.

She shook her head, almost angrily. "The idea of being in the presence of her thoughts again—oh, god, Nick, I wanted it so much. And he used that."

"He such a sick bastard," Nick said. "All that crazy stuff he said, you know it's not true, right?"

"Actually, some of it might be. My mother never lied to us, but I also realize there's so many things she didn't tell us," Astra said. Nick looked down at his beer and felt his face grow warm.

"I just keep thinking—was he planning this all along?" Astra continued. "What would he have done if Phoebe had been there? Maybe when I showed up alone, he just saw an opportunity and took it. I think—I think at first he just wanted to see me and Phoebe up close, and then it became something darker. Like he wanted to get back at her."

For a second, Nick didn't know who she was talking about, and then he realized, of course, she meant Thea. He reached out and took Astra's hand, and she let him, she didn't draw hers away.

She looked away, out toward the pier. People were all around them in bright leggings and short, boxy T-shirts, walking their dogs, rollerblading, going for jogs on a Tuesday afternoon.

"If I actually think about it, about what could have happened—" She stopped talking and took a deep breath. "I'm sorry, I'm just trying not to lose it again." Her hand was still in his; he was very aware of this as he sat across from her, holding her silence.

"When I was trying to open the door, it was the first time in my life I've thought my life was in danger, at least from another human," she said finally. "The only other time I've felt that much fear was with that bear I ran into before my sister's wedding. Do you remember that? But that made sense, it was a bear."

She made a face, a sort of grimace, but it was funny, it reminded him of her telling him the story, all those years ago. It would have been easy, in this pause, to slide her hand out of his, but she didn't.

All the words Nick could think of to say sounded so toothless, so clichéd. A part of him that just wanted to be angry, to tell her *I could go there and kill him*. But that would make this about him.

"Can I tell you what I was thinking about most as I was trying to get that door open?" she continued. "I was thinking about how he wanted to hurt my mom, to take something from her, and I couldn't let him. And as awful as it was in there, whatever he wanted out of me, I don't think he got it."

"Can I say something, that maybe will sound strange?" Nick said. "I know I didn't spend a lot of time with your mother, but I felt—well, I felt like I saw her in this very specific way. Even now, even as you have to process all this *shit*, you remind me of her. You got yourself out of there; you kept your cool. Whatever Cutter wanted to take from you, you're right, he didn't get it."

She started twisting a ring on her right hand. She had finally drawn it back, in the most natural way, while he was speaking. Her expression had softened as he spoke; there was a slick of tears on her eyes.

"I'm glad you came, Nick," she said. "I'm glad you're here." She said it with a simplicity that moved him.

"Your mom—she believed in you so much," he went on. "I just think . . . well, she would have been proud of you today."

Astra was looking at him intently, and then she leaned forward and took a sip of her drink.

"Is that what she told you?" Astra asked.

"What do you mean?" Nick asked.

"Did my mother tell you that? Before she died? Because let's be honest, it makes no sense that my dad has your number. Did my mother ask you to give it to him?"

Nick could see Dr. Erickson as clearly as he could see Astra across from him as she sat in that old Italian restaurant in her navy cardigan with the brass buttons, her face puffy from the chemo. He remembered her eyes, clear and urgent. She'd expected him to say yes, and he did. *Promise me, Nick.*

He took a deep breath.

Chapter Fifty-Six

For a few seconds, running from that brazen tomb of a house, Astra had thought she was seeing things, or maybe even that she was dead. These felt like more likely explanations than the fact that Nick Rosenfeld was here, in Malibu, at Cutter Nesbit's house.

As he'd driven them away from the house, Astra had watched Nick from the passenger seat. He looked the same, she thought. His hair was longer and softer, almost curling at the ends, and he was wearing scrubs. He had made it to medical school after all, she thought. After she'd told him she couldn't see him anymore, she had felt too embarrassed, or hypocritical, to ask after him, so she had never known, and with the death of their mother, Patty had slipped out of their lives. These were all things she thought as Nick had raced down the narrow road.

Her family and Adrian had wanted her to come home immediately. They had even gotten on their computers to research flights. But she told them it was okay, she would fly back tomorrow—she was too tired to go to the airport now. This was both the truth and not the truth.

And now she sat across from Nick, under a vined pergola strung with fairy lights that had started to light up like fireflies in the dusk. She was wearing the same belted navy dress she had put on this morning, and she thought of how carefully she had dressed, wanting to make a good impression on Cutter. That part of herself that was so eager to please—she wanted to cut it out of her, to surgically remove it like a cancer. That was the word that came to her mind. Cancer.

"Did my mother ask you to, Nick?" She repeated herself, softly. His face looked so anguished; it had the look of someone who was about to confess a secret.

"Your mom called me, right before Thanksgiving, that last Thanksgiving before she died," Nick said. He paused. "She asked me to meet her for dinner. To be honest, I thought she was going to tell me how disappointed she was in me about everything that happened at the wedding, or how much I'd hurt you. I was bracing for it. But she surprised me."

Astra had had two margaritas, but she didn't feel the slightest bit drunk. She looked at Nick carefully.

"She told me she had been having dreams since the wedding, really vivid dreams, and she felt they were some sort of warning," he said. "She wasn't sure, but she felt they were about you." Nick was looking down at his empty beer, white knuckling the glass. Astra's throat felt hot; she both desperately wanted to hear what Nick was going to say next and feared it.

"She told me she was a little embarrassed, because there was obviously no grounding in science, but after the bear—" He smiled a little as he said this and looked up at her. "And after Allie almost drowned, I think she realized that something bad could happen to you and she wouldn't be around to help."

Nick looked so nervous that Astra wanted to say something, to try to put him at ease, but she found she could not speak.

"She said you would never ask for help, Astra, because you would always overestimate the cost of asking. So she asked me to promise—she said if there was ever a situation where you needed help, whether it involved a plane, or driving through the night, or, I think she said, even if it involved impersonating some official, that I would do it, and that if money were needed, your dad would pay for it. And she made me promise that any time I moved, I would make sure your dad had my new address and my new phone number so he could always reach me."

Nick took a deep breath and looked at her. Her mind churned with a universe of questions, but there was one she needed to ask first.

"And she wanted you—you specifically—to help me?" she said.

"Well, I've had a lot of time to think about this, about why she asked me. Part of it was she knew I'd say yes. Your mother was practical that way. But the other part—well, she said she knew she could ask me because of the way I felt about you—" He held her gaze as he said this; he didn't look away. "But she also just told me, 'It needs to be you, Nick. I don't have any backups in mind.'"

Nick paused. He wondered if it was unfair to tell her this, if there was some part of him that wanted this knowledge to influence her. But he was not trying to manipulate her. He owed her the truth, and this happened to be the truth. "But she was clear that this wasn't about you needing saving, she knew how capable you were, Astra—"

"I know that, you don't need to tell me that, Nick," Astra said, and there was a sharpness in her voice.

Astra looked down at her hands. Her mind was trying to let in the idea that her mother had met with Nick, had had dinner with him, and never told her. And then had asked this of him! She felt her mind fighting the thought, fighting the idea of this concealment on her mother's part, but alongside it was another feeling, a different feeling. Her mother had known, had somehow *felt* what was going to happen to her here. Her mother, the doctor! Her love for Astra, for her daughters, for her family, had proved more powerful than a lifetime of rationality, of calmly weighing evidence and data. This stunned her. It stunned her.

Finally, she spoke.

"Nick, are you saying, what, my mother had a *premonition*?"

"I don't really understand it either," he said. "I thought she was maybe just having dreams about her children because she was dying, and of course she would worry about you. That seemed natural to me. But she was really serious about it, Astra, and she asked me to promise. She told me she knew she couldn't control things after she was gone, but she would feel better—more at peace, I think she said—if I promised her."

"But how did she sound? Did she sound like herself? With all the treatments she was exhausted, I just wonder—"

"Astra, she dreamed about you running down stone steps," Nick said.

"What?" Astra's voice shook.

"She said she could see you running down stone steps," Nick said. "But she couldn't see what you were running from or what kind of danger you were in. Whatever was happening with her, it wasn't—it wasn't the medications, or paranoia, or anything like that. She seemed comfortable just—just accepting that her dreams were a warning, even if she didn't fully understand them. She was not going to take a chance."

"That's what she told you?"

"Yes."

Astra brushed her hand across her eyes, almost angrily.

She reached out and took Nick's hand. "I'm sorry, I'm just having a little trouble—" And she stopped.

"I don't really understand it either," he said softly. "All I know is that the force of her love for you is why I'm here right now. Why I was there at Cutter's house today. I think that's—whatever this situation is—I think that's sort of extraordinary."

Astra thought about her mother sitting across from Nick and telling him her dreams. What did it mean that Thea had been so deliberate in entertaining a thought that, Astra believed, would have felt absurd to her when she was healthy? Astra had come here, to Los Angeles, because she had wanted a window into her mother as a younger woman, a person she had not known. Instead, it was not the journal that Cutter had dangled, it was Nick, this man sitting across from her now, who was showing her a side of her mother she had not seen before.

She felt she might cry again.

Nick was sitting there quietly, saying nothing. *The force of her love for you is why I'm here right now.*

It came back, in the end, to love. Her mother had loved her enough to hold, alongside a lifetime of science, another idea, a sense that there might be something beyond her, beyond explanation. Her mother had loved Astra enough to listen to that voice. Maybe even now, Astra could expand her idea of who her mother was. Her mother, head of surgery, had asked Nick to help her because of a dream. Her love was that ferocious. And so was Astra's for her.

"You know what's so lovely about being with you, Nick?" she said. "You knew her. You really knew her, and you know her still. I realize the older I get, the fewer people in my life will."

Chapter Fifty-Seven

"What if everything had been fine when you arrived at the house?" Astra said. "What would you have done?"

They had walked from the patio bar to another restaurant on the beach, a small, airy bistro with windows that opened onto the ocean.

"Other than wish the ground would open up under my feet and swallow me whole?" Nick said.

"Yes." She smiled.

"I guess I would have made something up—Phoebe had a message for you, whatever."

"God, that might have been even worse than what actually happened."

They both laughed. Astra imagined they must seem like two young people on a date, early on in a relationship when it was still new, but there was an ease to things. She thought how naturally Nick moved between lightness and seriousness. He would have a wonderful bedside manner as a doctor, she thought.

A waiter brought over the bottle of wine they had ordered, and as he held it with a white cloth and twisted the cork out, they smiled slightly at each other and then clinked glasses after he poured.

"Cheers to you for getting yourself out of that weirdo's house," Nick said. "If it were me, I'd probably be locked in the basement right now."

"Well, you're the one who drove the getaway car," she said. "Thank goodness. You're like the only New Yorker I know who can actually drive."

They laughed again. On the walk over they had been quiet, neither of them feeling like they had to rush into the silence. She'd thought about her mother's dreams, the vast strangeness of this trip. She had not gotten what she'd come here for, she'd not gotten the journals, and yet her mother felt so close to her now, in an utterly different way. It was like she'd had to turn herself inside out to find her. The mother of her heart. Amid all the anguish of this day, that felt like a gift.

"We've spent all night talking about my mother's possibly psychotic ex," she said. "Let's talk about you! You made it to medical school. You live in Los Angeles? Even with everything else that happened today, this is big news!"

He smiled, almost shyly. "Well, I guess I really did want to be a doctor, and it wasn't just a nervous breakdown, like my father feared."

"I always thought you would go to med school," she said, and it was the truth. "What is it actually like?" she asked.

"Oh, god, it's so hard," he said, and laughed. "It's like impostor syndrome at every turn. But then you realize that's the point, that's what they're training you to do. You are never going to know it all, you can't, and so you have to be able to hold that discomfort and still rely on your judgment and training."

"That's such an interesting way to put it," she said. "I wonder if my mom felt that way. Growing up, I always thought my mother knew everything, like God."

"Well, they do call it a God complex, Astra," he said, and smiled.

"But you like it?" she said. "It's what you feel you should be doing?"

"Yes," he said. "I love it. And in a way, it's not so different from any other job where you work with people all day. I like people. Not everyone does."

She smiled. "And people like you," she said. "That helps."

She raised her glass to him. "You did it, you made this big change," she said.

"Well, tell me about you," he said. "I want to know what your life looks like now." She shook her head, waved his question away with her hand. "I can't do a normal conversation yet," she said. "Not from my end. But I do have a question for you—do you know the feeling when something really crazy or different happens—it's like there's a tiny window, before everything starts to feel normal again, to take stock?"

"Yes," he said.

"I think about that sometimes—after Allie almost died, after my mom died, after what happened in that horrible interview—" She paused. For the first time, thinking about what happened in that black room didn't fill her with shame, as if the power of that story to hurt her had blunted and changed. "What if those things hadn't happened? What if my mom never got sick? I guess what I'm trying to say is—sometimes I can't decipher what's me, and what's those things," Astra said.

Nick was quiet. "I think there's a difference between taking away pain and taking away the things that make us who we are," he said finally. "I think about the night of the wedding all the time. What if Allie had died? I don't think I could ever have gotten over that; I'd be a different person. But what if the accident had never happened at all? I'd probably be a lawyer."

"So, you don't regret it, anymore?" she said.

"No, of course I regret it," he said. "I lost you, didn't I?"

He looked so sweet vulnerable in that moment, as if even he were surprised by his words. And she thought of what she'd told him at the end of that terrible night, after Allie had gone to the hospital. *I wish I was the person who could get over this, but I'm not.* She'd been so hard on him. And she'd never called him, even after what Allie confessed to her, the night of her graduation.

"Nick—"

"I shouldn't have said that," he said.

"No, I—I also have regrets about that night," she said.

Nick looked at her closely.

"There's something I should have told you earlier—" she said.

"Wait, let me guess," he said. "You're going to say that you have to leave dinner now and then I'm not going to see you for another four years."

"Nick!"

He spread his palms and smiled, a slow, sad smile. "I just want you to know I'm ready to be dismissed at any time."

Outside the sun was getting low in the sky, reflecting red on the water. His voice was not accusatory, or bitter—it was affectionate, as if all the emotion had cooled out of that memory for him. But it was also as if he was trying to be playful, to hold off what she was going to say. And she could, she could hold off. She could match his tone, and move on, and he could take her back to the hotel, and she could fly back to her family and Adrian. She would never have to tell him.

"Allie talked to me, the night of my college graduation," Astra said. "She always told us she didn't remember anything about that night, but that wasn't true."

Nick was sitting completely still.

"She told me you kept trying to get her to come back inside; you wanted to find me. She didn't blame you at all, not the way I did. She told me the reason she singled you out is she felt jealous, watching us together." Astra's voice faltered a little over those words. "She was—she was completely honest. She made no attempt to defend herself. And I wish—" She hesitated.

"What do you wish, Astra?"

"I wish I'd known," she said. "I wish—you'd tried to tell me."

Nick lifted his glass, looked at it, put it down.

"I'm not sure that's fair, Astra," he said, though there was nothing angry in his voice, it was just quiet, thoughtful. "I don't think anything I could have said that night would have helped. What was I going to say? Oh, your cousin was really good about lying about her age, and by the way I think she was trying to manipulate me? I had done enough

I wasn't proud of to feel horrible, and then I get it, you filled in the blanks, but it almost felt—" He stopped.

"You can tell me, Nick."

"It felt like you wanted to interpret my actions in the worst possible light. Like it was almost a relief, for you to not have to struggle with wanting to be with me. And I was so terrified Allie could have died, because I didn't stop her, that I accepted it."

Astra didn't speak for a few seconds. She felt the way she'd felt that night all those years ago, when they were talking on the dance floor, but reversed. He understood the things she liked the best about herself, and the things she liked the least. He knew her.

"You're right," she said. "I'm so sorry."

Nick's voice was hoarse with emotion when he spoke. "You know, I used to think you might call me again. When your mom asked me to promise—I was so excited, I wanted a reason to stay in your life. And I figured, if she was asking me to do this, it meant you didn't hate me. I held on to that for a long time."

"I wanted to, Nick. I wanted to so much." Her voice had risen, so that one or two people even looked over them. She had lost her bearings; she wasn't sure, anymore, what conversation they were even having. "I should have called you after I talked with Allie. I should have called you after I told you what happened with Cross & Key. There were a few times I almost did."

He was looking down at his hands now, and for a moment she was scared he would leave, and she didn't want that. How desperately she didn't want that.

"What stopped you?" he said quietly.

"I had—I had just started seeing someone," she said. She had not meant to hide Adrian from Nick, but it had also not felt like there'd been any natural place to bring him up. And she didn't know, Nick might be in a serious relationship too. She didn't want to assume. "I'm still seeing him; it's serious. And I thought if I called you, back when

Adrian and I started dating, this new thing that made me really happy would end."

He looked up, startled. "What are you trying to say, Astra?"

What was she saying? She was so far out on a limb now, and while she was not betraying Adrian, it still felt wrong, she was filled with the wrongness of what she was doing. And yet she would not take it back, this time with Nick. It was like she was trying to occupy some in-between space, and try on this other life, for a time at least.

She took a deep breath. "I'm saying I've never felt the way I felt with you the night of Phoebe's wedding. Not with anyone else."

Nick kept his eyes on the table for so long she thought he was never going to speak, and when he finally did, his voice was raw.

"When I think about the wedding, I always return to that moment when you told me you needed to go back to the tent, and I didn't go with you. The truth is, my ego was bruised. I was angry because I understood it, your loyalty to your family, and I envied that you had these amazing people you wanted to return to. For years, I've thought, if I'd just gone with you, if I hadn't let my pride or my anger over my parents' divorce or whatever hold me back, everything would be different. Anyway, I always wanted to tell you that, and now I have."

He was still holding her hand, and he ran his thumb across her palm, lightly, and then drew back.

"Nick—"

"It's okay, Astra."

"Adrian—I love him, it's real. But when Allie told me the truth, I couldn't—you were part of my before life. You knew my mother, my family. It felt too painful to go back. Adrian was a way to turn the page."

"I still wish you'd called," he said, and his eyes had filled with tears. She'd never seen him cry, not even on the dock, before the ambulance came.

"Nick, I—"

"But you're happy?" he said, cutting her off. "You seem like you're happy."

What she thought, as she looked at him, was that yes, in the three years she had been with Adrian, she had been happy. With Adrian, everything was new, and this newness was so light, so filled with possibility, that it was like a drug. He was not afraid to hear about the hard things, he loved her in part because of the way she was shaped by her loss, but she was a slightly different person with him, and she liked that. But sitting across from Nick now, she felt the ghost of that other girl, the one she carried with her. And she missed her. She missed that girl.

"Nick, when I think of that other girl, the one I'd be if Allie hadn't almost drowned, if my mother were still alive . . ." Her voice had gotten very quiet, he had to lean in to hear her. "Well, I always think she's with you."

He looked down at the table, like he was struggling to compose himself. "I can't believe how good it makes me feel to hear that," he said, and then he raised his eyes. "And it fucking breaks my heart."

Chapter Fifty-Eight

Neither of them spoke while Nick drove her back to the hotel, and when they pulled into the parking lot, Astra felt a sense of dread, sharp enough to cut herself on.

She thanked him, said goodbye, stepped out of the car, and stood there, holding on to the door handle. She got back into the car.

"Will you come up with me Nick, just for a minute? I feel a little scared to walk into my hotel room alone."

He took his hand off the gear shift and pulled his keys out of the ignition. "Sure, Astra," he said quietly. He didn't look at her.

Inside her room, the bed was turned down, her pajamas neatly folded on the pillow. She felt Nick take in the room, and then he said, "Do you feel okay being here alone? Because I think I should go, Astra."

"Yes, I'm fine," she said, and then she started to shake soundlessly, and she had to sit down on the bed and let the sobs come, as if the grief of all the un-cried-out places was rising within her.

And then he had his arms around her, and he was holding the back of her head, resting his cheek against her hair while he pressed her against his chest. "It's okay," he said, in a voice so devoid of anything but gentleness it almost did not sound like him. "It's okay, I'm here."

When she looked up at him, she felt something collapse inside her, and then she kissed him.

For a few seconds they stayed like that, just their lips touching, she could feel him draw in his breath, and then he kissed her back. He bent her head back over his arm and kissed her mouth, her ear, her neck, and then her lips again. She felt his arms tighten around her and then, with a sort of groan, he released her and stood, lightly crossing his wrists in front of him, as if he needed this distance.

"Astra," he said, and he was breathing hard. "I want this more than anything, but—fly back home, be with your family. If you want to call me, I'd love to hear from you. But this—you have a boyfriend you love. You escaped from that awful man today. You're leaving tomorrow. This wouldn't be right. And to be honest, it's just too hard for me."

She looked at this man, this person who was so entwined with both her past and who she was now, and she saw that he had traveled further than she had since the wedding. He'd lived his mistake out in the open. Nick had changed his life, not on a whim, not because he was running from something. Out of the ashes of that night he'd discovered something about himself.

He'd taken all the things that happened to him and carried them forward. And what had she done? She'd locked up a part of herself, left it behind. That girl—the one who stood on the dock, the one who walked into the pitch-black room, with trust and hope—that girl could be loved too. She knew that. She knew it because Astra loved her still.

Chapter Fifty-Nine

Adrian was waiting for her at the gate at JFK, right as she stepped off the jet bridge. His face, his dark hair, the way his expression changed and opened as he saw her, brought her love for him back to the surface. It didn't change the events of yesterday—they still pulsed just underneath her thoughts—but seeing Adrian was a reminder of home, of the life she'd made these past three years. And that was real too. He waved both hands over his head, and she found herself running toward him.

"Adrian! I thought you were going to pick me up at the curb!" she said, her face flushed and surprised.

"Well, that was the plan before yesterday's total creepfest," he said. "Today it's a full service operation."

"Adrian!" She hugged him, and he lifted her slightly off the ground, swung her around. She could feel people looking at them, and felt a tiny echo inside her, the memory of Eli spinning Phoebe around at the rehearsal dinner.

"God, I'm so glad you're okay," he said, when he set her down.

When they got in the car, he turned to her. "Start from the beginning," he said. "Tell me everything."

She tried. She told him, with more detail, about the terrifying encounter with Cutter, all the things he had said, running from the house and Nick driving her away. She did not tell him about Nick's promise to her mother, or what happened between them. She felt she needed to be home to get her bearings before she attempted it. She was still struggling to understand what she would say, but she knew she couldn't lie to him. She would have to explain, somehow, what happened with Nick, but that also, she was still the person he loved, who loved him. That was true.

When they reached their apartment building, Adrian parked and sat for a few seconds in silence. "I could go there and kill this Cutter guy," he said in a quiet voice. "That is some screwed-up, Norma Desmond, *Sunset Boulevard*–style shit, Astra." His voice vibrated with anger.

"I'm okay, Adrian," Astra said, and Adrian turned to her, with an expression she couldn't fully read. His face was flushed.

"I'm so sorry I wasn't there," he said, and his voice sounded so miserable, she felt a wrenching guilt.

"Adrian, you can say it. You wanted to come and I told you no. You thought it would be harder than I did, and you were—well, you were right."

She thought that would soothe him, but as soon as they got back into the apartment, he started again, more agitated than before. "I just hate that it wasn't me, driving you away from the house," he said. "I keep playing it over and over in my mind."

She reached out and took his hand and laid it against her cheek. "Adrian, there's nothing you could have done from New York. You're here now."

"I know. But I can't stand that Phoebe had to call up some stranger, basically, to help."

She hesitated. "Nick's not a stranger," she said. "I've known him since I was a child."

He looked thoughtful, as if he was trying to figure something out. "But you never talk about him," he said.

She felt a fist of unhappiness in her stomach.

"We weren't really in touch, after my mother died," she said.

"Did you guys hang out, afterward?" he said casually. "Or did you just head back to the hotel. I was so worried about you, I thought you'd call again."

Astra's heart was going so hard, she thought he must hear it, but he was only looking at her with kindness. "Nick and I went out for dinner," she said. "It was so late your time when I got back, I didn't want to wake you."

"Okay," he said. "How was the dinner? What did you talk about?"

"We talked about the strangeness of feeling, in spite of everything, disappointed that he didn't actually have my mother's journals. We talked about my mother a lot . . ."

She could not go on, and she knew Adrian could feel it, her discomfort.

"Astra, I'm so sorry, I don't mean to do twenty questions after what you've been through," he said. "I just feel like you were acting a little weird, so I was being weird. I'm sorry." He started to kiss her then, to wrap his hands in her hair, and he whispered, "Are you hungry, or can we skip dinner?"

She kissed him back, and then they started moving toward the bedroom, but instead of the desire she usually felt, her sense of misery grew and grew. She stopped and stood back from him.

"Adrian, I get why you feel weirded out," she said. "I should have told you right away, but Nick and I had a thing. Years ago."

She and Adrian almost never fought, it was a strange thing about them, and sometimes she actually worried about it. He was usually the one to bring them back from the brink, and she had always found this surprising. Now he looked at her seriously and said, "Did anything happen that I should know about?"

"Nick and I—" She could see the words in front of her, she just had to speak them. "The night of Phoebe's wedding, we got together. Just for that night. But it was really intense, and confusing, all wrapped up with what happened with Allie, and that's probably why I don't talk about him. So, I can see why it's a little disorienting for you."

As she spoke, she saw something flash over his face—a nervousness that was unlike him, even fear. Then it vanished, like a fissure closing.

"Okay," Adrian said. He was watching her closely.

"And then, last night was so emotional. The reason Phoebe called him was because of something my mother had asked him, years ago, that I never knew about. He drove me away from Cutter's, and then we talked about that . . ."

"Did something happen, Astra?" Adrian asked.

"Yes, something did happen," she said. "We kissed, at the end of the night. I'm so sorry, Adrian." Her voice was very quiet. "I'm so sorry I didn't tell you right away, I've just been so confused—"

"Did you stop it, or did he stop it?"

"He stopped it," she said. "I was the one who kissed him. He wouldn't do that." She thought she would be crying, but her eyes were hot and dry. Amid her guilt, she also felt, that after all the events of yesterday, perhaps she would be allowed this one mistake. Perhaps Adrian would try to understand.

She saw his expression narrow; he looked like he was trying to figure something out. "Sounds like he's a really decent guy," Adrian said. "And just so I'm clear, this is the guy who, like, almost killed your cousin at the wedding, right? This is the guy you kissed?"

She stared at him. She thought after the shock of yesterday she would never feel such astonishment again, but she did, now.

"What are you talking about?" she asked. "He pulled her out of the water."

"And before that, he gave her those drinks, he let her wander off to the pond, right?"

She paused and really looked at him. "I never told you that," she said slowly.

"Of course you did. You told me what you said to him, after Allie almost drowned. You said you wished you were the kind of person who could get over what he did, but you weren't! I even remember thinking, god, that's so generous of you!"

The air went dead in the room. Astra felt everything tilt slightly on its axis, as if the furniture might start sliding across the floor.

A realization was slowly taking shape within her, a sort of dull horror that part of her wanted to ignore, but another part, the stronger part, refused to. She thought she might be sick, she leaned against the doorframe for support. She wanted to close her eyes, but Adrian was still talking, his voice rising.

"So, what did Nick promise your mother?" he said. "What did she make him promise after he almost killed her niece?"

She didn't speak, couldn't speak.

"You're not going to tell me?"

"No," she said.

"I can't fucking believe this," Adrian said. "Why are you defending him? Why are you acting like you didn't say that about him?"

"I did say that, Adrian," she said. "But not to you." The silence that fell between them was total, and she did not stop looking at him until he looked away.

"You took Deacon Green's class," she said.

Adrian stared at her. "What are you talking about? I told you I always regretted not taking it."

"It must have been so exhausting for you to worry about it coming out all the time, Adrian," she said. "You could have told me you'd taken it, you know. I still wouldn't have figured it out. It would not have occurred to me in all my life."

"I told you, I never took his class! Jesus, Astra!" He was angry, really angry, she could tell this, and she found it so interesting, how offended he was. He was about to say something else, but she held up her hand, and something in her face stopped him.

"You liked it so much, it blew your fucking mind," she said, and for the first time, she saw real fear in his face.

"Astra—"

"You're right," she said quietly. "I did tell you."

Chapter Sixty

She walked into the bathroom, locked the door, and ran the tap. She let the cool water run over her wrists and splashed it onto her face and neck. Her face was so hot she thought the water would scald off it, like steam. Then she sat down on the edge of the tub, letting the drops run down her neck and soak into the collar of her shirt.

After the Cross & Key disaster, she'd never told anyone else the full story of what happened between her and Nick the night of the wedding. Keeping that story secret was like a sacrament to her. She remembered the first time she had poured it out, in all its rawness, to her mother, and as this thought settled upon her, she burst into tears.

Adrian had been in the pitch-black room. He'd heard the story of the wedding; he'd heard about Nick. He'd listened as she confessed her most forbidden, confusing thoughts about her mother's death so they would think what a brave girl she was. The shame of that memory had burned so hot for so long, but she was tired of feeling that way. She slowed down, let her mind rest on it.

The girl in that room had just lost her mother. She'd believed these people wanted her to be a part of a group, the kind of group that had given her mother a lifelong friend. She could forgive that girl; she realized she already had. But Adrian? The shape of his betrayal was still coming into focus, it felt so unbearable.

She and Adrian had been together for three years. Three years. That was real history, and he loved her, she knew that. There was always a grateful quality to his love she had never understood, but now she did, because her loving him, him making her happy—it absolved him from the worst thing he had ever done. Which, to be clear, was not torturing her in a pitch-black room after her mother died because Cynthia told him to. It was that he had used all the things he knew about her but shouldn't know to bind her to him. Maybe he hadn't intentionally, but one of the reasons she'd fallen in love with him, in those early months, was because he seemed to understand so instinctively the raw and tender parts of her.

What would it mean to forgive Adrian? *So sweet and deferential,* that's what Cutter had said about her. She'd hated him for saying it, but she'd also felt fear, the bell of recognition. If she went back to Adrian now, she would tolerate for herself what she'd never tolerate for another person. She would accept something she would have been too ashamed to accept if her mother were alive. What did it mean to carry her mother forward? What would her mother have said to her now? She had to do this without her. That was the terrible, terrible freedom of being a motherless girl.

Her first serious relationship had come out of the ashes of the most humiliating thing that ever happened to her. She knew, if she decided to stay with him, she would extinguish a part of herself.

~

She opened the door. Adrian was sitting on the bed, with his head in his hands.

"Astra, please, please just listen to me," he said. "I always wanted to tell you, but in the beginning, I thought you would just leave, and then all of a sudden it was too late—I'd waited too long. I don't know if there was ever a moment I could have told you when you would have stayed, but I definitely knew when it was past that. And I was in love with you, completely, for who you are, and the more I got to know that the more awful it was to know what we had done to you. It was like turning a screw."

"Who were they, the other two?" she said.

"What does it matter now?"

"Are you seriously not going to tell me, Adrian?" she said.

He looked down at the ground. "It was Cynthia, you already guessed that, and Josh Larraby."

She nodded. She'd known Josh slightly, he would say hi to her on Cross Campus, nod to her at the library. Humans were so strange, in the ways they were cruel to one another.

"So, Atticus wasn't there. I always wondered."

"No. He and Cynthia got in a huge fight after what happened in that English class. They broke up a few weeks after—after what we did to you. I think she always blamed you for that too."

"Good to know," she said.

"Astra, I just want you to know, the moment you started talking in that room, I knew what a terrible mistake I'd made. You know Cynthia—she could be so convincing, so charming, that this was just a joke, that you had it in for her and needed to be taken down a notch. She was weirdly jealous of you. And then it was so awful in there, I thought I was going to throw up."

"You could have stopped it," she said.

"I wanted to—I didn't know what to do. It was so fucked up in there."

"I know that, Adrian. You don't have to tell me what it was like in there."

He was quiet. "Please," he said simply. "If you give me another chance . . . you know I'm not that person in that room. You know I'm not."

"I know you're not the person in the room, Adrian," she said. "I know that. But who would I be? Who would I be if I stayed with you?"

"Astra, I promise—"

"How many times do you think it's made me feel sick to think that these strangers, these people I didn't know, had my stories? That I'd opened up the most intimate and painful parts of my life to them? It was right after my mother died, and I thought, maybe this exciting thing is happening, something good, because I'm so sad and I've tried to muddle along and be such a *good girl.*" She paused, as if she needed to catch her breath.

"And instead, it's a trap," she said. "And the worst part is that it's a trap I willingly participated in. I couldn't believe I'd do that. It made me doubt myself; it almost made me change my idea of who I was. And now, to know it was you—not only you who hurt me, but you who used my stories to get close when we started dating."

"Astra!" he said, and there was so much pain in his voice. "I know how wrong that was. But those stories are part of what made me love you. I didn't use them to my advantage, or to try and manipulate you." She was surprised, how he was still fighting for her. "I hated myself, but I didn't take your stories," he said quietly. "I swear."

It hurt her, how much part of her wanted to forgive him.

"Maybe you think you didn't, but it was there, between us, from the beginning," she said. "It was the thing I could never figure out. You wanted to tell me, that dinner we had before graduation."

"Yes."

He looked like he might start crying, but he did not. "You know what's funny?" he said. "If you hadn't been honest about kissing Nick, this would never have come up. It took you twelve hours to come clean about this thing you did, while I've held on to this massive fucking betrayal for years."

She was silent.

"Do you think he's a better person than I am?"

"Adrian, don't do this."

"Do you think he's a better person?"

"I think you are a good person who made an awful mistake."

"Please tell me. Do you think he's a better person than I am?"

She thought of Nick, of how devastated she'd felt, doubled over in the grass after he told her what had happened between him and Allie. She remembered how part of her wished he hadn't, that she could just be allowed some happiness. Nick couldn't stand there and hear her praise him for saving Allie and say nothing. There was the kind of person who could move through the world carrying a secret like that, and there was the kind of person who couldn't. Adrian could. Yes, he felt guilt, he felt awful, she saw that, but he could do it, and Nick could not. That didn't make Adrian a bad person; she didn't hate him, not at all. But he was asking her a question, and she knew the answer.

"Yes," she said. "I do think he's a better person."

He nodded. "Thank you for saying that," he said. And then he looked around the room. "I can just leave now, if that's what you want."

"Okay," she said.

This surprised him, he opened his mouth to say something, then closed it.

"Are you going to tell people what I did? Are you going to tell your family?"

"I will tell my family," she said. "They won't tell anyone. I don't know what I'll tell other people."

"Tell them whatever you want," he said. "It will feel good, in a way. To not get away with it anymore." He started walking toward the door. "I'll get out of your way for a few hours, and then I can come back and pack, or whatever you want." He went to the door and opened it.

"Adrian," she said, and he stopped. She walked up to him and put her arms around him, and they stayed like that for a long time. Then he left, softly shutting the door behind him.

Astra sat down on the bed. She wondered if she were in shock or just numb from the last two days. The full sense of Adrian's betrayal had not hit yet, and she did not want to think right now about what it would mean, the unwinding of their life together. She would stay with Phoebe tonight, and they would peel back these scalding revelations—the encounter with Cutter, Nick's promise to her mother, what happened with Nick in the hotel room, Adrian's deception—one by one. They would do it together. She would go to her family.

That decision made, she lay back on the bed, exhausted. Adrian's books were stacked up on his side, his clothes were in the closet, the vintage posters and photographs they had picked together were still hanging on the wall, but he was gone. He was gone and she was devastated. But underneath that pain, she felt something else.

A prick of relief.

Chapter Sixty-One

When Astra looked at the clock again, almost an hour had passed. She had not slept, but she had drifted, trying to let her tangle of emotions settle. She needed to pack, she wanted to be gone when Adrian returned, but she found it almost impossible to focus. Her mind kept circling the hard strangeness of what had happened.

She went to her suitcase and opened it, rummaging around for the crumpled-up piece of paper on which she'd written Nick's phone number. Then she sat on the bed for several minutes, holding it.

When she dialed the number, she was not expecting an answer, but Nick picked up.

"Nick, hi, it's me," she said quickly. "I didn't think you'd be home."

"I just finished my rotation, actually, so I have a couple days off," he said. "I'm so glad you called. How was the flight home?"

"It was easy. I just wanted you to know I got in safely," she said, and paused. "And to say thank you, again, for everything."

"How is your family? Have you seen them yet? How is Adrian?"

She thought of Nick, standing at the phone in the kitchen, next to his fridge with nothing in it, asking after her boyfriend. She took a deep breath.

"Well, as of an hour ago, he isn't my boyfriend."

There was a long silence on the phone, and Astra was about to say something when Nick spoke.

"Is it—is it because I was there last night? Nothing happened; or I mean, nothing really happened—I can tell him that."

"No, that's not the reason. I found out—" She didn't really possess the words to describe what she had found out. "I found out he was one of the people, in that blacked-out room—back in college." There was an awfulness to speaking the words out loud, and she felt them register with Nick, heard his intake of breath.

The line was quiet, and she wondered if the connection had dropped. Maybe it was for the best. It felt crazy to call Nick now, when she wasn't even thinking straight. This was the kind of decision you weren't supposed to make after a loss, and that is what her breakup with Adrian was—a loss, even a kind of death. She still loved Adrian, you couldn't just turn that off, like putting a lid over a flame. Lying on the bed after he'd gone, she'd even pictured what it would be like to change her mind, to throw her arms around him when he got home and see the look on his face. She'd followed this idea through, and then she put it aside, like pushing back a darkness.

And in that moment, the person whose voice she'd most wanted to hear was Nick's. The man who had sat across from her mother all those years ago and given her his promise.

He still had not said a word. She was about to say his name, and then Nick spoke.

"I'm leaving for the airport now, Astra," he said. "Can I come see you?"

Astra put the phone down on the bed, wrapped her arms around herself, and then picked up the receiver.

"Yes," she said.

Epilogue

November 2002
New Jersey

Astra heard the car returning from the train station, sooner than she'd expected. From the window in the kitchen, she saw her father walking toward the house, with Nick and his mother, Patty, just behind them. Nick was laughing at something her father said.

She ran outside, still holding the wooden spoon she had been using to stir the gravy. Her nephew Jeremiah, a sturdy three-year-old with a thick sweep of ginger hair, hustled behind her. When he reached her, he raised his arms in an almost imperial gesture, and she lifted him up.

"Granddaddy!" Jeremiah said, pointing to Tom who waved at his grandson with the energy of a castaway trying to flag down a passing ship. "And Nickeee!"

Even after all these years, Astra still felt a jolt of electricity when she saw Nick. He was holding his mother's arm now as Patty navigated the flagstones; she looked lovely in a belted wool coat and scarf patterned with vines and birds. Patty had worn it a few years ago at Thanksgiving, and when Astra had complimented her on it, she'd touched her neck and said simply, "your mother gave it to me." Now Patty wore it at every holiday.

When they stepped inside the door, they almost bumped into the table, which was awkwardly long this year, angled so that part of it stuck out from the dining room into the entryway. Last night, Astra and Phoebe had set it for sixteen. They didn't have enough forks or plates or glasses from the same set for all the places, so it was a mismatched jumble, including a few coffee mugs. "I think this is my favorite table ever," Phoebe had said, and Astra had smiled, because Phoebe said this every year.

In the warm hubbub of greetings—Farris and Mrs. Friedman were at the stove, and Grandy came up to Tom and Patty with small glasses of sherry—Nick and Astra slipped out the side door for a moment alone. They started walking toward the pond, like they always did. The first time he'd come back to the farm, she'd wondered if it was hard for him, but he'd grown to love it the way she did. The sharp edges of the wedding night had been sanded away, the memories rearranged and reconstituted. Though he still made a point, whenever they were in the gazebo together, of kissing her.

It was cold for November, and there was a skim of ice on the pond now. "I always miss her, when we come here," Nick said. Astra looked up at him, and then she took two fingertips and traced his face, from his hairline to his temple, along his jaw and down to his neck. He shivered, and she pulled his head down and kissed him.

"That's not the first thing I love most about you, but it's probably the second or third."

He looked down at her and smiled, pulling her next to him with his arm. "We should get back to our family."

~

When they got back to the house, Mrs. Friedman announced that it was almost time to eat, and Astra went to look for Phoebe. She knocked quietly on her sister's door and pushed it open. There was a tote bag on the floor, spilling out diapers and swaddles and tiny socks, but her sister was not there.

She walked back down the hall, to the spiral staircase that led to her parents' room. Phoebe was sitting on their mother's side of the bed, by the window that overlooked the lower field that skirted the water.

When she turned, Astra saw that she was holding her tiny daughter in her lap. "She's sleeping," Phoebe said with a smile.

When Phoebe's daughter had been born, Astra had expected Phoebe to name the baby after their mother. She'd even imagined crying in happiness and a tiny bit of sadness when her sister told her. But Phoebe didn't. "Alice Loomis Friedman," she'd said, with an exhausted smile, as she'd held her tiny dark-haired daughter to her. And then, in answer to the question Astra hadn't asked, Phoebe had said quietly. "I wanted you to have it." And then Astra did cry. Her older sister, who always went first, was giving her this gift.

Astra settled down beside Phoebe. "I saw you and Nick walk down to the pond," Phoebe said. "Have you finally picked a date?"

"Phoebe," Astra said, drawing out her sister's name, the way she did when she was a kid. "Maybe we'll just elope, and I'll tell you afterward, okay?"

Phoebe laughed. "Ha! As if."

Alice opened her eyes and yawned, and both sisters leaned toward her in one movement.

"Can I tell you something I've been thinking about, while I've been sitting up here?" Phoebe asked. "You know how I was so happy about having a girl, but also scared, like it would be harder somehow?" Astra did remember. She and Phoebe had talked about it several times, the joy but also the terrifying intimacy of mothers and daughters. Would Alice be a mirror for Phoebe, for all her fears and vulnerabilities, in a way that Jeremiah wasn't?

"But it's not. I was wrong. Sometimes when I'm holding her, I imagine I'm Mommy, holding me as a baby, and it actually helps." Phoebe paused. "Does that sound crazy?"

"That doesn't sound crazy at all," Astra said.

They were quiet, and the baby made small, snuffling noises. Astra took her in her arms and breathed in her warm, grassy smell. Sitting next to Phoebe, on their mother's old bed, Astra could feel the girls they used to be, and the women they were now. She could feel the shape of her mother's love, in the room with them. When Alice moved, Astra was startled by the warmth of such a small body against hers, and thought, as always, how happy her mother would have been, at this unremarkable, beautiful business of living.

Phoebe reached out and took Astra's hand, and they stayed like that, not saying anything, until their father called up that it was time for dinner.

ACKNOWLEDGMENTS

This book exists because of my mother, who died when I was seventeen and whose competent, lively, ferociously loving spirit fills these pages. She not only gave me my love of books, but she was the first writer I deeply admired.

I am eternally grateful to my agents, Rick Richter and Caroline Marsiglia at Aevitas Creative Management, who supported this project with such enthusiasm, rigor, and happy relentlessness. Thank you, always, for believing in this book.

Pippa White, my editor at Lake Union, not only championed this novel but understood it down to its atoms and made it better. It's an honor to be on this journey with you. I am so grateful to Pippa, Carmen Johnson, Darci Swanson, and the entire team at Lake Union for their professionalism and deep expertise that made this book stronger every step of the way. Thank you to Angela Elson for keeping the trains running on time; Tree Abraham and Addie Lutzo for their wonderful design; and Elsa K, Aimée Hill, and Andy Hodges for their eagle eye.

Mackenzie Huynh, you were my first reader, and not only did your feedback shape every part of this story, but you actually believed this could be a novel. Thank you.

Suzanne Zuckerman, I will save the screenshots you sent me of this manuscript forever. Thank you for reading this book with such intelligence, thoughtfulness, and humanity.

Thank you to Gerd Thomsen for telling me I wasn't done yet.

So many mentors and editors helped me on this journey, but special thanks to Honor Brodie, Dave Kalstein, Sam Adams, and Kerry Cullen; my high school English teachers Kolia O'Connor and Ann Klotz; and my college professors Amy Bloom and, in memory, Robert Stone. To my West Coast magazine family—Lisa Trottier, Rachel Levin, Nino Padova, and Mackenzie Huynh—thanks for always being there for the group chat.

So many people were generous with their publishing expertise, but special thanks to Jenny Rosenstrach, Kemper Donovan, and Robby O'Connor, for their steadfast advice and support. Robby, thank you for understanding the journey, always.

To James Prosek, my oldest creative friend, your generosity and advice as I tried to get this manuscript out into the world cannot be repaid. I'm so grateful for our friendship.

Tonya Kaltenbach and Greg Neukirchner, thank you for your patience and wisdom in helping me with the medical details in this book. Erin McClam, your deep dive on the AP remains a delight. There's no one I love talking about writing with more. Mark Hatzenbuehler, thank you for just being you and believing in me.

Julia Powell, you understood what it meant to put so much creative struggle into a project I wasn't sure would ever see the light of day. The joy you took in seeing this book get out into the world was such an act of love. Thank you for the sisterhood.

This book is about families, and I am so lucky to be part of several, including the wonderful, endlessly supportive Thompson Poindexter clan (special thanks to my niece Madison for being my social media strategist), and my mother's extended family, who always kept her memory alive and made a place for me. To my TQF community, you are beloved.

Sam, thank you for being the kind of older brother who always lifted me up; you're my model for what an older sibling should be. I loved sharing the childhood that was so much a part of this story. Joan,

I'll never forget not just your feedback on this book but your kindness when I had a creative setback.

Dad, thank you for always encouraging me to write, and for reading us everything as kids, especially every last word of *The Lord of the Rings*. I hear your storytelling voice, always. You loved us in a way that made us believe in ourselves. And to my stepmother, Janet, thank you for always believing I'd write a book and telling me you would throw the party. I can't wait.

To Brant, William, and Olivia Rose—you supported me and believed in me every step of the way. Being part of this family has given me a happiness I never imagined. You know I love words, but I actually don't possess the ones to explain how much your love and belief in this book has meant. Thank you. This is for all of us.

ABOUT THE AUTHOR

Photo © 2025 Darcy Hemley

Anna Nordberg is a journalist and culture writer whose essays have appeared in *Slate* magazine, *The Washington Post*, *The New York Times*, and the *San Francisco Chronicle*. She grew up in New York City and now lives in San Francisco with her husband and two children. *When She Was Ours* is her first novel.